Ten Percent
-Hollywood Can Be Murder

by
DL Bruin

Acknowledgements:

This book exists due to the love and support of a few good human beings.

Lefty -Thank you for teaching me how to read and write, and for pointing me in the direction of the library.

Diane -Thank you for your love and support.

Stevie Nelson -Wife, best friend, editor, my partner in crime for these many years, and my toughest audience -thank you for never losing faith.

Stephen King -Thank you for penning the work "On Writing". That book changed my perspective on storytelling, renewed my passion and strengthened my resolve.

Thom Steinbeck -Thank you for your friendship, encouragement and advice.

For my fellow kid actors who spent their childhoods toiling away in The Hollywood Dream Factory
-You know who you are.

PART 1

THE COYOTE MURDERS

"A kingdom like Oz".
-Adela Rogers St. Johns

1

December 2012

On this particular December evening, Los Angeles was lit up in her holiday finery. Rain-slick streets reflected ripples of multi-hued neon. Windows in stores and restaurants were festooned with Christmas decor and fake snow. There were acres of tinsel and miles of blinking colored lights interspersed amidst the palm trees and tropical flowers. And on every other street corner there was a sullen-faced Santa clanging away with a brass bell at passersby.

The scene was Norman Rockwell on acid. An airbrushed portrait of an aging prostitute, best viewed under moonlight and from a proper distance.

*****

They were parked on a fire road off Mulholland Highway in the hills overlooking the San Fernando Valley. It was just past midnight when the rain began to morph into a fine steady mist. On the CD player Travis Tritt was singing about Livin' on Borrowed Time.

The girl looked twenty. Pretty in a hard way, with close-cropped blonde hair framing a heart shaped face.

When The Man had asked her name she'd told him it was April.

He knew she was lying. They all lied.

The air inside the cab was dank with the distinct tang of sex mixed with spilled malt liquor. April's skirt was hiked up around her thighs and her panties lay in a tiny heap on the floorboards. She straddled The Man and moaned profes-sionally as he thrust himself in and out of her.

When she felt him start to climax she reached down with one hand and adroitly massaged his scrotum. That did the trick... as they say.

As he started to cum the muscles in The Man's jaw con-stricted and a series of grunts escaped between clenched teeth.

April pulled her blouse down without ceremony and bent over to collect her panties. The Man grinned, reached over and goosed her ass. The girl sprang up, smacked her head on the underside of the dashboard.

The Man laughed.

"Goddamnsonofabitch!!" she swore. "That fucking hurt!"

"That the same mouth you talk to your momma with?"

April rubbed her head and sneered. "It's the same mouth that was suckin' your dick a few minutes ago and you didn't seem to mind it much then."

She glanced down and noticed his latex-covered prick was rigid once again.

"Geez, mister, you been snortin' Viagra or somethin'?'

"Or somethin'," the man replied, grabbing for the girl's breast.

With a practiced agility April managed to evade his grasp.

"You wanna play again, you gotta pay again, Cowboy. Those're the rules."

"Nah, I don't think so," he drawled.

He grabbed her, yanked her towards him, pressed his mouth forcefully on hers, kissed her hard.

April pulled away, repulsed. "I told you not to do that!"

"You gotta lot of rules for a nasty little street tramp," he taunted, tightening his grip. Then he kissed her again.

The girl's adrenal glands kicked into overdrive as she struggled fiercely.

"Get off me you sick fuck!"

The Man released his grip and backhanded her across the face.

April exhaled a stunned gasp and pulled as far away as the confined space allowed. She touched the back of her hand to her crushed lip, glanced down and saw blood, began to tremble.

"Nobody does that to me! Nobody!" She lunged at him.

At first The Man made no attempt to shield himself from the girl's rage. He accepted the punishment with an amused grin. Then, in one fluid motion, he snatched her hands and forced them to her side. His strange smile remained fixed as he held her arms pinned. He glared malevolently into her eyes. The Man's gaze penetrated, chilled the fire right out of her.

And then, in the space of a single heartbeat, April understood...

Time became elastic, slowed like cold molasses, down to the millisecond. The Man felt his heart rate increase and his erection strain. He inhaled deeply, feasting on the aroma of the young woman's fear.

If he were ever required to narrow it down to just one moment, this was it; that marvelous expression of unbridled terror they all seemed to have in common... once they came to realize the depth of their miscalculation. How he savored this.

The rain began once again, this time in earnest. And the sound drowned out the screams.

It was a considerable time before the truck's motion

ceased. And then, just for the briefest of moments, the only sound to be heard was that of the sheeting rain; a droning that encompassed all, washing away dirt, smog and sin.

The passenger door opened and moments later April's lifeless form dropped onto the muddy roadway. She came to rest face down, extremities all askew, a macabre rag doll.

The door squealed as it was yanked shut, and then a few seconds later the big V-8 cranked over.

The Man strapped on his seatbelt and turned up the volume on the old Pioneer deck. He paused to check his reflection in the rearview, picked something from his teeth, then slipped the gearshift into drive and crept the two hundred yards to where the fire road joined up with Mulholland Highway. He switched on the headlights and pulled onto the deserted roadway, accelerated to cruising speed, all the while singing along with Travis.

2

It was the kind of mid-December morning that took your breath away. The sky was an incredible shade of cobalt and the air was fresh and crisp. A rare day indeed for this so-called City of Angels. The storm in the flat-lands had drifted east during the night, flocking the local mountains with nearly a foot of snow.

Maxine "Max" Calderas stood on the balcony of her fifth-floor North Hollywood apartment; warming her hands on a mug of coffee and watching the clouds drift by.

Aretha Franklin wafted from the living room and a clock indicated the time as 7:15. A pile of newspapers littered one corner of a dining table, and on the opposite end, a .40 caliber Smith and Wesson semi-auto slept snugly in a ballistic nylon holster. A collection of family photos hung on the wall by the table, one of which, a portrait of a teenage girl, was framed with black crepe paper.

Even at fifty-one, Maxine "Maximum" Calderas was one Los Angeles Police Detective that was especially easy on the eyes. Thick salt and pepper hair and ex-pressive wide-set green eyes complemented high cheekbones. Standing five-nine on an athletic frame, Max was formidable as well as attractive. She'd ac-quired the handle 'Maximum" at the police academy, the explanation for which varied depending on to whom one was speaking. In any event, the handle had remained. Even her grandkids referred to her as Maximum: Granny Maximum.

Her shift started at eight and this was her 'Quiet Time'. Her time to relax and contemplate the day ahead. Quiet Time was a survival skill Max's mother had taught her at an early age. One of a multitude of character traits they shared in common was the absolute requirement for space away from The World.

Max eyed the traffic on Lankershim and breathed in the fragrant steam rising from the mug. She returned to her thoughts.

Life had been so simple once upon a time, back in Momma's kitchen, with all those fine spicy aromas and kettle juices sizzling on the old iron stove. Max and her sister, Bernie, older by four years, helped out with food preparation, chopping onions and carrots and celery.

Feeding a household of eight was a full-time job all by itself, but there was still laundry and grocery shopping and guitar lessons for Alonzo on Tuesdays after school, and a whole litany of other chores and obligations, all of which Momma Calderas juggled with a perpetual smile.

Max had enjoyed school, excelled in English and anything related to sports. By age sixteen she had developed a marked preference for one-on-one competition and became infatuated with the sport and art of archery.

There was just something so elegant about the entire experience. The tension of the bow. The stillness and concentration. The release of the string and the transfer of energy to the aluminum shaft. The wickedly fast flight, a sunlit reflection of quicksilver and blurred feathers, The sound of the strike, the shaft burying itself in the wired bale of hay.

Max swallowed the last of the coffee and stepped inside the apartment, locked the sliding glass door behind her. She crossed to the dining area, lifted the shoulder

holster from the table and strapped it on. She camou-
flaged the rig with a rust colored blazer, checked her
reflection in the mirror, made some last minute adjust-
ments, and exited the apartment.

*****

Greg London didn't hear the alarm go off at seven. He
was lost in a tropical dreamscape, cavorting with buxom
young women aboard a sleek yacht.

At 7:30, the blaring of the second alarm clock finally
roused him as it echoed off the tiles in the master bath.

Greg mumbled profanities as he swung a leg over the
side of the bed. He padded barefoot toward the bathroom, smacked the alarm silent, and checked out his
reflection in the mirror.

Detective Greg London was thirty-nine, with a mostly
full head of nutmeg colored hair, and a baby face that
belied his true nature. He'd been married and divorced
twice, and after his last experience at the hands of the
California Family Courts, swore an oath to God and
Universe that there would never be a third Mrs. London.
However, his current squeeze, Denise, a twenty-four year
old pre-school teacher, had different plans entirely.

Greg glanced at the time. "For fucks sake."

He kicked in the afterburners, showered and dressed
in record time. Then, as was his custom, he headed for
the automatic drip coffee pot that had been set the previous night to begin brewing at six a.m. sharp. Fuck stroll-
ing around on the moon. As far as Greg London was
concerned this was the epitome of Mankind's technology.

In his hurry, Greg overfilled the coffee mug, and then
compounded the gaff by attempting to slurp the overage.
Having sat in the pot those extra thirty minutes or so had
turned the liquid molten.

Greg jumped back, knocked the mug across the counter, and splashed hot coffee all over the silk tie Denise had just given him for his birthday. Worse still, he didn't have a clean replacement or time to go digging through the laundry hamper for a less soiled alternate. He hadn't been up an hour yet and already he was in a foul mood.

Less than five minutes later, on the way out of the apartment building, he stepped off the stairs at an angle, twisted his ankle and very nearly completed a full face-plant.

And of course, when he finally got to the station house, Max was waiting for him by the cruiser. She glanced down at her watch.

"Sorry, Max. Goddamn alarm didn't go off."

"Nice tie there, Chief," she smirked, always happy to add insult to injury. "Let's shake it. We have a call."

London climbed into the passenger seat and clicked on the seatbelt.

"Another long night?" Max queried.

London pretended not to hear her.

Max continued the needling. "You should marry that girl before she wises up."

"Like I really need to hear this shit first thing in the morning," Greg replied with a caustic tone.

Max chuckled.

Twenty minutes later, Detective Calderas nosed the cruiser off Mulholland Highway onto a dirt fire road that had been marked off with crime scene tape. The prior night's storm had reduced the roadway to an impass-able mud hole. There were a couple of black and white prowlers on scene as well as a coroner's wagon and a four-wheel-drive news van. The muscles in London's jaw tightened as he surveyed the panorama.

"Ever have the feeling you should've just stayed in bed?"

"Frequently," Max responded.

Beverly Crescent, newscaster for local channel six, along with her crew, was shooting a sequence for the evening news. Just a few yards behind her the blanket-shrouded remains lay in plain sight.

"Hello, I'm Beverly Crescent, and you're watching channel six news. Early this morning, a local man out for a jog made a grisly discovery; the body of a young woman apparently dumped here sometime during the night."

The cameraman adjusted the depth of field on the lens and tilted the camera in such a way as to take in as much of the body's exposed extremities as possible. Death was always good for ratings. Death by homicide, even better. Throw a dash of kinky sex into the mix and we could be talking Pulitzer here!

The newscaster continued her monologue. "Police are refusing to speculate if this is the latest victim of the serial killer who's been terrorizing Los Angeles; the elusive stalker known only as 'The Coyote'."

Beverly's pause was dramatic. "For those of you keeping count, in just the past two months the bodies of four young women have turned up in semi-rural locations throughout the county."

At that instant detectives Calderas and London came into Beverly's field of view. The newscaster was quick to capitalize on the opportunity, shoving a microphone under London's nose.

"Excuse me. Excuse me, detective London. Is there anything you'd like to say to our viewing audience?"

"As a matter of fact, there is," Greg replied. Then he looked directly into the camera and smiled all warm and toothy. "Change the channel, folks. These people are fuckin' ghouls."

Beverly's lips stretched back over artificially whitened teeth into what could only be described as a snarl. But always the consummate professional, she managed to regain her composure in just under a nanosecond.

"Thanks a lot, London. Now we're going to have re-shoot the entire sequence."

"Uh, no Bev. I don't think so," the detective replied. I think what you're going to do is pack up all this crap and vamanos the hell outta here. You're standing right in the middle of a crime scene for chrissakes. I can't have you and your crew contaminating the scene and destroying evidence."

"What about the people's right to know?"

"Inform the people," London continued. "Be my guest. Just do it from the other side of that tape."

Beverly opened her mouth as if to say something pithy in reply, but her brain engaged before her tongue did. She turned on her cameraman instead.

"Alright Les, you heard the detective." Her voice was cold, taking on a tone not associated with her on-air persona.

London shook his head.

"Is there something else, Greg?"

"Yeah Bev, as a matter of fact, there is. You know, ever since I got handed this assignment there's been one thing eating at me."

"And what might that be? How you've managed to rise to the lofty rank of Lieutenant despite your obvious lack of competence?"

"Actually Bev, you're not even close. What I was wondering was where you come up with those moronic names? I mean 'The Coyote', what the fuck is that about anyway?"

"The last girl had bite marks…"

"So the media alleges," London snapped back.

"People saw the body Greg…"

A sardonic smile spread across London's face. "That's right, Bev. 'People' did see the body. But as you know, people frequently don't know what the fuck they're looking at. There are a lot of ways for a stiff to get marked up."

Looking for a way to end the conversation, Beverly opted for candor. "It was either going to be 'The Coyote' or 'The Grim Raper'. I made an executive decision."

"Really? You mean to tell me you made up that shit on the spur of the moment?" London asked, utter amazement in his voice.

"That is what they pay me for Greg," Beverly replied icily, annoyed with the banter.

London turned to Calderas. "Damn, Max, I was wrong."

Calderas raised an eyebrow.

"Whoa, there. Hang on a minute, Beverly. This is a real piece of late-breaking news. Greg London has just admitted to being wrong. I've never heard him use those three words in a sentence before."

London shrugged. "What can I say? There has to be a first time for everything, no?"

"What are you talking about?" Beverly demanded.

"Well Bev, I was sure that a select group of you media jackals got together at the beginning of the year around some waterhole, and picked names out of a hat. You know, like the weather guys do with hurricanes."

Calderas smiled at the insult.

"If that's your idea of comedy Greg, I hope you plan to keep your day job," Beverly retorted.

"Nice talking with you Bev."

Detectives Calderas and London picked their way across the muddy access road and approached two uniforms.

"You guys first on the scene?" detective Calderas queried the older of the two.

"Actually the snow queen over there beat us in," he replied, referring to the news team.

"Find anything interesting?" Calderas continued.

"We found a purse. Got the vic's ID."

The officer handed detective Calderas a plastic baggie that contained an Oklahoma driver's license. Max scanned it.

"Ellen Pomeroy, D.O.B. March 21, 1993. Jesus Greg, another baby."

"What can I say, Max? This prick likes them young."

"All men, regardless of age, race, creed, religion, or infirmity seem to like them young, Greg," Calderas responded acidly.

"Aw shit Max. Don't go getting all gynocentric on me."

"When I was growing up I always wanted to be Someone.
Now I realize I should have been more specific."
-Lily Tomlin

3

(A couple of days later)

The morning sun illuminated the traffic that was backed up outside the office building at the corner of Hollywood Boulevard and Ashleigh way.

In its heyday the building was occupied by the likes of Herman Cardell, the world-renowned attorney-for-the-stars, and Jake Epstein, Hollywood agent turned Hollywood producer; the very first of the breed. But that was a long time ago, way back in the mid-fifties, before crack babies and drive-by shootings. It was a time when the neighborhood was considered upscale and its proximity to the major studios, desirable.

That was then. Today nothing is the way it was: not the Town, not the Industry.

Currently the building's occupancy rate hovered in the neighborhood of twenty percent, which gave the owners little in the way of motivation regarding upkeep. The few tenants that remained were a reflection of the times.

The entire bottom floor was home to ZT Systems, an answering service bureau utilized by the entertainment industry since '79.

On the second floor there was a company called Keyhole Investigations. Keyhole was directly across the hall from an outcall massage service, the sign on that door read: PRIVATE in oversized, blood red lettering. At the end of the hallway, a large, five-room suite was currently being utilized as a dental clinic, the primary clientele being illegal immigrants; people used to paying cash for services rendered and ignorant of their rights under personal injury law.

On the third floor there was an accountant, three attorneys, and one low-rent talent agency. The sign on that door was in an elegant script more befitting Rodeo Drive. It read: MONROE TALENT GROUP, LTD.

On the wall right beside the door some artist wannabe with too much time on his or her hands had spray-painted a primitive rendition of a penis, in day-glow neon pink, along with the catchy phrase: PORNO MEAT RENTAL CO.

The Monroe Talent Group's offices consisted of three rooms. First, there was a tiny reception area dominated by a battered green naugahyde couch. In front of the couch, at the perfect shin-crunching distance, there was a decrepit coffee table with months-old copies of the Hollywood Reporter and Actors Log strewn about.

Referring to the second area as a 'room' was an out and out fabrication concocted by a rental agent of questionable repute. In reality it was the size of a large walk-in closet and served only to store the 'Files'. The Files were large vertical cabinets containing mostly pictures and resumes of the current clientele, along with various contracts and the like. This entire system was a remnant of the prehistoric time before submissions became mostly digital in nature.

The room where the actual work got done was about three times the size of the reception area but felt cramped nonetheless. Two large desks faced each other at one end of the room. And at the opposite end there was another beat up couch. The walls were a nicotine-tinted shade of eggshell, and the earth tone carpet was pitted and water-stained.

Such are the stuff Hollywood dreams are made of.

Shelly Ilene Monroe sat at her desk gazing out the window at the alley below, a Camel filter tip dangling from her lips, and a phone cradled between shoulder and doughy cheek.

"...Of course he can scuba dive. It's right there on his resume for chrissake... It's not?"
Shelly improvised as she adjusted the bra that was cutting into the ample flesh of her bosom.

"Has to be some sort of computer glitch. What do you think, Bruce, I'm going to risk my reputation sending you someone who can't deliver? ...Of course not, sweetheart. No problem. I'll have him there tomorrow at five-fifteen. Ciao for now."

Shelly glanced across her desk at her lone employee, Irv, who was calmly losing a hand of solitaire. "Irv, get me that lox Jimmy Bodine on the phone."

Irv looked up from his cards and blinked. "That wasn't Jimmy you were hyping to Bruce Kanter just now?"

"Sure as hell was. What about it?"

Irv removed his gold wire-frame glasses and nervously polished the lenses. "But Shelly, Jimmy Bodine doesn't know how to swim."

Shelly's eyes narrowed to slits as she bored a hole through Irv's forehead. "Yeah, so? What's aqua ability got to do with the price of tea in China? Jimmy Bodine doesn't have a fuckin' prayer. You read the breakdowns. He's all wrong for the part."

"Then why are you wasting Bruce's time sending him Jimmy?"

Shelly shook her head, and as if addressing a slow child, continued, "Let me explain it to you. The rumor going around town is Bruce and his most recent fuck-buddy are on the outs. So I figure what the hell. I know for a fact Bruce's taste in men leans toward big, dumb country humps like Jimmy. So I..."

"You thought you'd set the two of them up?" Irv interrupted.

Shelly fluttered her eyelashes. "There could be romance in the air."

"But Jimmy is straight! What're you thinking, Shelly?"

"Give me a break! Jimmy-Fuckin'-Bodine grew up in the hill country of Tennessee for chrissakes. Didn't you ever see Deliverance?"

"As I recall, that film took place in Georgia."

"Tennessee, Georgia, whatever!" Shelly fumed. "If I tell him it'll be good for his career, trust me, Jimmy'll show up at the interview wearing a wetsuit and kneepads."

While Irv blinked a silent response Shelly dialed out on another line. "God if only we had a couple more clients like Cody Clifton..." Shelly added dreamily. "That boy's got winner written all over him."

"Let's not forget who brought him over," Irv reminded.

"You're right, Irv. We should give credit where credit is due. Jimmy-Fuckin'-Bodine may be a lox, as well as a colossal pain in the ass, but he did bring us Cody. God bless him for that."

Shelly turned her attention to the telephone. On the other end of the line a machine picked up after the fourth ring. "Cody, darling, this is Shelly. Give me a call as soon as you get this message. I have an interview for you. Another callback for Chuck Dallas, Private Investigator. I'll give you the details when I hear back from you. Ciao for now, honey."

Irv Birnbaum was forty-eight years old. He'd started working with Shelly back in '96 when they were both schleppers for the Spielman Agency. Over the course of three decades in the Entertainment industry, Milt Spielman had cultivated a reputation as a tyrant as well as a tight-wad. Under his tutelage Shelly and Irv learned the ropes of the talent agency business. And for that privilege they were ruthlessly overworked and severely underpaid.

It was Shelly who dreamed of bigger things and always kept her eye on the ball.

Then in 2002, Shelly's mother, Lillian Monroe nee Him-melstein, did the only unselfish thing she'd ever done in her entire life; she died suddenly, leaving all her worldly pos-sessions to her only child, Shelly Ilene.

The inheritance hadn't been much, but it had been enough to tell Spielman where he could stick his shitty job. She'd emptied her desk and opened her own shop and asked Irv if he'd care to tag along. He'd agreed, and spent the following decade with Shelly, eking out an existence pimping, what is referred to in the Industry as, day players.

Irv's great ambition in life was to become a full partner in the agency. An equal. A peer. But Shelly liked things the way they were, with her name on the top line of the fran-chise.

"Shell, how many callbacks does this make?" Irv asked.

Shelly held out her hand with all five plump fingers fully extended. "The casting director told me the writer loves Cody's delivery."

Irv's face took on a sour expression. "Who cares what the writer thinks? Writer's are the bottom of the food chain."

"In this particular case the writer also happens to be one of the producers."

"Oh my!"

Shelly continued, "The bad news is he's only one of four."

"There's always bad news, isn't there?" Irv responded, once again removing his wire-rims for a quick polishing.

"Just the same, I'm starting to get excited. The Network's so completely apeshit over this show, they actually gave the producers a deal for a guaranteed thirteen episode run!"

Irv adjusted the nose piece on the spectacles and his eyes grew wide, magnified four-fold by the lenses. "Are you serious?"

Shelly beamed a smile. "Serious as a heart attack. Brings back sweet memories, doesn't it?"

The corners of Irv's mouth curled upward in a faint smile. "The good old days, eh Shell?"

"That's right Irving, The good old days. Back before a show got bought for six and canceled after two."

Shelly sat back in the chair and propped her feet up on the desk, gazed out the window into the distance.

"And you know what it'll mean if Cody hits, don't you?"

Irv chuckled nervously. "No more wrestling with the junkies to get out of the parking lot?"

Shelly didn't even hear the response. Her mind was off planning the future.

"It'll mean the Monroe Talent Group's name will be on the lips of every power broker in town! That's what it'll mean! After all these years scratching I think we finally got a 'Contender'."

Shelly turned her eyes toward Irv. "And Irving, doll, do you know what the best part's gonna be?"

Irv's lower lip quivered. "Tell me about The Rabbits again, Shelly."

Her grin broadened. "The best part's going to be when I negotiate a five year deal for our young Mr. Clifton, so that no matter what big agency the ingrate prick eventually leaves us for, we'll continue getting paid each and every episode."

Irv sat back in his chair and put his feet up on the desk, emulating Boss lady. "And let's not forget about the residuals!" Irv added.

Shelly laughed. "No, Irv, we most certainly won't forget the residuals. God, how I love this Business!"

4

Cody Clifton stood in the bathroom of his quaint, old Hollywood duplex, brushing his teeth. Cody's companion, Blue, a five year old floppy-eared hound of dubious ancestry, was sprawled on the floor nearby, snoring.

Cody had come across Blue in Ozona, Texas, on his way driving out to Hollywood. He'd pulled off the freeway and coasted up to the pump at a Shell station. And then, while he was checking the water level in the old truck's radiator, this scruffy flop-eared dog approached and began sniffing at Cody's boots.

An attendant appeared and Cody handed the man a couple of twenties.

The dog barked.

"Nice dog, buddy. What's his name?" Cody enquired.

"I have no idea. Mutt's been hanging around here for about a week now. Coupla kids dumped him."

Cody kneeled and scratched the dog's neck. The dog licked Cody's hand.

"Looks like you just made a friend, mister."

Cody smiled and opened the door to the pickup. "Dog, you wanna come home with me?"

Without missing a beat the dog jumped into the truck and curled into a ball on the passenger seat.

"I think I'll call you Blue."

And the rest is history.

Cody continued his ritual, vigorously rubbing his perfect pink gum tissue in an up and down motion. When he finished he replaced the toothbrush in its cup, and patted his face on a towel. He reached for a hairbrush on the edge of the john and began brushing the damp hair off his forehead.

Cody stood six-one on a lean and athletic, one-hundred-seventy pound frame. Genetically blessed, one might say. His eyes were of an unusual brown hue, almost golden in the right light, with tiny flecks of green encircling the perimeter. His smile was pure riverboat gambler.

Fifteen minutes later, clad in grey sweats and generic sneakers, Cody stepped into the morning. He squinted at the overcast and slid on a pair of Ray Bans, brushed a palm over his wavy blonde hair.

Striding the short distance to a dented green Toyota sedan, he fished in a pocket and produced a key ring with about a dozen keys on it. He rooted around some more and came up with another key, this one attached to a white plastic insignia. He stuck it into the door lock on the Toyota and twisted clockwise.

"Alright Blue dog. Time's a-wastin'."

Blue leaped into the car and took up a position on the front passenger seat, tail wagging savagely. Cody slid behind the wheel and closed the door. He reached over and scratched the pooch behind the ears.

"You're a good ole dog, Blue. Yes you are. You're a good boy."

Blue woofed an agreement and sat down, tongue lolling to starboard.

They arrived at the park fifteen minutes later and proceeded toward a well utilized running track. Blue paused now and then to sniff at messages on the moist grass.

21

Cody began his stretching ritual concentrating primarily on his calves and quads. After a few minutes warming up he called to Blue, who seemed to have found something of profound interest in the bushes by the baseball diamond.

Cody put two fingers in his mouth and whistled. The hound paused and lifted his head, then took off at full gallop in Cody's direction.

"What're you up to, you sneaky beast?" Cody demanded, bending down and scratching the white blaze of fur on Blue's chest. "C'mon, time to burn some calories."

Cody loped off in a counter clockwise direction with Blue right at his heels.

*****

When Cody and Blue returned from their morning run they were greeted by the upstairs neighbor, Mrs. Valletti. A sweet old Italian lady with a penchant for cannoli, Mrs. Valletti was recently widowed. Cody was reasonably certain it was Mrs. Valletti's high-cholesterol cooking that had killed Mr. Valletti.

"Good morning, Cody. Did you and Blue get in a good workout today?"

"Yes ma'am, we certainly did," Cody replied, adjusting the towel around his neck "And how are you feelin' on this lovely mornin'?"

Mrs. Valletti made a gesture with her hands. "A little stiff in the joints, but I guess that's to be expected at my age... Listen Cody, I was wondering..."

Cody's left eye twitched. Over time it became plain that whenever Mrs. Valletti preceded a statement with: "Cody, I was wondering", it ended up costing him money.

"Ma'am?"

"The senior center is having its annual raffle in two weeks. First prize is a weekend for two in Las Vegas, all expenses paid... and that includes transportation!... by bus, of course."

"Well ma'am, I'm not much of a gamblin' man..."

"Did I mention that proceeds are going to the Children's Hospital?" she added, turning up the charm. "C'mon Cody, tickets are only five bucks apiece. How many can I put you down for?"

Cody scratched his chin. "Well I guess if it's for charity and all, I'll take four of 'em off your hands."

Mrs. Valletti beamed. "You're such a wonderful boy, Cody. Your mother must be very proud."

Cody blushed. "I'll get that money right up to you, Mrs. Valletti. Just as soon as I get cleaned up."

He crossed to the front door.

"Take your time, Cody. I'm not going anywhere," she called after him, chuckling.

*****

Cody kicked off his sneakers and padded across the oak floor in his socks. As he was about to head off to the shower Cody noticed the flashing red light on the answering machine. He paused beside the kitchen counter and pressed 'play'.

"Cody darling, this is Shelly. Give me a call as soon as you get this message. I have an interview for you. Another callback for Chuck Dallas, Private investigator. I'll give you the details when I hear back from you. Ciao for now, honey."

Cody reached for the phone and punched a speed-dial button.

"Hey Irv, It's Cody. Is Shelly around?"

"Acting is an empty and useless profession."
-Marlon Brando

5

Jimmy Bodine could easily have passed for Cody Clifton's brother. The resemblance was uncanny. He was just under six feet tall and a stockier one-hundred, ninety pounds. His hair was a few shades darker and a bit longer than Cody's, and his nose was broader at the bridge. Jimmy and Cody were born within sixty days of each other, in towns one county apart, separated by a state line. There was even the distant possibility the two were related; fifth cousins, or some such nonsense.

Jimmy sat across the desk from Shelly, clad in worn designer denim and expensive gray ostrich cowboy boots, a crumpled copy of 'Actors Log' poised in his lap.

"... And as far as I know they haven't cast the part of the hitman yet. So what do you think, Shelly? Can you get me out on it?"

Irv interrupted, "Shell, Cody's on line three."

"Hang on a second, Jimmy. I gotta give Cody an interview."

She picked up the phone and punched the button with the flashing light.

"Cody, darling. Got a pencil handy? ...Good. They want you at bungalow 33 tomorrow at eleven. Use the south entrance to the lot. There'll be a drive-on pass waiting for you at the guard shack. Get there early, and don't forget to check in with me after. Knock 'em dead, kid."

Shelly hadn't even hung up the phone before Jimmy Bodine started in again. "So what do you say, Shelly? Can you get me out on the gig in 'Actors Log'?"

Shelly suppressed the sudden urge to reach for the .38 snub-nose in her purse and permanently silence his incessant questions. Taking a deep breath, she forced a warm smile.

"You know Jimmy, we had that in the 'breakdowns' over a month ago, and if I would have thought you were right for the role I would have submitted you back then."

"What's wrong, Shelly? Don't you think I could play the part?"

"This isn't a question about acting ability. It's a purely physical thing. Jimmy, there's just no way in Hell you could ever pass for Italian."

Jimmy thought about that for a moment, and then came up with what, in his mind, seemed like a plausible solution. "What if I put a really dark rinse on my hair?"

Shelly chuckled and shook her head. "Jimmy, even if you had your septum surgically removed, I still couldn't sell you as a wop hitman. Get a grip already."

Jimmy's expression wilted.

"Now don't go getting all puppy-eyed on me," Shelly snapped. "Jimmy, what you have to understand here is, I'm the agent and you're the performer. My job is to get you interviews and negotiate the deal when you land a role. But in order for me to do my job, casting directors have to trust me. And if I send them Joe Pesci when they've requested Clint Eastwood, they're going to stop trusting me. And if that happens, all my clients, including you, will suffer... Are you beginning to get the picture?"

Jimmy Bodine sat there quietly digesting the information. "Gee Shelly, I never looked at it like that before."

Shelly smiled inwardly. Actors were just like little children. Sometimes you just had to draw them a picture.

"Well what about this one?" Jimmy asked, shoving the 'Actors Log' under Shelly's nose. "It says here Randolph Foods is lookin' for a spokesperson, and they're interviewing southerners for the job."

"We had that one in 'breakdowns' two weeks ago. And if you'd take the time to read a little further down the page, you'd learn that Randolph Foods is interviewing actors in their sixties!"

Without missing a beat Jimmy shot back, "No problem, Shelly. With a little makeup and a grey rinse I can play sixties, easy."

"There are two classes of people in this world: there are those who prey, and those who are preyed upon."
-Mr. Jacques

6

The room was windowless and cold, harshly lit, and possessed with the sharp smell of disinfectant.

Ellen Pomeroy aka April Waters lay on her back on a stainless steel table. Over the course of the past several hours, her body had been opened, and each of her internal organs removed and inspected. Samples of urine, bile, blood, CNS fluid and stomach contents had been collected. A diamond-bladed surgical saw had circumnavigated her cranium, and its contents removed en masse. Slices were taken from various sections of her cortex and slides were prepared.

The dead don't complain.

Doctor Cecelia Chao stood over the corpse tying off sutures along the lengthy vertical incision. She worked meticulously while a digital recorder captured her verbal commentary.

"...And the cause of death is asphyxia, the proximal result of a crushed trachea. Death to be ruled a homicide."

A knock on the lab door distracted her. She paused the recorder.

"Yes?"

Detectives Calderas and London stepped into the autopsy room.

"Ah, good morning, detectives. So sorry you didn't get by earlier," Dr. Chao said, peeling off latex gloves.

"We've been busy," Calderas explained.

"I understand."

London asked, "So what's your professional opinion, Doc? Are we looking at number four?"

Doctor Chao crossed to the stainless steel basin and turned the faucet on hot. She proceeded to scrub her hands, paying scrupulous attention to each individual digit.

"Similar method of strangulation. Obvious signs of intercourse without the presence of semen. The biting behavior. Yes, detective, I would have to say that in all probability, this is the fourth victim."

Calderas folded her arms. "Imagine that. A serial killer who's into safe sex. Go figure."

"This guy thinks he's clever. He wears a rubber so he won't leave DNA evidence behind," London commented.

"Guess our perp missed the outcome of the O.J. Trial... the first one." Max quipped.

Doctor Chao finished drying her hands.

"I'll be sending the case file to Doctor Ehrnquist at the forensic odontology lab for review."

London frowned. "This hump's raped and strangled four women..."

"That we know about," Calderas interjected.

"Four women that we know about," London continued, "And all we have are a set of tooth prints... Now how often do you see that?"

Max glanced at the girl's corpse and grimaced. Her instincts told her that the predator responsible for this had more going for him then mere luck. He was smart. And he was cagey. Cagey enough to blend in when he was on the prowl for hookers, and smart enough to know that water washes away all sins.

The northern branch of the jet stream had dipped seven hundred miles south of where it should typically have been, resulting in a freakishly wet November and December for Los Angles. All four victims were found in hilly areas, and all had been left out overnight in the rain. It hadn't taken long to wash away hair and fiber evidence, as well as DNA, footprints and tire tracks.

The only physical evidence linking killer to victims was a set of dental impressions, and the detectives would hate to base a multiple-murder case on that alone.

*"My only regret in the theater is that I could
never sit out front and watch me."*
-John Barrymore

7

Trevor Stone's Acting Workshop in Hollywood was
founded in 1996. That was precisely two years after Trevor's once white-hot star had dimmed, and right around the
time the creditors started seizing assets.

Trevor's rock bottom came the day the bank repo'ed
his beloved Mercedes. Considered the ultimate pussy-magnet of its era, the sleek, black BMG-converted 600
series sedan was Trevor's pride and joy. The thought of
life without 'Herr Heimlich' was almost too much to contemplate.

As he leaned against the doorjamb and watched the
tail lights of the tow truck descend the driveway of his
Hollywood Hills home, Trevor knew something had to be
done. And right away.

The very next morning Big T hit the street, a man
with a plan! By mid-afternoon he'd forked over nine crisp
Benjamins in exchange for three months advance rent on
a bungalow, a block off Hollywood Boulevard. The price
was steep for the area, but Trevor could hardly quibble,
given his current credit history.

A couple of days later, Trevor utilized several more
Benjamins from his rapidly diminishing stash. This time
the cash bought him a full back-page ad in 'Actors Log', a
film industry rag sheet read by every wannabe in town.

Ten Percent -Hollywood Can Be Murder

The ad copy announced the Grand Opening of The Trevor Stone Acting Workshop. It hyped Trevor's recent TV show, 'Bear Mullen', as well as his extensive background in legitimate theater.

Hollywood is a major breeding ground of fantasy. Always has been. Always will be. And because of this, it should be no great surprise to anyone that the town attracts more than its share of the psychologically impaired, as well as the gullible and naive; folks who not only believe 'Miracles Happen Every day', but are willing to shell out large sums of cash in pursuit of one particular Miracle of Miracles: Stardom.

Everybody wants to get into the act, and talent, or lack thereof, is purely in the eye of the beholder. And in 'Actors Log', the neophyte thespian can find anything he or she needs: From headshots to answering services, from dialect coaches to lists of theatrical agents. It's a money-making juggernaut that feeds on ignorance, greed, ego, and hope; four commodities of which there exists an apparent endless supply.

And Trevor Stone was about to jump onboard.

When the ad hit the street the following week a funny thing happened; the phone started ringing.

And the rest, as they say, is history.

Seventeen years had come and gone and little had changed. Trevor's classes were still held in that same shabby bungalow he'd started teaching in back in '96. And the very same ad continued its weekly run in 'Actors Log'. The only difference was it was no longer on the back cover. The ad now took up about one square inch of page real estate, lost amid a plethora of ads for acting coaches and alleged photographers, offering twenty-five dollar headshots.

31

Stardom is strictly a Seller's market. Caveat Emptor, baby.

*****

Jimmy Bodine stood at the center of the stage sweating beneath the lights. He could feel his heart rate climb as he neared the end of his self-written monologue.

"... And when I looked up I saw my mother, standing in the doorway. She had an expression on her face like a deer staring into the headlights of an oncoming car."

Jimmy waited a beat for the laughter that never came. "It was then that I realized things would never be the same between us. Elizabeth pulled the blankets up, shielding her bare breasts."

He paused, closed his eyes and concentrated hard on visualizing the image, but the gum-smacking and fidgeting wafting from the 'audience' rattled him.

"The only thought that entered my mind was... Why couldn't Mom have come home ten minutes later? Just ten minutes later... Just ten-fucking-minutes!"

Jimmy lowered his head, signaling to one and all his scene had finally concluded. The spotlight dimmed and the 'house lights' were brought up.

Returning to their senses and realizing their suffering was over, the audience responded with applause. Not raucous, happy clapping. Merely the minimal-effort, relieved, politically correct variety.

Jimmy started to slink from the stage.

A rich baritone voice projected from the back row freezing him where he stood. "Mister Bodine. Where, young sir, do you think you're going?"

"I just figured class was runnin' late and..." Jimmy began.

32

"And? And what, Mister Bodine? Did you honestly believe that you could leave this theatre without receiving critique? Is that what you thought, Mister Bodine?"

Trevor Stone rose from his chair and stretched to his full five feet, nine inches. Though forty pounds heavier than he was in his prime, his hair was still thick and imitation honey blonde. He turned his attention toward the class.

"So does anyone have any constructive criticism for Mister Bodine?"

He scanned the room for volunteers.

"No one has anything to say? Megan, how about you? What did you think of Mister Bodine's performance?"

Megan McKinnon was an extremely pretty redhead in her late-twenties who'd been attending the workshop for nearly a year. Her acting talent was nil, but the girl was an amazing performer, nonetheless. So much so in fact, Trevor had made 'special' tuition arrangements with the young lady. The lesser part of their arrangement had to do with Megan helping out in class.

Megan rose from her seat and addressed Jimmy, one freckled hand constantly fiddling with her hair.

"I like what your scene is saying, Jimmy. I really respect your honesty. The subject matter had to be extremely difficult for you."

Megan flashed a most sincere smile and returned to her chair. She thought Jimmy was kinda cute.

Jimmy nodded his head.

Trevor cast a heavy browed glance in Cody's direction.

"And what about you, Mister Clifton? Is there anything you might have done differently?"

Cody tilted his head and placed a hand to his chin, feigning intense concentration. After his brief dramatic pause Cody replied, "Well Trevor, If it were me, I'd've politely asked Mom to clear outta my room so I could finish what I'd started."

As usual, Cody's delivery was perfection.

The entire room erupted into paroxysms of laughter. Everyone except Jimmy Bodine, that is.

Cody continued, "Honestly, I think Jimmy did a good job with the material. The writing needs some polish is all."

Polish.

The visual that ran at twenty-four frames a second across Trevor's vivid imagination was that of three sweating Mexicans Simonizing a giant frozen turd. What came out of his mouth was: "Thank you Mister Clifton. I concur." Then he turned his attention to Jimmy who was doing his utmost to maintain a quiet dignity.

"I would like you to run the last few lines of your monologue once again. But first, I want you to do a visualization exercise with me."

Jimmy's preference was to vacate the stage post haste, but he realized that was completely out of the question. Trevor Stone was famous for his volcanic temper. On more than one occasion Jimmy had witnessed the verbal barbecuing of a student who'd managed to get on Trevor's bad side. As worn as he was, this student had no desire to incur the Coach's wrath.

"Close your eyes Mister Bodine and visualize the color black."

Jimmy did as commanded and tried to make the room disappear.

"Very good," Trevor continued. "Now, I would like you to picture Elizabeth in your mind."

Jimmy smiled.

"Ah, excellent," Trevor enthused. "You are both naked, laying beside each other on your bed... Her hair smells of cinnamon and she is the most perfect thing you have ever seen."

Jimmy's smile grew broader as he manifested the image in his mind.

Trevor's tone was soothing, almost hypnotic.

"Her body is so warm. She kisses you. Your tongues touch."

Trevor exhaled an "ahh," and paused for effect.

"You taste the inside of her mouth and feel your heart race. She reaches down and strokes your cock. It's your first time and you're so excited you almost forget to breathe... She directs you. And just as you're finally inside of her, you hear a noise downstairs. Nobody is supposed to be home for hours! How do you feel, Mister Bodine?"

Jimmy's eyes remain clamped and beads of perspiration accumulate on his upper lip.

"I'm scared. I don't wanna get caught."

"That's good. At first, you're scared. But you are enjoying this encounter with Elizabeth, are you not, Mister Bodine?"

"Hell yes."

Some of the girls sitting in the audience giggled, but Jimmy was oblivious. He'd suddenly made the transition that Great Actors achieve at will...

...He was fifteen years old, and back at his family's ranch, just outside of Memphis. He could see the gold-grey light of early afternoon as it filtered through the dogwoods and spilled across the desk.

As he gazed out the bedroom window of his adolescence he became aware of the subtle fragrance of cinnamon. He felt her touch and turned to face her.

Elizabeth's eyes were the color of the autumn sky at twilight, and they glittered when she smiled. She took his hand and placed it on her pussy, moaned softly as he slid a slender finger inside.

"Oooo Jimmy, just like that," she cooed into his ear.

They explored one another with racing hearts, breathing together in pleasant gasps. So engulfed in their mutual pleasure, neither heard the the front door open downstairs. Or Jimmy's mother's footsteps crossing the living room and then ascending the stairs.

Jimmy became peripherally aware something was wrong when he heard the squeal of the loose floorboard outside his bedroom door. He didn't even have time to panic before his mother called out.

"Jimmy? Jimmy, are you in there?"

Elizabeth let out a gasp as the door swung open and Jimmy's mother stepped into the room. It took several beats for his mother to fully comprehend what she was seeing.

"Oh. My. God!" She screamed in horror. "You dirty, dirty boy! How could you do such a thing!?"

She glared at her son, envisioning everything she detested about the Male of the species. An image blazed across her mind. It was an unspeakable memory of her own drunken, abusive father.

Jimmy looked into his mother's hateful eyes... and heard Trevor's voice.

"So what are you feeling, Mister Bodine?"

"I feel ashamed," the fifteen year old Jimmy responded.

Trevor's expression soured. "For what? For doing what Nature intended? What's wrong with you Mister Bodine? Where are your cojones? Now think, Goddamnit! What else are you feeling?"

Jimmy looked into his mother's eyes and felt the rage begin to grow. Those awful eyes, always watching him. Always judging him.

"I'm angry!" Jimmy screamed.

"Goddamn right, Mister Bodine! You're enraged!! And you have a right to be! You're in your room; your private area. You're not doing anything wrong. You're not hurting anyone."

Jimmy looked at his mother's scowling face.
"I'm not doing anything wrong. Elizabeth wanted me to."

"That's right Mister Bodine. It's the most natural thing in the world. And your mother's home early from her charity work. She just walked in on you and your sister's babysitter. What are you feeling, Mister Bodine?"

Jimmy's face contorted, and he wailed, "Get outta my room!!!"

"There it is! Now use all that anger and do the last lines of the scene."

Trevor took a seat in the front row beside a curvaceous blonde named Paula, placed his arm around her chair back.

"Begin," he commanded.

Jimmy Bodine opened his eyes and saw his fifteen year old reflection glaring back at him from a fun house mirror. The words came out of him like poison churned from the depths of his bowels.

"Why couldn't mom have come home just ten minutes later? Just ten minutes..."

He closed his eyes and tears began rolling down his cheeks, mingling with the sweat around his collar.

The guttural noise began from a spot so deep he'd never accessed it before. The sound grew in intensity until it became an eerie, pitiful howl; something not quite human. Jimmy Bodine spat the last line like it was burning hot bile.

"...Just ten minutes..."

The room was completely silent as Jimmy lowered his head and emerged from character.

Trevor stood up and began a slow, rhythmic applause, In short order everyone was on their feet joining in. And this time it was real!

As he stood there on the stage Jimmy's spine began to tingle. As the applause reached a crescendo he felt a rush of adrenaline course through him. It was the most amazing feeling he'd ever experienced in his thirty-eight years on the planet. It was better than sex.

As the applause died down Trevor stepped up on the stage and put an arm around Jimmy's shoulder. His tone was avuncular. "You've made an important breakthrough tonight, Jimmy. Savor it, and remember it always. Acting is 'being', and it all begins with visualization... and that, ladies and gentleman, is all the time we have for this evening. I'll see each and every one of you next week. Same time. Same station."

As Trevor walked Jimmy off the stage half the class dashed for the front door, collars up, hats on, cigarettes at the ready. Three hours was a helluva long time to go without a nicotine fix. But that was another of Trevor's rules. No smoking in class, and no interruptions.

Cody stepped up to Jimmy and clasped him on the shoulder. "That was mighty impressive."

Jimmy smiled. "Thanks, buddy. It sure felt good."

"Feel like splittin' a pitcher?"

"Why not?" Jimmy replied. "But first I gotta drain the lizard."

"I'll be outside."

Cody headed for the front door stopping briefly to schmooze with one of the students.

Megan was standing at the corner of the stage chatting with her pal, Lisa. When Cody crossed toward the exit the girls's attention was diverted. Lisa gave Megan a gentle push.

"Go on girl."

"I don't want to look too aggressive," Megan argued limply.

"Trust me, honey. Men love it when a woman gets aggressive. Go on now. No guts, no glory."

Megan shrugged and walked off. She stepped into the damp and drizzly night and felt her nipples harden from the cold. She came up behind Cody and tapped him on the shoulder.

"Hey stranger."

Cody swung around, faced the lovely redhead, and unconsciously wrinkled his nose. She was wearing a flowery scent; a fragrance he somehow found disagreeable.

"Well, hey Megan. What's cookin?"

"I uh... I was wondering if we could get together tonight. Maybe grab a beer or something."

Cody scratched an ingrown hair on his neck.

"Sorry, darlin'. I've gotta make it an early one tonight. Maybe next week, okay?"

Megan tried to hide her disappointment. "Sure, Cody. Next week..."

Megan was a great looking young woman with a body that could stop traffic. Only problem was the girl had red hair. And Cody made it a point to steer clear of red-headed women. Bad Mojo.

8

Looziana Pete's was a popular neighborhood bar on the Westside. It was loud and dark and reeked of stale Budweiser. The pitted oak floor was littered with sawdust and peanut shells. Redneck chic. At one end of the room there was a jukebox. A Dixie Chicks CD blasted a banjo and fiddle duet through two-thousand dollar, state-of-the-art speakers.

At the opposite end of the bar there were three well-used pool tables and a couple of pinball machines. A group of college kids monopolized the games, all the time laughing and knocking back 'Buds'.

Cody and Jimmy occupied one of the booths across from the pool tables. They commiserated over a pitcher. It was not their first.

"...And then the girl said..." Jimmy switched into the voice of a southern girl. "Next time, I'd like it better if you'd keep your cowboy boots on."

The alcohol was starting to make Jimmy's left eyeball wander in the direction of his right eye socket. That, in conjunction with his ridiculous southern falsetto, was too much for Cody to take. It was everything he could do to keep from blowing brew out his nose.

When he'd recovered enough to speak he said, "I guess she liked her men ridin' high in the saddle."

Jimmy cocked his head and peered at Cody through glazed eyes.

"Ya know, I never thought about it like that before... I thought the bitch was sayin' she didn't like how my feet smelled."

Jimmy's comedy timing was perfect... and he wasn't even aware of it.

When Cody'd stopped laughing he refilled their mugs and raised his.

"You one alright guy, Jimmy Bo. Here's to success. Yours and mine."

Jimmy lifted his glass with a lopsided smile plastered across his face.

"Fuck all that! Let's drink to the real thing! Let's drink to fame!"

They proceeded to clank mugs and swallow down the beer that didn't wind up splashing on the table.

Jimmy wiped his mouth with a shirt sleeve and set the mug down. His expression became comically serious.

"Talkin' 'bout success... ya know, I had the weirdest dream the other night..."

Cody paused and tried to determine if Jimmy was bullshitting him or not. When his radar proved useless he tested the water. "Weird how?"

Jimmy's expression showed discomfort. "Well, for one thing, you were in it."

Cody shifted in his seat.

"I wasn't naked, was I? 'Cause if I was naked, I don't wanna hear any more about it, okay?"

Jimmy's expression soured. "You ain't that good lookin' and I never been that drunk before."

Cody laughed and switched effortlessly into a passable German accent. "So vhy don't choo lay down on zeh sofa and taill me about your dreamz?"

"it Just felt kinda weird is all. Like Halloween. We were working on a show together. I'm not sure what show, but there was a crew and camera truck, and each of us had a decked-out RV. I'm talkin' big screen, Jacuzzi tub, the whole nine yards."

"Doesn't sound weird to me," Cody interjected. "Sounds downright ...successful."

"Well, things were goin' along real good until they were ready to shoot this scene, see? And then, all I can remember after that is being chased. And then it wasn't a show anymore! People were really out to kill me!"

Cody paused, stroked an imaginary goatee. "Ah, zis iz veddy interestink but I'm afraid your time iz up. Pay ze zecretary on ze vay out."

"Seriously, Cody, what do you think it means?"

Cody dropped the German accent. "What do you think it means, Jimmy? That's what matters."

"I don't know. Maybe it doesn't mean anything. Maybe I've just been watching too much late-night cable."

Cody thought about that for a moment. "Was it the first time?"

"First time?" Jimmy repeated.

"Ever had that dream before or was it the first time?"

"First time I ever been chased," Jimmy replied. "I'm on film sets and sound stages in a lot of my dreams."

"Yeah?"

Jimmy chuckled self-consciously. "Fuck yeah. Actually, most nights I'm this major star with my own hit show. I've got all these hot babes hangin' on me, and everywhere I go I get treated like royalty."

"Sounds like a sweet dream, Jimmy Bo."
The muscles in Jimmy's jaw flexed.

"If it's so sweet, then why do I wake up every morning feeling pissed off?"

Cody looked confused.

"I'll tell you why, buddy," Jimmy slurred, starting to get agitated. "It's because that life is the only thing I ever wanted. It's the only thing that means anything to me."

"Now that's fuckin' nuts," Cody responded. "I mean

what if you won the lottery? Would you still wanna be fuckin' around in Hollywood?"

Jimmy laughed. "For me, it's not about money."

Cody rolled his eyes. "Bullshit it ain't about the money. What the fuck do you think it's about?"

Jimmy stared unsteadily at his friend. "Christ, buddy, look around you. This is America in the twenty-first century. Any fool can make or steal a fortune. You don't even hafta be educated. But the one thing your money don't get you, my friend. And that's the Grand Prize."

"The Grand Prize?"

"Fame! Celebrity! A-list parties. Hangin' out with Jack and Bruce, Scarlett and Uma. Prime seats at the finest restaurants. Pussy up to your eyeballs. And I'm talkin' the thousand dollar a night stuff. Fast cars, boats, a Lear jet! All of it! I fucking want all of it!"

Cody laughed. "Everybody needs the proper motivation, Jimmy Bo. Sounds to me like you got yours in spades."

Cody lifted his arms over his head in an abbreviated cat-stretch.

"I hate to be the one to break up the party but I oughta be gettin' outta here 'bout now. Gotta get my beauty rest before that callback, tomorrow."

Jimmy caught the cocktail server's eye and she came over.

"Can I get you gentlemen another pitcher?" the young woman enquired.

Cody shook his head. "Just the check."

She produced a handful of tabs from a rear pocket and picked through them. She placed the appropriate one on the table and Jimmy reached for his wallet.

"Forget about it, pal. It's my turn tonight," Cody insisted.

Jimmy slapped his friend on the back. "Tell ya what, good buddy. You can pay for the next ten bar tabs after you land that part tomorrow. What do ya say?"

"Do I have a choice?" Cody asked.

"No, not really." Jimmy pulled a wad of bills from his wallet, peeled off a couple of crisp twenties and handed them to the server.

"Need change?" she asked hopefully.

"Nah, keep it," Jimmy replied, rising from the table.

"Thanks a lot, mister," she said, pocketing the bills. "Have a nice night."

"You, too," Jimmy replied, flashing a wink.
Then he turned toward Cody. "Good luck tomorrow. I'll be thinking positive thoughts for you."

"Thanks Jimmy Bo. You be sure and drive safe."

Jimmy started to pick his way through the crowd toward the front door. Just as he was nearing the exit he felt a hand reach out and grab his crotch. "What the...?"

"Hey Jimmy?" the slender blonde with the diamond stud in her nose said, pressing herself against him. "Long time, no see, baby."

"Kathy, me love, how the hell are ya?" Jimmy replied, reaching around and grabbing a handful of the young woman's muscular ass.

She pressed harder and whispered in his ear. "Hot and wet, cowboy."

"Well, we're gonna have to do something about that right away, aren't we?"

Jimmy slid an arm around Kathy's waist and the two of them sort of leaned against each other as they exited the bar.

They walked half a block to Jimmy's pickup, and then groped one another on the front seat for a few minutes, before Jimmy put the truck in gear.

Just as the tail lights of the old Ford disappeared around a corner, Cody Clifton stepped from the bar onto the slick sidewalk.

He walked the sixty paces to where he'd abandoned the piece-of-shit, slime-green Toyota. Just as he was about to unlock the door an unfamiliar voice called out.

"Hey handsome. You in the mood for a little company?"

The girl was blonde with light cappuccino colored skin, and looked to be about twenty. She was dressed in a tight blue mini that accentuated her superb flanks, and a white halter with nothing underneath. A cold breeze made her nipples strain pleasantly against the material.

Cody looked the girl over and smiled. "Who could possibly say no to you?"

The girl flashed a feral smile. "It'll cost you a hundred."

"What's your name, darlin'?"

"I used to wonder if there was a sub-human species of womankind that bred children for the sole purpose of dragging them to Hollywood."
-Hedda Hopper

9

When Shelly Monroe moved into the shabby, cramped North Hollywood house, nine years ago, the paint on the bedroom walls had been a 'Pepto Bismol' pink. In the near decade that followed, her three-pack-a-day tobacco habit had dimmed the shade down to a sickly opaque flesh tone.

The master bedroom was located at the back of the house. Its clutter was dominated in one corner by an enormous Queen Anne high back chair. Upholstering the chair were layer upon layer of Shelly's clothes.

Perched atop Laundry Hill, curled into a huge silver ball of fur and attitude, napped Boris, Shelly's seven year old Blue Point Himalayan. One rear paw twitched as the feline dreamed of chasing field mice under a swollen July moon.

When Shelly's key snicked in the front door deadbolt, two pointy cat ears snapped to attention, sensing dinner-time close at hand. When he heard the door open and the alarm's beep tone sound three times, his suspicions were confirmed.

"Boris? Shelly cooed, crossing toward the bedroom. "Boris, sweetie. Mommy's home."
Boris lifted his massive head an inch and opened his eyes to green slits. He coughed half a meow.

Shelly stepped into the master bedroom.

"There you are, baby. Are you ready for your supper?"

Shelly glanced at the mountain of clothes and wondered how they managed to accumulate so damn fast. She thought briefly about sorting through the mess and then thought again.

"I'll do it this weekend," she told herself, knowing full well she wouldn't get around to it until she was down to her last clean caftan. There just never were enough hours in any given week.

She scooped Boris up, hugged him to her breast and scratched him behind the ears.

"Mommy loves her baby Boris. Yes she does."

When they reached the kitchen, Shelly set Boris on the tile counter and removed a can of Supercat tuna flavor from the pantry. She opened the can and spooned the fragrant meat into Boris's bowl. Shelly set the bowl on the floor and Boris began to chow down.

"That's a fine cat," Shelly crooned.

Shelly crossed to the fridge, removed a Tupperware container and a corked bottle of cheap cabernet. As she scooped the prior night's pasta Alfredo into a ceramic dish, congealed creme sauce slopped to the gold linoleum.

Moving remarkably fast for a creature of his dimensions and physical conditioning, Boris lunged for the clot of gravy.

Shelly stepped gracefully over the cat and slid the bowl of pasta con cholesterol into a microwave. She punched a couple of buttons on the timer and returned to the waiting bottle of vino. Shelly proceeded to fill a water stained wine glass to within a millimeter of the brim.

An hour later, she was stretched out on the couch, in front of the TV, with Boris curled up beside her. This afternoon's DVR'ed episode of All My Children flickered on the screen and Boris purred contentedly while Shelly stroked his neck. Just a couple sips of wine remained in the bottom of the glass. It rested beside the empty bottle of cab on the formica table. A Camel filter-tip smoldered in an ashtray that was overflowing with butts. On the opposite end of the table was a stack of scripts spread out, each of which was tattooed with different colored sticky notes.

Shelly pressed a button on the remote and fast-forwarded through another series of commercials. God how she loved her DVR.

By the time the show was over Shelly's eyelids were at half mast. Boris plopped from the couch and strutted toward the bedroom.   Shelly yawned, switched off the TV and levered herself from the couch.

Time for the nightly Rituals.

It took fifteen minutes to wash off all the makeup and brush out her hair fifty strokes. Then she flossed her teeth, swished mouthwash from cheek to cheek, bent over the sink and spat. She switched off the faucet and dried her hands on a cloth.

Shelly crossed into the master bedroom, folded back the covers, sat down on the bed and leaned against the upholstered headboard. She closed her eyes and smiled. Another day done.

After a few moments she opened her eyes and reached across the cherry wood night stand. One more ritual to go. Her fingers brushed across the grips of the Smith and Wesson .38. She lifted the weapon from the night stand and held it up to the light, popped the cylinder and checked to see that it was properly fanged. Satisfied that all was well, she snapped the cylinder shut and dialed it in. She returned it to its spot on the night stand and turned off the light. Fifteen minutes later she was comatose.

*****

As she slept she time-traveled back to 1978. She could hear Eric Clapton singing Lay Down Sally, and she was nine years old once again...

...The waiting area was unusually quiet. Only two other Movie Mom/PHB (Precocious Hollywood Brat) combos were present. But then again, this was the seventh call-back for the role.

Lillian Monroe had read the script cover to cover at least twenty times. She'd run the lines with her daughter so often she could see the words when she closed her eyes. And according to the script's description of the character, Sarah, Shelly was dead on the money.

Lillian always knew her daughter had talent. Talent was never the issue. To hear it from Lillian, all of the Monroe's were gifted. The problem was there weren't a lot of roles for short, "big-boned" girls with frizzy brown hair and unfortunate noses.

But the second lead in 'Thunder Duck' was described as a short, pudgy, offbeat nine year old with frizzy hair. Lillian remembered re-reading the character description several times looking for something she'd missed.

Sitting across the room from Lillian and Shelly were the other two contenders, although Lillian was certain the one little girl simply had to be there reading for another show. After all, Lillian had never noticed her on any of the past interviews, and she was completely wrong, physically, for the role. The little girl was a nine year old blonde 'Lolita'.

The third mother/daughter team sat on a couch adjacent the receptionist station. From Lillian's estimation that had to be the competition. The little girl was taller than Shelly, and maybe twenty-five pounds chunkier. Her hair wasn't frizzy, like the script called for, but was of a particularly curly variety. And as for the little girl's features; let's just say that in the homely department she was at least Shelly's equal.

The suits had already seen the kids perform. All that was left was the waiting.

Little Shelly gazed dreamily out the window to the streets of Hollywood below and fantasized her future. She saw herself at twenty-four, and in her imagination she looked just like Sandra Bullock. She was dressed in black satin and lace, sitting in the front row at the Academy Awards. Her boyfriend was Brad Pitt's evil twin.

Looking up, she notices that the man in the tuxedo at the podium greatly resembles George Hamilton, all mahogany leather skin and shiny big teeth. Toothsome George tears open the envelope and removes the slip of paper from within.

"...And the winner for best actress is... Shelly Monroe!"

Evil Brad gives Shelly a big kiss for the cameras and the applause begin in waves. Shelly moves gracefully toward the stage touching outstretched hands as she ascends the stairs to accept her award. She steps in front of the podium and beams a smile to the house. She clasps the Oscar in her left hand and raises it above her head.

"Thank you. Thank you, one and all..."

"Shelly..."

"Huh? What the…"

"Shelly!" Lillian whispered harshly into her daughter's ear, yanking her back to the there and then. *"Did you remember all your lines?"*

"I already told you."

"Tell me again," Lillian insisted, wiping some schmutz from Shelly's nose with a saliva-moistened finger.

Shelly pulled away. *"Maaa! Stop it. You're driving me crazy."*

"Then tell me again," Lillian demanded.

"Grown men were crying, Mother. I was perfect."

The door to the casting office opened a crack, and all eyes shifted in that direction. Laughter and overlapping voices emanated from within.

The casting director, an effeminate man in his early thirties with a pencil-thin mustache and brown tasseled loafers entered the waiting area. He smiled wanly at Barbie's mom and proceeded to glide across the burgundy carpet toward the 'competition'.

Shelly held her breath and prayed harder than she ever prayed before. *"God, if you just let me have this part I promise you, you won't be sorry. I'll be good. I'll be sooo good you won't even recognize me…. What I really mean is…"*

And right beside her, Lillian prayed to her own version of a Savior.

"God, I know you haven't heard from me in a while, but I think it's time that we talked. You know, I've never asked for much. Always figured you had more important things on your mind. But today I'm askin'. Lord, today I'm begging! Please give this part to my daughter!. If you do this one thing for me, I promise I'll never ask another favor. And I'll start going to Temple every Saturday… Well, not

next Saturday. I have tickets for the Lakers, next Saturday, so if it's all the same to you, Lord, I'll start the Saturday after that..."

Brown-tassels came to a halt in front of 'the Competition' and offered his soft white hand to the mother.

"Thanks for bringing your daughter in, Mrs. Frumkis..."

Shelly and Lillian exchanged a knowing look.

"Yes!" Shelly thought to herself. "I am the best!! I knew they'd all come around some day."

'The Competition' and her mother lumbered from the building as Brown-tassels directed a glance in Shelly's direction.

"Thank you for bringing your daughter in again, Mrs. Monroe. Can't tell you how much we appreciate that."

"Oh, no problem at all," Lillian replied, positively radiating.

"Shelly's a marvelous little actress. Simply marvelous. She has so much potential, " Tassels continued.

"What do you have to say to the gentleman, Shelly?"

Shelly looked up and smiled. "Thank you."

Tassels bent neatly at the waist and patted the little girl on her frizzy locks. "No. Thank you, Shelly."

Then he straightened and faced Lillian. "Yes, your Shelly's one terrific little actress alright... but the director's decided to take the role of Sarah in a different direction."

It took Lillian several seconds for the words to register.

"A different direction?"

Lillian thrust the script beneath Tassels's cheesy mustache and fanned the pages.

"Different, how? You mean different from the writer's description in the script?" Lillian demanded, her voice strident.

"The script is merely a suggestion," Tassels tried explaining.

Lillian opened the script to one of many dog-eared pages and began to read aloud:
"Sarah is a plump and precocious nine year old with dark frizzy hair."

Lillian slammed the script shut and glared at tassels.
"The writer is describing my Shelly, is he not?"

"I'm sorry, Mrs. Monroe," he soothed. "But it is the director's decision after all."

Shelly looked up at Tassels hard-eyed.
"Yeah? Well the director's a schmuck! C'mon, mom, let's get outta here."

Shelly reached out and took Lillian's hand and mother and daughter exited the office, heads held high.

*****

Shelly awoke the next morning feeling pissed off. As usual, she had full recollection of the dream. She rose from the bed, crossed to the bathroom and gazed upon her visage in the mirror. Shelly inhaled deeply, thrust out her chest, squared her shoulders.

"The fuckin' director was a schmuck! Goddamnit! I am the best!

"All great successes are the result of cool consideration, long silence and waiting, strict self-control, and above all renunciation of intoxication and exhibitionism."
                                    -Oswald Spengler

10

The apartment building was located on the fashionable westside, with the average two-bedroom unit renting for forty-five hundred a month. Jimmy Bodine's unit was on the ninth floor, with a balcony and an ocean view. He paid seven grand a month for the privilege, or rather, the family trust did.

Frances James Bodine, Jr., forever 'Jimmy' to friends and enemies alike, was born in Memphis, Tennessee. His father, Frances, Sr., was a respected dentist with a practice that catered to the well-heeled. Doctor Bodine was three months shy of his forty-second birthday when he'd married Jimmy's mother. Janet Poe was sixteen at the time. She gave birth to Jimmy six-and-a-half months later. Three years after that, sister Katie was born.

Jimmy's childhood had been idyllic. At least the first fifteen years had been. The family had lived in a spacious house on a five acre parcel of lush green land. But childhood came to an abrupt end the day Jimmy's dad keeled over, a victim of heart disease compounded by hypertension. He was only fifty-seven.

Janet Bodine's descent into depression was rapid and complete. She was thirty-one, reasonably attractive, wealthy, and extremely available. And she couldn't remember a time when she'd felt more miserable. So Janet decided she'd do what so many others had done before her; she'd surrendered her life to Jesus and the refuge of the Church.

Janet became a regular at the Four Square Church of Jesus Christ Our Savior. She began attending Bible study classes four evenings a week and insisted that Jimmy and Katie accompany her to Sunday services.

Jimmy's little sister went along with the program, anxious to please her mother. But Jimmy was another story.

While his mother was in the throes of her religious transformation syndrome, Jimmy was seeking out his own internal Salvation; he was developing a keen interest in the opposite sex.

Then one night, in early August, Janet Bodine was behind the wheel of her Jaguar, enroute to a bible study class. Katie, as usual, was seated in the passenger seat. They were three blocks from their destination when a drunk in a three-quarter ton Dodge pickup rocketed through a red light. The authorities had estimated the truck's speed at better than sixty when it had broadsided the Jaguar, reducing it to a crumpled pile of steel, glass and plastic.   The woman who had been driving the pickup suffered minor abrasions and was able to walk away from the collision. But it took firefighters the better part of an hour to extricate Janet and Katie's mangled bodies from the wreckage.

The day after the funeral, Jimmy's non-stop party had commenced, and twenty-three years later was still going strong.

*****

The apartment floors were covered with deep plush carpeting, and the eighteen foot high cathedral ceiling in the living room was the perfect spot for 'Elvis'.

Elvis was an eleven foot tall, stuffed grizzly bear Jimmy had purchased during one of his more whimsical moments. Elvis served as the quintessential conversation piece. In honor of the holiday, tinsel hung from his ears and paws, and tiny colored lights twinkled in his pelt.

Off to the right of Elvis, there were two overstuffed couches, as well as a marble coffee table. As usual, the table was littered with marijuana droppings, as well as a collection of empty beer bottles.

On the floor beside the coffee table there were stacks of porn DVDs for viewing on the seventy-two inch Sony, high-definition flat screen.

The Bodine master suite was directly off the living room and nearly as spacious, with a king-size, four-poster bed at its center. The blankets lay in a heap on the floor.

Jimmy was still sacked out, naked and face down on the mattress. It was almost eleven and he was just beginning to come to, roused to consciousness by an overfull bladder.

He raised himself from the bed and swung his legs to the floor. He winced, touched a finger to the fresh gashes that striped his back, then remembered how they got there. He grinned at the memory. He padded across the carpet to the master bath where he examined his wounds in the mirror.

Bitch tore his ass up real good. But then again, he'd certainly reciprocated.

*****

Jimmy stepped from the bathroom with his hair dripping, clad only in a black towel. He crossed to the walk-in closet. Shirts and vests were hanging, all tailored, and in every color imaginable. Above the shirts on a shelf, were Jimmy's collection of Stetsons. Jimmy's extensive shoe wardrobe was split evenly between high-end sneakers and cowboy boots; from the most basic leathers to the most exotic, in every color a man could ever need.

It would be fair to say that Jimmy Bodine was the Imelda Marcos of shit-kickers.

Jimmy stepped from the closet holding a pair of jeans and a tee-shirt. Dressing, he crossed to the night stand beside the bed. Picking up the rolled 'Benjamin' from the mirror, he inserted one end into his right nostril. He bent his head down to the mirror and inhaled. The two-inch line of sparkling white powder disappeared.

As the cocaine rush began to clear the fog from his brain, a smile spread across Jimmy's face.

11

Cody Clifton stepped through the door to bungalow 33, on the Universal back lot, at precisely 11:15 and approached the receptionist. As he glanced around the room he saw a total of three other potential Chuck Dallas's' and a contingent of twenty-something blondes he assumed were auditioning for the role of Chuck Dallas's secretary, Cassie. People were spread out around the waiting area seated on couches and chairs. Some leaned against walls.

"Good morning, Mr. Clifton. Anita will be with you in just a few."

Cody crossed to an empty seat beside one of the young blondes. "Mind if I sit here?"

"Not at all," she replied, sliding over to give him a little room.
Cody eased into the seat, held the script loosely on his lap.

"My name's Lydia" she said, extending a delicately boned hand.

Cody took the young woman's hand in his, looked into her eyes and smiled, dialing up his cowboy charm. "Cody Clifton."

"Pleased to meet you, Cody Clifton."

Despite herself, Lydia was blushing.

"Pleasure's all mine," he replied, eyes sparkling.
Lydia giggled and lowered her voice to a stage whisper. "You'd make an amazing Chuck Dallas."

Cody cupped a hand and bent his head to whisper a reply.

"And you would be my right-hand girl, Cassie."

"From your mouth to God's ears, Cody Clifton."

The spell was broken when the door to the casting room opened and a red-headed gnome of a woman stepped into the waiting area. Her heavily lidded eyes were focused on a clipboard. She lifted her head, squinted, spotted Cody sitting across the room.

"Cody, you're up."

Cody stood, script rolled into a tight crescent held in one hand.

"Break a leg, Cody Clifton," Lydia whispered.

Cody flashed her a wink, crossed to the casting office door and disappeared inside. Anita Kasabian stepped into the office behind Cody and closed the door.

"Cody, I'd like you to meet the executive producer for 'Chuck Dallas', David Bloom."

Cody had never actually met the man before today, but he knew exactly to whom Anita K was referring. David Bloom was a major player, a well-known face in industry circles. Totally upper echelon.

David Bloom was forty-eight years old, with the physique of someone who was no stranger to the gym. Exercise relieved stress. At least that's what his cardiologist had told him. His pepper hair was perfectly coiffed, and when he stood up and offered his hand, his smile was insincere and perfect.

"Pleased to meet you, Cody. I've heard a lot of good things about you."

Cody nodded an acknowledgement.

"And these are the producers, Cody," Anita continued.

Cody's attention was directed toward a trio seated on the butter creme kid leather. None appeared much older than thirty.

"Eric Taylor."

A soft round man with a pink face and a receding blonde hairline stood and offered a hand to Cody.

"Nice to meet'cha."

The man smiled thinly and returned to his position on the couch. It was evident by his body language that Cody wasn't his choice for the role.

Cody smiled at him with feigned warmth and wondered which of the actors in the waiting area was blowing him.

"And this is Susan Schneider,"

The woman rose from the couch and gracefully extended a hand to Cody. She was tall and well proportioned, dressed in black.

Cody took her hand.

"Pleased to meet you, Susan."

"Cody."

"And you already know our writer/producer, Tom Harvey."

At thirty-six, Tom was the eldest of the trio. His beard was calico, and he wore his sandy brown hair moussed up into little nerve endings. He waved from the couch.

"Hey, Cody. Long time. No see, eh?"

Cody returned a crooked smile.

"So shall we get started?" Anita queried.

"Ready when you are," Cody responded.

Anita sat down on the love seat next to the executive producer.

"Alright. Let's try the scene that begins on page eighteen. I'll read Gail's lines."

"Great," Cody lied convincingly. He'd never met a casting director yet who could act, and Anita K was no exception. Her delivery was as dry and sterile as a medical school textbook.

Cody sat down on the chair that was positioned opposite Anita K.

"You come highly recommended, Mr. Dallas."

"And how may I be of service, Mrs. Caitlin?"

"I think someone's trying to kill me."

Anita turned the page.

"If you don't mind me askin', What makes you think so?"

David Bloom held up a palm. "Hold up a second.... I want you to take it from the top Cody. And this time give me more of a feeling that Chuck's a Southerner."

Cody's expression was confused. "You want more of an accent?"

Not at all sure what it was he, in fact, wanted, the executive producer responded, "Yeah, I think that's what it needs."

Cody flashed a thumbs-up and Anita began again.

"You come highly recommended, Mr. Dallas."

"And how may I be of service, Mrs. Caitlin?" Cody's accent was now ratcheted south of the Mason-Dixon Line.

"I think someone's trying to kill me." Inwardly he thought: "I'd like to kill you myself, you no-talent cunt. You're makin' me look bad! And that ain't easy to do!"

Cody arched an eyebrow registering concern. "If you don't mind me askin', what makes you think so?"

"I think someone took a shot at me yesterday, and today the brakes on the Bentley failed."

"That sure don't sound like coincidence to me, Ma'am. You got any idea who might want to harm you?"

Cody's delivery was flawless. He made the tired dialogue seem fresh.

"I think my husband may have something to do with it," Anita droned on.

"Why do you think your husband's involved, Mrs. Caitlin?"

"He thinks I'm having an affair."

Cody looked deep into Anita's eyes searching for truth. "Are you?"

"Mr. Dallas, I married my husband when I was barely eighteen years old. He was fifty-four at the time."

Anita suddenly changed tempo, rushing the dialogue like she was late for an appointment with her Vicodin dealer.

Cody took a thoughtful pause before responding. "Ma'am, you seem to be avoidin' the question …I don't do domestic cases. They tend to get complicated."

Having seen what he needed to see, David Bloom stopped the proceedings.

"That was very good, Cody."

Having been cut off mid-scene Cody was panicked. He thought briefly about reaching over and slapping Anita K for her 'performance'. And just as a million thoughts of failure and desperation started to rush at him, Susan Schneider spoke up.

"Cody, would you mind doing the scene once again," Susan Schneider began. "Only this time make the accent a bit more Texas and a little less South Carolina."

And then Eric Taylor added for the record, "And I'd like

to see the energy notched up a few degrees."

"Absolutely!" Anita K agreed. "Jack up the energy!"

It took every ounce of Cody's self-discipline to keep him from reaching over and throttling her.

Not wanting to be left out, Tom Harvey chimed in. "And keep in mind, Cody, Chuck Dallas is very attracted to Mrs. Caitlin."

Gazing at Anita K, Cody realized he'd have to channel Clooney to make that believable. But at least his fears were held at bay. The fear would roll down and crush him eventually. But not today.

"No problem," Cody replied easily, flashing his heartbreaker smile.

*"I've had the same goal I've had since
I was a little girl. I want to rule the world."*
                                                    -Madonna

12

The alarm went off and Shelly rolled out of bed with a groan, each individual frizzy hair on her head pointing in a different direction. Boris meowed impatiently and ran figure eights between her ankles. Shelly grunted, squatted and rubbed a palm across Boris's arched back.

"Give Mommy just a minute, sweetie-pie," she purred. "Boris will get his breakfast right after my coffee."

After breakfast Shelly said her farewells to Boris, locked up the house behind her and crossed to her beloved automobile; a 1982, bone white Mercedes Benz 280SE that looked like it had at least a million miles on it. Shelly adored the old Benz, and refused to take notice of any of the little idiosyncrasies that chronically plagued the machine.

"That's the way it goes when you drive a classic," Hans the mechanic had told her repeatedly over the years. He chanted it like a mantra every time she pulled into the garage. Hans adored Shelly and her vintage '82 Benz. She'd singlehandedly paid for more than half of his daughter's orthodonture.

Shelly shifted the Mercedes into drive thinking today was going to be a good day.

*****

By four o'clock Shelly's eyelids were at half mast and she was wishing she was somewhere else, anywhere else. Since returning from lunch, she'd suffered through two dismal acting scenes presented by 'friends' of various clients. And there were still three more sets of hopefuls in the reception area waiting to be seen.

As the young man and woman struggled to an anti-climatic finish Shelly rubbed a palm across her face.

"That was excellent Dana, Perrin. Really great! Didn't you think so, Irv?"

Irv blinked behind round lenses. "Absolutely," he agreed quickly.

Shelly stood up and offered her hand. "Someone from the office will be in touch with you shortly."

Perrin, a skinny teenager with horrific acne and a weak chin, grinned broadly at Shelly. He placed a headshot with an attached resume on her desk.

"I got my home phone, cell phone and email address on the back." He said in his nasal twang.

"That's very professional of you," Shelly replied off-handedly while ushering the pair to the exit.

"I'm picking up a batch of new headshots, tomorrow," Dana chimed in. "Would it be alright if I dropped one by?"

"Sure. Of course, dear," Shelly lied. "Just be sure and give a ring first, okay?" She thought, "So we can be conveniently out of the country."

"Whatever you say, Ms. Monroe."

Once she'd closed the door on the pair Shelly turned and glared at Irv.

"What?" he asked innocently.

"That was awful."

Feeling relieved, Irv continued, "You mean we're not going to sign them?"

"Oh fuck you very much, Irving."

And then the phone started ringing.

Shelly and Irv exchanged a long glance.

The phone continued to ring.

"So are you going to answer that, or what?" Shelly snapped.

Irv lowered his head and picked up the phone. "Monroe Talent, Irv Birnbaum speaking."

After a long pause Irv's delicate eyebrows hoisted above the frames of his glasses. He swallowed dryly. "Just one moment," he finally managed to croak.

He punched the red 'hold' button and looked up at Shelly, his eyes blinking rapidly.

"Well?"

Irv could barely get the words out of his mouth. "It's Anita Kasabian's office. They want to make a deal for Cody Clifton!"

Shelly dropped to her knees, arms raised to the sky. "Hallae-fuckin-Looyahhh!"

She looked up towards the ceiling, apparently seeing something there nobody else did.

"Thank you, Lord. I promise I'll keep up my end of the bargain."

She stood on wobbly knees and crossed to her desk, sat down. She took a deep breath and picked up the phone, leaned back in the chair.

"Anita, darling. How's my favorite casting director doing this afternoon?..."

"Fabulous, dear. Just fabulous. And you?"

"Holding my own," Shelly replied. "So what's the story?"

"The story is Cody Clifton's got the part. David Bloom gave his official blessing this afternoon."

"So maybe now's a good time to get down to the details," Shelly suggested as matter-of-factly as possible. "What are they offering?"

"Seventy-five thousand an episode," Anita replied.

Shelly felt her heart palpitate and made an unspoken oath to quit smoking once and for all... well to cut down, anyway.

"It sounds a little low to me, Anita," Shelly began noncommittally. "Wasn't I just reading the other day that CBS agreed to pay Peter Grogan a hundred and a half an episode?"

"That's hardly a fair comparison," Anita argued, "Fair Play is in its third season."

"Yeah, but it's an ensemble cast, and it's only a half-hour show," Shelly countered.

Anita tried another tack. "Mmmm... So what kind of quotes do you have on Cody?"

'Quotes' was Industry-Speak for a client's highest veri-fiable salary, with 'verifiable' being the operative descrip-tor. Shelly knew Cody had never worked a job for much over scale-plus-ten in his entire career, but that wasn't something she was going to confide to Anita K. So she did what any agent would do under similar circumstances; she punted.

"I'll have to get back to you on the numbers," Shelly lied. "We've been having computer problems all day."

The casting director knew Shelly was stalling. If Cody's quotes were anywhere in the vicinity of seventy-five grand a week, Monroe Talent would be in a different area code.

"You know it's a guaranteed thirteen episode run?" Anita added.

Shelly calculated the math in her head and nearly had an orgasm right there, sitting in the chair. Ten Percent of seventy-five thousand came to seven thousand, five-hun-dred dollars. Multiply that by thirteen episodes, kah-ching, kah-ching, and you come up with a total of just under a hundred grand. Ninety-seven thousand, five-hundred dollars, to be exact! The agency had never grossed that much in a single year since... well since never. And Shelly knew if the studio was offering seventy-five as an ice-breaker, she could probably negotiate up to ninety, maybe even a hundred grand an episode. And then, with just a bit of luck, the show would take off, and Shelly would be in the driver's seat.

"I think one-ten's more in line with today's market," Shelly stated, the numbers already crunched in that calculator brain of hers.

*****

A DVD of Clint Eastwood's Unforgiven spun in a Chinese Sony knock-off. At times the resulting image on the old school thirty-two inch tube was slowed and filled with digital artifacts.

Cody sat on an overstuffed garage-sale couch, chowing down on a dinner of chicken enchiladas from Marguerita's down the block. Blue sat at attention at his master's feet concentrating with all his being on the steaming plate of enchiladas. Cody chewed a forkful of savory chicken. He looked past the hound, his attention riveted on the scene playing on the screen.

Blue barked.

"Hush up, dog! Can't you see Gene Hackman's kickin' the shit out of Richard Harris??!! For chrissakes!"

Then the phone rang.

"Shit!" Cody cursed, clicking the remote to pause the film. He sprang from the couch and made it to the kitchen counter in six long strides, picking up the handset on the third ring.

"Hello," Cody grumbled into the receiver.

"Cody, darling, it's Shelly." The voice on the other end dripped honey. "Am I interrupting something?"

"No, not at all, Shell. Me and old Blue dog were just watchin' a movie is all. What's up?"

"Cody, are you sitting down?"

"No. Should I be?"

"Yes Cody, you definitely should be. God forbid you hear the news and pass out, hit your beautiful face on the floor."

"Oh Jesus," Cody exhaled, realizing what it was Shelly was telling him. "Oh my God, Shelly! Did I get the part?"

"Hundred-thousand an episode. Thirteen guaranteed! I'm looking at a print out of the deal memo as we speak. Studio just emailed it over. I assume it won't be a problem for you to come by the office tomorrow, say around four?"

"Jesus, Shelly, I can't believe this is happening!"

"Oh it's happening alright," Shelly assured him. Then her tone shifted, became serious. "I know you're going to think I'm some kind of superstitious fool, but I want you to be very, very careful, Cody. I don't even want you opening your own mail. You could get a paper cut and it could get infected. Hear what I'm saying?"

"C'mon, Shelly. I'm as healthy as a horse."

"You know what I mean," Shelly insisted. "No unnecessary risks, capeesh?"

There was an edge to her tone that Cody had never heard before. It reminded him of... he wasn't sure.

"Don't worry about me. I'll be extra careful," he lied. "And I'll see yah tomorrow."

"Ciao for now, darling."

Cody hung up the phone, opened up the refrigerator and took out a bottle of Miller Genuine Draft. He popped the cap and took a long swallow.

"Hey Blue, old buddy. Looks like you and me are gonna be eatin' a lot better real soon. What do you say?"

Blue gazed at him.

Cody grinned and pushed the plate of chicken enchiladas across the coffee table, directly under Blue's nose. The hound didn't move a muscle. Not a twitch.

"Well go ahead, Blue dog. It's okay."

Cody grinned as Blue wolfed the enchiladas and then proceeded to lick the plate clean. He marveled at his pal. That was one dog with a whole lot of self control. More than most people he knew.

*"Obscurity and a competence-that is
the life that is best worth living."*
-Mark Twain

13

Max sat at her desk going over the case file for the umpteenth time. Her expression was tense.

Greg London and Max Calderas were the detectives assigned to investigate what turned out to be the first of the so-called 'Coyote' homicides. That was a little more than two months ago but it seemed like two years to Max.

The first victim's name was Lily McAllister, known on the street as 'Flower Girl'. She was just three weeks shy of her twenty-first birthday when a couple of teenagers out riding mountain bikes discovered her body.

She had been dumped by the side of a road. The date was November 10th. The previous night, a squall line had drifted in along the coast, soaking the city and generally wreaking havoc.

When the detectives had arrived at the scene and viewed the victim, the first thing Max noticed was how young the girl appeared. Fair of face and skin, she reminded Max of a favorite child's doll that was broken in a fit of rage, and then carelessly discarded.

It was London who had noticed the bruising around the victim's throat and the too-familiar red-eyed stare. The coroner later confirmed manual strangulation as the method of death, showed the detectives exactly how the killer had placed his thumbs against the girl's windpipe.

London knew from his years of experience that the cause of the victim's red eyes was exploding capillaries in the viscous jelly behind the cornea. The official medical term was petechial hemorrhaging.

When the detectives ran the victim's name through the system they found two priors for prostitution and not much else. Lily McAllister aka 'Flower Girl' was a ghost. Her last known address was a transient hotel off Lincoln. The case had appeared clear cut. Flower Girl had simply picked up the wrong trick. Shit, as they say, happens.

The fact that the coroner's report stated the victim had been bitten on her breasts, neck and buttocks was an interesting side note, and nothing more. That is until two weeks later when victim number two turned up.

Christine Peters aka 'Spinner', twenty-four years old, with a history of arrests for prostitution and drugs, was found dumped in brush at the side of a dirt road off Malibu Canyon. The date was November 25th. An inch and a quarter of rain had fallen in the twenty-four hours prior the discovery. The autopsy had confirmed that victim number two had been beaten, raped and sodomized, and eventually died from asphyxia. Jagged bruises, later determined to have been caused by human teeth, marked her breasts, neck and buttocks. Impressions and detailed photographs were taken of the wounds. These items of evidence were sent to one Doctor Franz Ernquist, Chief of Forensic Odontology at the State Crime Lab, in Sacramento.

Then, on December 9th, victim number three was found.

Maria Reposa, nineteen, worked part-time as a receptionist for a cosmetics company in the valley. When her body was discovered in a hilly area overlooking Hollywood, the detectives were, at first, perplexed. Even though she had received the identical bite wounds as the other victims, Ms. Reposa didn't seem to fit the profile. At least, not at first.

When they'd run the young woman through the databases she'd come back clean. Not so much as a traffic ticket. But then, upon further digging, it began to make sense. Little Maria, the girl who had so reminded Max of her older sister that it had ached to look at her, had been living well beyond her means. When the detectives had checked out her apartment, it had been obvious that her gig at the cosmetic company wasn't covering the rent, let alone the payments on the BMW convertible parked in the underground garage. Victim number three had been living a double-life. Calderas and London had concluded that she must have gotten careless in her choice of benefactors. It only takes once. The El Lay P.D.'s caseload was concrete evidence that there were a lot of freaks roaming free out there.

After the third murder there was the usual talk of inflating the investigation to Task Force status. The Mayor and the Police Chief simply couldn't have a maniac running around slaughtering working girls. It was bad for business.

'Task Force'. London had always considered the terminology a joke. The LAPD wasn't a whole lot different from the military in that regard. 'Task Force' was synonymous with 'Cluster Fuck' as far as he was concerned. But still, the overtime would be great. And if he just kept on working sixty, seventy hour weeks, he might even get caught up on back alimony before he reached mandatory retirement age.

And then the fourth victim, Ellen Pomeroy, was found just eight days later on December 17th. It appeared The Coyote was getting bolder and killing with greater frequency. And each of his victims had been more severely savaged then the last. The Police Psychologist consulting on the case had warned of this. They were all ominous signs of a psychopathic personality approaching critical mass.

And only eight more shopping days until Christmas.

*****

The homeless woman who discovered Kathleen Becker's nude and mutilated corpse on December 21st, ran screaming into the night. Several concerned citizens had notified authorities about a raving woman running down Laurel Canyon, near Old Mulholland, and a prowler was dispatched. Within fifteen minutes a black and white was pulling up alongside a curb where a bedraggled woman of indeterminate age, lay crumpled, vomiting her dinner into the gutter.

When she was able to speak the woman told the officers what she had seen and where. With some gentle prodding reinforced by the promise of a reward, the uniforms managed to coax the woman into the backseat of the cruiser. Ten minutes later, Officers Crenshaw and Regan called in a 'one-eight-seven'.

14

When Cody stepped into the agency's shabby reception area at a little after four he could hear Garth Brooks wailing on the stereo on the other side of the wall. When he rapped on the door that separated the reception area from the main office Shelly called out.

"That you, Cody?"

"Yes Ma'am," Cody replied to the closed door.

"Well c'mon in," came the response. Cody opened the door and did an immediate double-take. Then a broad smile spread across his face and he shook his head.

Shelly stood before him. In one hand she held a half-empty bottle of Dom Perignon.

Irv grinned goofily and handed Cody a champagne glass.

"Congratulations, Cody!" Irv said. "I always knew you were going to hit."

"Thanks, pal. That's mighty nice thing to say," Cody replied, accepting the glass.

Shelly reached over and filled it to the brim and then refilled hers and Irv's. Then she hoisted her glass.

"A toast!" she began.

Irv and Cody raised their glasses.

"To Cody, and the Good Life!"

"Here, here," Irv agreed.

Cody smiled, and they clanked glasses. He swallowed some of the effervescent liquid and felt his nose tingle.

"Mmmm, this is real tasty stuff, Shell."

"Drink up now Cody. You got a lot of catching up to do," Irv advised in an ever-so-slightly slurred voice.

They knocked down the first bottle in a manner of minutes and were well into the second when Shelly began her gentle segue into the subject of business.

"Now Cody, I want you to sit back and listen very carefully to the things I'm about to tell you. Will you do that for me, honey?"

"Absolutely," he replied, easing into the orange sofa.

"The first thing you're going to need, my dear, is a publicist. Abby Singer is top-notch. So is Freddie Mendez over at MPL."

Cody slapped back the remaining Dom in his glass and held out his arm to Irv for a refill.

"Jesus, Shelly. Can I afford that kinda thing right away?" Shelly put a damp palm on his shoulder. Her expression was all business.

"Cody, my darling, you can't afford not to! This show is the opportunity of a lifetime. We have to capitalize on it, ride it for all it's worth. And besides that, you're going to need all the write-offs you can get."

As the truth of his impending financial success was beginning to sink in, Cody's eyes started to mist up. With an embarrassed swipe of a shirt sleeve the emotion was once again stifled. He put his arms around Shelly and gave her a hug.

"None of this would be happening if it weren't for you," he stated honestly. "And I promise you Shelly, I'll never forget it."

Shelly thought: "Goddamn right you'll never forget! You're signed, baby. I own your ass! ...Well, Ten Percent of it, anyway."

"That's such a sweet thing to say," Shelly began. "But all I did was send you out on an interview. You're the one who beat out every actor in town for the part."

"You shouldn't be so modest, Shelly," Irv interjected. "You did a lot more than send Cody on the interview. You also negotiated one helluva deal for him."

Irv hoisted his glass once again.

"A toast to the Mother of all Negotiators and the Prince of all Cowboys. Mazeltov!"

They all laughed and clinked glasses and sloshed back more champagne.

"But seriously, Cody," Shelly continued. "You just concentrate on being the best Chuck Dallas you can be and leave the rest to me. I'll make sure you have all the right people watching out for you."

Cody looked directly into Shelly's eyes and spoke from the heart.

"I won't let you down, Shelly. I promise I won't."

Now that he was sufficiently lubricated Shelly felt it was time to unload the rest of the speech on him.

"If you want to promise me something, Cody, promise me this. When you've become a superstar, I'll never hear anyone saying what a colossal prick you turned into."

Cody flashed his riverboat gambler smile. "That'll never happen, Shelly. I promise."

"It happens all the time in this town, Cody. People start believing what the press write about them and their egos over-inflate. I've seen a lot of careers wind up in the toilet because of just that kind of stupidity. An example that comes immediately to mind is your beloved acting coach, Trevor Stone."

Cody looked at Shelly with stunned disbelief. "What about Trevor?"

"You ever see his show, Bear Mullen?"

"Sure," Cody replied. "They're still re-running it on cable."

"Back in '91, when Bear Mullen went into production, young Mr. Stone was a rising star. The hair, the eyes, the voice. The man had winner written all over him. Everything went well the first season and Trevor was a pleasure to work with. He made an all out effort to treat everyone with respect. Didn't matter if they were a P.A. or an A.D., Trevor was a gentleman to everyone.

"So what happened?"

"He got hot is what happened and the show took off. Ratings blew through the roof! And by the time the show was halfway into the second season things began to change. Trevor changed. He started missing his call times, and soon progressed to not showing up at all. He cursed and belittled the crew, and generally made enemies of everyone. And it was right around then that he left the agent who'd discovered and nurtured him, and went over to William Morris. Didn't even have the class to tell her in person. He had his attorney send her a letter."

Cody absorbed her words. "Jesus Shelly."

"And soon thereafter a rumor started circulating that old Trevor had a serious drug problem."

"So that's what it was," Cody said, shaking his head back and forth.

"Not in and of itself, it wasn't. This was the nineties, remember? Cocaine was considered de rigueur for the era and would have been overlooked if not for all the enemies he'd made. By the time the show got cancelled, after the third season, most of the crew had moved on. Several had moved up. One of those people on The Ladder was a man by the name of David Bloom."

Cody's eyebrows raised. "You talkin' the same..."

Shelly cut him off with a nod of her head. "David Bloom bailed after Bear Mullen's second season and took a job in development. Within a year he was producing and Trevor Stone was just one more unemployed actor. Trevor couldn't even get arrested after that, let alone land a speaking role. Lucky thing for him he had an aptitude for instructing, otherwise good old Trevor would be signing autographs in Reno shopping malls by now."

Cody just kept shaking his head. "Yah know Shelly. I never could figure out why a talented guy like that wasn't getting out."

"Well now you know. Just remember, the toes you crush on the way up are often attached to the asses you kiss on the way down. I trust you're a smart enough boy not to make the same mistake."

"C'mon Shelly. You know me better than that."

Shelly's smile was completely false as she stared through the cowboy actor. "Yes I do, Cody. I surely do.

15

Calderas and London worked into the wee hours of the morning at the Fryman Road crime scene. It had been a complete and total cluster fuck due to the fact that both the Hollywood and Valley divisions claimed jurisdiction. It took the detectives nearly an hour to sort through the red tape, and that was before they even got a look at the body.

The dead girl's wallet had a California Drivers license that was issued to one Kathleen Leonore Becker, age twenty-three. The photograph was of a fresh faced blonde girl who looked like she could be in toothpaste commercials or print ads for beach wear. Calderas had a hard time putting the face from the photograph to the face of the victim at her feet.

Max got home just before three. She undressed and climbed into bed, stared at the ceiling for what seemed like hours, before she finally gave up on sleep. She spent the next several hours padding around the apartment, running on nervous energy. She tried picking up a novel to get her mind onto something other than sex and death, but found she couldn't concentrate. The faces of murdered girls kept floating in her mind.

*****

Kathleen Becker's autopsy was scheduled for the afternoon. Doctor Chao and her assistant had just begun taking scrapings from under the victim's fingernails when detectives Calderas and London were ushered in.

"Ah, good afternoon detectives," Chao began.

"Afternoon, Doc," London replied. "You sounded excited on the phone. What's up?"

Doctor Chao looked up from what she was doing. "Our killer is getting sloppy. This time he left something behind."

For the first time in two months Max felt the curtain of clouds begin to lift.

"What did you find?" Calderas enquired.

Doctor Chao removed a pair of glassine envelopes from a tray and presented them to Calderas.

"In envelope one there is a single strand of blonde hair that was found entangled with one of the victim's earrings. And in envelope two there are several blonde hairs collected from the young woman's scalp."

"And?" Calderas coaxed.

"In sample number two, the color came out of a bottle. Not so for sample number one. That hair is natural. Unfortunately there is no root attached, so there is no way to DNA type."

"It's a start," London replied, returning the evidence envelopes to the coroner.

"Good work, doc," Calderas congratulated. "Give us a holler when you get the results back from the toxicology lab."

"Will do, detective," Chao replied, waving a latex covered hand.

Calderas's expression was pensive as the two detectives walked through the building. She didn't utter a word until they'd reached the cruiser.

"We have to get this son of a bitch, Greg. He's starting to   keep me up nights."

"Don't worry Max. We'll get him," London replied with total conviction.

Deep in her heart Calderas knew her partner spoke the truth. They'd throw a net over this sicko sooner or later, and that was a certainty. The problem was Max didn't know how many more dead girls she could look at and still manage to keep her soul intact.

"A fan club is a group of people who tell an actor he is not alone in the way he feels about himself."
-Jack Carson

16

The celebration at Shelly's office continued into the evening until at one point Irv suggested they consider getting dinner. Anything to help sop up a portion of the alcohol they'd consumed.

Cody had begged off, promised them another time, soon. Shelly wanted to call him a cab but Cody told her he'd planned to walk.

As soon as he'd stepped from the office building into the cool night he began to feel better. He hadn't noticed before today, but Shelly's office had a definite odor to it; something musty and not altogether clean. Sitting in there for so many hours with the lousy ventilation and Shelly's heavy perfume had given Cody a monster of a headache.

He walked east down the boulevard massaging the back of his neck with one hand. After he'd traveled several blocks the neighborhood began to change. The store fronts became closer together and the graffiti more colorful. Pawnshop windows displayed all manner of electronic gear, from the latest and greatest in grey market gaming consoles and cell phones to vintage electric guitars.

A few blocks further the heavenly scent of Thai Coconut Curry overcame Cody's thoughts, and he spent the next couple of hours at Madame Shu's Thai Food Restaurant. He feasted on Shrimp Panang and Pad Thai and drank copious amounts of sake and Thai iced tea.

And he contemplated his future.

One-hundred thousand dollars an episode! Cody would be trying to wrap his mind around that one for awhile. One-hundred thousand dollars was more money than he'd ever made in a year, let alone in eight days. At this point it was just too many zeros for a country boy to comprehend. The one thing he knew for certain was his life was about to change, and change Big Time. It was going to take awhile for the numbness to wear off. He just had to allow himself the luxury of Time.

*****

It was just after midnight when the banged up green Toyota pulled up along the curb in front of the duplex. Cody unfolded himself from the vehicle and stepped through the yard, headed for the front door.

No sooner was the key turned in the lock then old Blue began to bark. Cody opened the door and slid inside.

"Jesus, Blue! Shut the fuck up, already. You're gonna wake up the whole neighborhood."

Cody knelt on one knee and scratched Blue behind the ears.

"You been a good dog today, have you?" Cody enquired with a detectable slur to his drawl.

Blue looked up at his master, tail wagging.

Cody struggled out of a well worn pair of cowboy boots and padded into the kitchen. He noticed the flashing red light on the answering machine. He paused by the counter and pressed a button on the box.

Cody scooped some dog food into Blue's dish and set the bowl on the floor. As Blue dove nose first into his dinner the speaker on the answering machine chirped.

The first message was a wrong number. Someone looking for Barbara Fuentes. Cody received an average of

85

ten of those a week. The second message was from a salesman pimping some Hawaiian time-share. And then the machine started to play the third message.

"Uh Cody, this is Ernie, over at the garage. If you want to swing by in the morning, your truck will be ready to go. Parts and labor came to one-thousand, seven-hundred and eighty-eight dollars. Sorry buddy. All I can say is, if you're planning any more off-road adventures in the near future, you might want to start thinking about trading that old bitch in on a real four-by-four. Later."

"Thank God." Cody exclaimed to Blue. "I don't think I could stand one more day drivin' around in that Japanese rollerskate."

PART 2

CHUCK DALLAS, PRIVATE INVESTIGATOR

"Greed is Good."
                    -Gordon Gecko

17

The new Year (2013)

Cody was on payroll at a hundred grand an episode as of January 6th. And a week before that, Shelly gave the landlord thirty days notice of her definite intention to vacate the premises. The Monroe Talent Group, LTD., had finally arrived, or was just about to, and new digs was the first order of business.

"You have to have a classy office if you want to attract classy clientele," was how she'd explained it to Irv. "And besides, it's all deductible."

Irv nodded in agreement.

Shelly had noticed Irv was even more agreeable than usual and actually found it a rather attractive quality. They perused the real estate section of the local paper and made phone calls regarding leases in upscale buildings.

Decisions, decisions. Should it be a Beverly Hills address? Always impressive on fine stationery. Or perhaps Century City? Nah, too many goddamn lawyers. Studio City? Absolutely no fuckin' way!

The thought of moving the office to The Other Side Of The Hill had never crossed Shelly's mind. Owning a residence Over There was one thing; an accommodation based solely on taxation and economic factors, but never would she consider locating her business there!

After all, the idea was to attract a classier, higher-priced clientele, not the other way around. Now on the other hand, if she were thinking about opening an agency that specialized in Adult Entertainers, the hot, carbon monoxide choked San Fernando Valley would be her first choice. But that wasn't the case, so Shelly and her cohort checked out suites on the Westside and Santa Monica. Ridiculously overpriced square footage at half the asking price, but worth inspecting, nonetheless.

"Never know how things are going to shape up for the future," she'd confided to Irv. "If the show takes off, Cody could wind up becoming a superstar. Another Brad Pitt or George Clooney... Any idea how much George Clooney's agent made last year?"

"A shitload!" Irv answered correctly.

"Fuckin-a right!

It took them a little more than a week before they found a place that suited them. The building was located in the Beverly Hills zip, but only by mere inches. The imaginary dotted line that separated El Lay from Beverly Hills ran down the center of the street. Office buildings on the opposite side of the avenue rented for about a third less scratch. Shelly signed a one year lease with two, one-year options.

In one small leap the Monroe Talent Group, LTD. managed to quadruple their usable square footage while simultaneously increasing their monthly nut by a factor of twelve. But it was so very tasteful, and each of them had their own private office.

But what had really clinched the deal for Shelly wasn't so much the Beverly Hills address as it was the minis-cule balcony the larger of the offices opened onto. It was there that Shelly could smoke to her heart's (dis)content, without incurring massive penalties for violating OSHA workplace hazard laws; a document she was only vaguely aware of, and was now expected to live by. For the Monroe Talent Group would be expanding. And that, unfortunately, meant hiring employees. And with employees came payroll taxes and workmen's compensation insurance, as well as a whole litany of must-dos and can't-dos. The price of doing business, as they say.

Shelly had managed to avoid most of the red tape all these years by staying small, and by paying Irv as an independent contractor. But a new era was dawning for The Monroe Talent Group, LTD. Essential new employees would include a receptionist as well as a full-time book-keeper.

That delighted Shelly to no end. Shuffling papers had never been her forte. Drudgery, pure and simple, and well beneath the dignity of a Real Player like Shelly Monroe, Agent To The Stars...
But the thing that tickled Shelly the most was the fact that the staff were a deductible business expense.

Maybe she was riding Cody's coat tails into the Big Leagues, but how she capitalized on the opportunity was strictly up to her. It was all in the Follow-Through.

In every business the Players are judged by their plum-age, and the film industry is no exception. If you expected to play in the Majors, you'd damn well better be dressed in League-Approved attire. For Shelly, that meant no more Hawaiian-print caftans or high-top sneakers.

This was Shelly's big chance, and she had no intention of blowing it. So she made one of the smartest business decisions of her life. Not completely trusting her own taste, she contracted with Mister Julian of Beverly Hills, Stylist Extaordinaire. The man's hourly was beyond exorbitant, but he was the best in town, with a clientele studded with

Hollywood Stars and Power Players. If you wanted to turn a trout into a poodle, Mister Julian was your man, so to speak.

*****

The building on Camden Drive had a polished granite facade and four huge trees lining the sidewalk in front. Parked alongside the curb was a vintage seventies Rolls Royce convertible, glossy black lacquer over tan Connolly hides. The personalized plates read: 1JULIAN.

Shelly stepped from her Mercedes, fed the meter a fistful of quarters, and hurriedly crossed in the middle of the street. She opened the door to the establishment and stepped inside.

The reception area was stark, with white-washed walls and concrete colored furnishings. The floor, polished black marble, reminded Shelly of a mausoleum.

The receptionist greeted her. "My name is Kim," he said. "I will be assisting Mister Julian this afternoon."

Shelly clasped his hand. It had all the firmness and texture of a dead mackerel.

"Pleased to meet you, Kim. Take me to your leader."

Kim offered a thin smile. "The prep rooms are this way."

Shelly followed Mister Julian's assistant down a hallway, past a half-dozen closed doors. Kim turned the handle on door number seven and Shelly stepped inside.

"Mister Julian will be attending to you shortly," Kim offered with a polite smile. Then he excused himself.

Shelly glanced at her image in the full length mirror and immediately began having second thoughts. Did she really need to put herself through this? Was this expense really necessary? Or was there some other way?

It was at that very instant when Mister Julian made his Grand Entrance, accompanied by an entourage of assistants. They glided across the floor as a single unit and surrounded Shelly like a school of piranha.

At six foot-three, Mister Julian towered above his assistants. His limbs were long and his hands thin, and he was particularly narrow across the shoulders and hips. The Master Stylist's posture was that of an irritated heron. He possessed an olive complexion complemented by moist dark eyes and short, curly salt and pepper hair. He wore a pencil-thin mustache and an emerald stud in his right earlobe. The man was flawlessly attired in a truly elegant forest green Armani suit.

"Oh my God!" Mister Julian exclaimed as he gently probed Shelly's coif with an extended digit. "Whomever did that to her should be flogged and given a full Brazilian on National TV."

Mister Julian spoke as if the client wasn't present in the room.

Shelly flushed and turned her head, rubbing a self-conscious palm across her wavy brown locks.

"And the color is all wrong! The woman's an obvious Winter. We need to lighten and tighten. Lighten and tighten!" Mister Julian proclaimed.

He tilted his head this way and that and slowly looked the new client over. Up and down, side to side.

Shelly felt like a cow at a livestock auction.

"Well then... I need the Prada and Armani samples right away. Manolo and Jimmy Choo, too! Shaakira, go. Chop, chop!"

A lovely young woman with high cheekbones and skin the color of milk chocolate scurried from the room.

"Okay, here we go," Mister Julian began. "One: Under penalty of public dismemberment, keep this woman away from all shades of red."

Kim lowered his head and began scribbling on a note pad.

"Two: Shoulder pads go in every one of her jackets to help balance out those hips."

Mister Julian shook his head. "But make a notation not to overdo! We don't want her to end up looking like Dwayne Johnson in drag."

Kim wrote furiously as Shaakira returned with an armload of sample outfits and shoe boxes.

"Three," Mister Julian continued. "No flat shoes. And I mean never! High heels only. The taller the better. We need to lengthen those legs! Let's try to create an illusion of height, shall we?"

Shaakira held up one of the sample jackets.

"Four: Call Clarence over at Andy Compte's. Tell him we're going to need more time than I had originally anticipated. If he whines, tell the bitch I'm calling in that favor... Something simply must be done with that hair."

Mister Julian stood back, placed his hands on his narrow hips, and squinted. In his mind's eye he could see what the "After" Shelly would look like. His lips drew into a slight smile.

Mister Julian simply adored a challenge.

*****

The move to the new offices went remarkably well, all considering. On a Saturday, at promptly eight am, four swarthy men, the smallest of whom was the size of your average Fridgidaire, showed up in front of the dilapidated Hollywood Boulevard office building.

Shelly supervised as the four men sweated and humped her inventory from the one building to the other and thanked god when the last box was slid from the dolly onto the fine grey carpet.

When the Beef brothers had departed with check in furry hand, Shelly popped a bottle of Dom and toasted the new location with Irv. It was the last leisure either of them would see for the next thirty days.

On Monday morning Shelly showed up at nine-thirty, dressed to impress, in an earth-tone Ralph Lauren Power Suit, matched with Jimmy Choo shoes that tortured her feet. Even so, Shelly was in particularly fine spirits as the task of re-organizing began.

After a staff had been hired, Shelly issued an edict calling for a severe culling of the client list.

"Gotta get rid of the loxes," was how she'd put it.
This was a particularly arduous task for Irv. He had heart palpitations every time Shelly made him send out one of those letters. So Irv would play the part of Lox Advocate, arguing each case with Shelly, who served as the penulti-mate judge, jury and executioner.

It was nice to be Queen.

"How about Tank Garcia?"

"Gone," Shelly replied without taking a beat.

"Cleo Hardy?" Irv continued, scratching a red check mark beside Tank Garcia's name.

"Outta here."

"Patricia Herndon?"

"Buh-bye."

"What about Ernie Higgins?" Irv queried, sharpie poised.

"Ya know Irv, I've got a soft spot for Ernie. He stays."

The fact was Ernie Higgins was a mediocre actor who had trouble remembering his lines. But he was also a wealthy older gentleman who delighted in presenting his friends and agents with extravagant gifts. Naturally, Ernie Higgins's favorite holiday was Christmas. Last year he'd sent the agency a case of Cristal. The year before that it had been a Baccarat crystal decanter and four tumblers. As far as Shelly was concerned, Ernie could remain a client just as long as she had a franchise.

Irv didn't start making nervous noises until the leather furnishings began to arrive.

"Jesus, Irv. Lighten up already," Shelly teased. But the price tag on the charcoal sectional caused Irv's eyes to momentarily leave their sockets.

"Eleven thousand dollars for a couch?" he stammered. "Isn't that a little over the top, Shell?"

"What's wrong, darling? Don't you think it's beautiful?"

Irv glanced over the piece with an appraising eye and had to agree with Boss Lady. It was stunning. Glove-soft tufts of top grain leather that simply shrieked luxury. And the smell! It was better than sitting in a new Bentley on a summer day with the windows rolled up. And then Shelly reminded him that the real beauty of it was the fact that every penny spent on office furnishings was completely deductible.

"Just pretend our sweet Uncle Sammy gave it to us as an office-warming gift."

What could he say? Boss Lady was right on all counts. Everything they bought that was even remotely business-related was fully deductible. And it was Shelly's star client, after all, who was covering the bills. Best thing for Irv to do was relax.

But as the new office continued to hemorrhage money, Irv started to hear that annoying inner voice, the one that always warned him not to strive too hard because his destiny was to be a failure.

On the opposite end of the spectrum was Boss lady. Shelly always knew she was going to Make It Big, never suffered any of the doubt that had plagued poor Irv his entire life. Shelly took it as a foregone conclusion and wasn't bothered by each passing birthday spent living in the nine-hundred square foot house in NoHo. She figured that with each year that Success passed her by, her fortune, when it finally arrived, would have multiplied to unspendable proportions.

She enjoyed many evenings elaborating on the theory to Boris the cat, who always seemed to be in full agreement.

*****

On March 3rd, in the middle of the morning rush hour, Shelly's beloved Mercedes stalled at a traffic light, and then refused to turn over. Two hours later she was having a face-to-face conversation with Hans. The mechanic offered condolences and informed her in the kindest of tones that the old Mercedes's engine had finally shaken apart. He'd smiled consolingly and assured her that he could rebuild the engine, or find a new one to replace it. He'd said he'd have to call around for prices, and that he'd get back to her in a couple of days.

Shelly left the garage feeling funereal.

When Hans got back to her four days later, the news wasn't good.

"Ah, it's not so bad Shelly. Nine thousand's a good price. Check around and you'll see how good. And you know when I do a job, it's done right."

Shelly recognized a sales pitch when she heard one.

"Let me get back to you tomorrow, okay Hans?"

"Sure. No problem. Tomorrow will be fine, just fine... Oh, by the way, did I mention the price includes new oil pump, new water pump, and all new gaskets and hoses?"

"Thanks, Hans. Talk to you tomorrow."

Shelly hung up the phone and pressed a red button marked INTERCOM. "Irv, darling, I just got the coroner's official word. My dear old Mercedes has crossed over to the other side. Arrangements will have to be made."

"Jeez, Shell, what're you going to do?"

"What do you think, schmuck? I'm going to get another car. I was hoping you'd accompany me to the local Mercedes dealer this afternoon."

"No problem," Irv responded evenly, over the objections of that inner-voice of his, that just kept getting louder and louder.

"The TV business is… uglier than most things. A cruel and shallow money trench… a long plastic hallway where thieves and pimps run free and good men die like dogs."
-Hunter S Thompson

18

It was still dark outside when the alarm clock by Cody's bed sounded. He opened one bloodshot eye and groaned in protest. Two minutes later, by sheer force of will, he rose from his cozy nest and trudged off toward the john. Blue raised an eyebrow half an inch in greeting just as the bathroom door smacked shut.

Cody stared into the mirror and wasn't pleased by what glared back. In just a couple of months' time his reflection had begun taking on a distinctly worn countenance. And when he looked close he could see faint lines developing around the corners of his eyes. The very same lines that, over the course of years, would multiply and etch deep, ushering in his transition from Leading Man to Character Actor…

Unless, that is, he got lucky. Will Smith or Tom Hanks lucky. Cody certainly had the potential. Getting There was the trick.

In the meantime, the schedule for Chuck Dallas was a real ball-breaker. Cody, being the title character, was in damn near every scene. This translated to fifteen hour workdays, and in Cody's case, the consumption of mass quantities of coffee.

As the weeks dragged on and Cody's energy flagged, he got wind of other stimulants readily available around set.

But then he'd remember.

It was as if every time he had an impure thought, this miniature Shelly, all loud clothes and attitude, invisible to everybody but him, of course, would suddenly materialize on his shoulder. She'd light up a tiny cigarette and start puffing away. And she'd warn him, in between exhalations of smoke, not to be a schmuck like Trevor Stone.

Shelly had become his personal Dragon-Lady Protector, and he felt a certain perverse comfort in the belief she was watching over him.

It was strange for Cody to allow someone to get so close to him. Especially a woman. The areas in his frontal lobes that allowed him to feel affection had atrophied long ago. It had been an unconscious act of self-preservation performed by a wounded and confused fourteen year old.

But that was the past. And the past was always best left buried… Besides, Cody had plenty to keep him occupied right here in the present.

His day began at six am, and if he was lucky he'd be home most nights by nine. From nine until eleven Cody would attempt to unwind from the day's grind while simultaneously studying the next day's dialogue. On weekends, when he should have been resting up, Cody was busy attending publicity events and A-List parties. It was a helluva way for a grown man to make a living, and the pace was kicking Cody's ass.

Cody developed small personal rituals as a defense against stress. For instance, after each episode of Chuck Dallas was completed, Cody would put a check mark on a calendar he kept on the wall in his custom Airstream trailer. After today, it was nine down, four to go.

Cody held that thought a moment and felt reassured. He smiled at his reflection because he knew he was going to get through this. Just hold on for another month was all.

The doorbell rang promptly at six-thirty.

"C'mon in a second, Felix," Cody called to the closed door. "I'll be right with you."

Cody's driver stepped inside.

Felix was a paunchy man in his fifties, with wavy, shoe-polish black hair and sorrowful eyes.

Cody crossed from the kitchen with a steaming mug in his hand.

"Like some coffee? Jamaican Blue Mountain. I just ground the beans a minute ago."

"Thanks, Mister Clifton. Don't mind if I do."

Cody scowled. "Felix, how many times I gotta tell ya? I'm not comfortable with folks callin' me Mister. Name's Cody.

"Right. Sorry Mist... er, Cody. I'll work on it, I promise," Felix replied.

*****

Jimmy Bodine opened one bloodshot eye and rolled over in bed. He was fully expecting to bump up against Megan's aerobicized ass with his good-morning hard on, but it wasn't meant to be. He grasped his organ and squeezed.

"Baby, where are yah?" he called out.

A minute later Megan glided into the bedroom clad

in black panties and a pair of shocking blue knee-high socks. The colors contrasted nicely with her fiery hair and fair complexion. In each freckled hand she carried a mug of coffee.

"Better get up or you're gonna be late for your call," Megan scolded, placing the mugs on one of the night stands.

Jimmy reached over and scooped her back into bed, planted wet kisses along her neck.

"Jimmy!"

He pressed against her with urgency. "You smell good."

"You're gonna be late," she warned.

"Don't care," he replied, massaging the silky material covering her mound.

Forty-five minutes later, Jimmy was behind the wheel of his pickup truck, inching along in traffic, enroute to the studio.

When he arrived at the guard shack he was directed to crew parking. He then spent the next twenty minutes endlessly circling the lot, looking for a parking space.

*****

At five minutes after seven, Felix pulled the Town Car alongside the sound stage. Cody and Blue emerged from the rear compartment and crossed toward Cody's trailer.

"Hey, good morning Cody."

The jovial voice that greeted him came from the assistant director, one Sterling Carpenter. Sterling was thirty-five and a mountain of a man. Everything about the man was on a grand scale, especially his appetites.

"Mornin', Sterling."

Cody's next stop was with the folks over at the Hair and Makeup trailer, universally known, among casts and crews everywhere, as 'The Fluff Brigade'. If you wanted the inside scoop on anything concerning the show, these were the people to dish with. Larry and Karen knew where all the bones were buried. And better still, in whom they were currently buried.

Lately, a lot of the conversations revolved around Cody and how he was looking a bit rough around the edges.

While Cody's face and hair were being prepared, dozens of other tasks were simultaneously underway. Lighting was being rigged and cables were being run. Microphones and booms were being tested and inspected. Notes were being exchanged and compared.

Episodic television was a collaborative effort, but with logistics that would give your average corporate comptroller an aneurysm. Seventy hour weeks were the norm. If the job took less, then that was a good week. And if it took more you'd suck it up and smile about it. Because Rule Number One was, and always would be: The Show Must Go On.

And then there was Rule Number Two which was almost as important: Nobody likes a whiner.

Followed closely by Rule Number Three: You can rest all you want when you're unemployed.

True, there are some major stars and directors who are complete prima donnas. But as a general rule, Show Business ain't for pussies.

*****

The director calling the shots on this episode was a gun-for-hire by the name of Reed Sloane. Reed was a diminutive man with an outstanding head of auburn hair and a deep baritone voice. He was known for his splendid eye as well as his fast and efficient technique. He was also a close personal friend of Executive Producer, David Bloom.

The company completed the first shots well before noon. But as they began prepping a daylight exterior walk-and-talk that would feature Chuck Dallas and the Guest Bimbo of the Week, one Maggie Sepulveda, it became apparent to one and all the shot wasn't' going to happen until after lunch.

Cody took the opportunity to retire to the privacy of his trailer and began making calls on the new I-Phone Shelly had given him as a present. Jimmy Bodine was slouched leisurely in a leather club chair, reading the Hollywood Reporter.

Cody had arranged with Tom Harvey to write a recurring role for Jimmy. It had been an easy sale once Tom and Jimmy got together.

"Incredible!" the writer/producer had exclaimed. "He could be your cousin."

So, in the first nine episodes, Jimmy worked a day here and a day there, always for Guild minimum Under-Five. Soon thereafter, Cody got the brilliant idea to put Jimmy on payroll as his personal assistant.

"Shit, Jimmy-Bo, you've been runnin' lines with me since the beginning. It's all deductible for me. Whaddah ya say?"

What could he say? For Jimmy, it was all about the action. Always had been. Always would be. And action was constantly swirling around Cody. He attracted it wherever he went. So, as a purely political maneuver, Jimmy agreed to Cody's offer.

*****

The fire engine red, S-Class Mercedes nosed up to the guard shack and one limo-tinted window slid silently into its sheath.

The guard glanced at the face of the woman behind the driver's wheel.

"Can I help you?"

"Yeah. Name's Shelly Monroe. I'm Cody Clifton's agent."

The guard gave his clipboard a cursory look.

"Mr. Clifton expecting you, ma'am?"

Why was it always a hassle with these gate guards? Was it something in their Union contract, or what?"

"Something wrong with your ears, Butch? I already told you I'm his A-Gent."

The guard's forehead visibly reddened beneath his black-billed faux-cop hat.

"Well, your name's not on the sheet."

At this point, Shelly was blocking the egress of three other vehicles that had pulled up behind her.

"Okay, so I'm not on your sheet. I guess you're gonna have to call over to the production office."

The guard picked up a phone and cursed under his breath. Three minutes later, Shelly and Irv were handed a drive-on pass and rumbled off in the direction of stage eighteen.

"Well I don't think it's particularly ethical," Irv remarked while checking his reflection in the vanity mirror. "But agents and managers have been poaching actors since the dawn of time. It shouldn't be a big surprise that Jake Brenner is sniffing around Cody."

"Not going to happen," Shelly insisted.

Irv laughed nervously.

"You find something amusing?"

"Amusing, no. Disturbing, definitely."

"Do go on."

"Come on, Shelly. You know how weak actors are when their egos are being stroked. What could you possibly do if Jake the Snake, or some other agent, tries to lure Cody away?"

Shelly slid the Mercedes alongside Cody's trailer and switched off the engine. She turned and looked Irv straight in the eye.

"Simple, Irv. I'd kill the pretensious bi-coastal cock-sucker."

Irv's expression was stunned. But only for a micro-second.

It was five minutes before noon when the duo strut-ted up to Cody's trailer. The pair were dressed to im-press.

Shelly was attired in a classy business suit, pale mocha in color, and a pair of excruciating Jimmy Choo heels. Shelly was certain the little sushi-eating bastard was a closet misogynist. On one plump wrist she sport-ed an eighteen carat gold, diamond-studded Rolex. On the other, a collection of gold link bracelets.

Irv was decked out in shark grey Gucci slacks and a mint colored Dior shirt. The ruby Pinkie ring on his left hand had been a bargain at six grand.

"Well, come on in!" Cody exclaimed when he opened the door.

The agents stepped inside the trailer.

"Jeez Shell, you look fabulous," Cody commented.

Shelly attempted a quick pirouette, halfway pulled it off.

Cody applauded. "You guys thirsty? Can I get y'all something to drink?"

"Got a cold Pepsi handy?" Irv asked.

"Absolutely. How 'bout you, Shell?"

"That'd be great."

"Hey Jimmy. Could you get a coupla Pepsi's outta the fridge?"

Jimmy slid from the club chair and slinked into the kitchen. Less than a minute later he returned with two cans of cola. He placed them on the coffee table and returned to his chair.

"I'm glad you guys came by," Cody began. "Angel's cookin' up fried chicken for lunch. The man's a true artiste. Y'all gonna stick around, aren't you?"

Shelly shook her perfectly coiffed head. "Actually, no Cody. I came by so we could have a short chat together... Could we maybe have a little privacy?"

All eyes turned toward Jimmy Bodine.

"No problem, Shell," Cody replied. "Hey Jimmy, do me a favor and check and see how long they're gonna be settin' up the next shot."

"Sure thing, pal," Jimmy responded evenly. "Nice seein' you Shelly, Irv."

The pair nodded politely as Jimmy exited the Airstream.

"So what's up?" Cody asked, an edge of nervousness in his tone. "Everything's alright, isn't it?"

Shelly chuckled.

"Alright? Let me tell you about alright... Got a call this morning from your Executive Producer. Do you want to know what David had to say?"
Cody blinked.

"I think that means yes," Irv interpreted correctly.

"David said the word on the set was you've been behaving like a Prince. He also said you were doing an outstanding job, and that the network was extremely pleased with the way the show was turning out."
Cody was relieved.

"I'm just glad everyone is happy."

"Jesus, Cody. Haven't you seen the ratings the past couple of weeks?" Shelly queried.

Cody laughed. The show had premiered as a mid-season replacement six weeks ago and he hadn't been home to catch an episode yet. He did have them DVR'ed.

"Right, Shelly. Like I got time to read the Trades. I'm up every morning at five-thirty, and I don't usually get home much before nine. Doesn't leave a whole lotta time for outside interests, like sleep and keeping up-to-date... But I did hear the numbers weren't too shabby."

"Jesus, Shelly. He really doesn't know," Irv responded, running one bony hand through thinning brown hair.

"Cody, Chuck Dallas, P.I. is a bona fide hit!" Shelly roared. "During our little conversation this morning, David told me he expected a back-nine pickup and a second season, guarantee."

The thoughts flooded Cody's mind and nearly overwhelmed him. His response wasn't what Shelly had anticipated.

"So how're they gonna work that out?" I'm still gonna get some time off after the thirteenth show, aren't I?"

"After the back nine episodes you'll have a couple of months to rest up before you start shooting the second season. That oughta be enough time for you to recharge your batteries, eh Cody?"

It wasn't an outright lie, just a mere omission of facts. Shelly actually had no idea how the producers might juggle the schedule. It was their show, and they called the shots. If Cody didn't get a break, that'd just be too damn bad! Inconsiderate, crybaby, cocksucker.

Shelly stood up and crossed to her prize client, put her arms around him and hugged him tight. At the end of the embrace she said: "Getting the word from the network is just a formality, and I wanted to be the first to congratulate you... And to tell you how proud I am. Not only are you doing an outstanding job, but everybody on the show loves working with you. And that makes me very happy."

"I told you I wouldn't let you down, Shelly."

"And you've kept your word."

Shelly signaled Irv, and they crossed to the door.

"We'll let you get back to work now."

"Keep it up, Cody," Irv said, holding up a thumb.

"Oh, almost forgot. These came for you." He handed Cody a stack of fan mail.

Cody placed the letters on the coffee table.
The agents descended the aluminum steps and brushed by Jimmy Bodine on the way to Shelly's new Benz.

"Shelly, if you've got a second there's something I want to ask you about," Jimmy began.

"Sorry, Jimmy. I'm late for an appointment," Shelly lied. "Call Raymond and have him schedule you a meeting."

"Sure thing," Jimmy replied. And the smile never left his face.

The Mercedes's doors sealed, and the engine hissed to life. Jimmy Bodine watched as it turned around a corner and disappeared like a bad daydream. He spat on the ground and crossed back toward Cody's Airstream. Once inside, Jimmy returned to his seat and settled back in.

Blue stood up and padded over, shoved his cold wet nose under Bodine's elbow.

Jimmy smiled and scratched Blue on the blaze of his chest.

"You one good old dog, you are."

Cody walked over to Blue and knelt beside him.

"He knows you're upset about somethin'."

"He's one smart hound dog," Jimmy agreed.

"Yeah? So what's the problem?"

Jimmy shook his head. "It's nothin' Cody. No problem."

"Look buddy, I don't got time for this bullshit right now. So if you don't wanna tell me what's buggin' you, that's okay. But I'm not gonna ask again…"

"I just wish Shelly would pay two percent as much attention to me as she does to you," Jimmy blurted.

Cody paused for effect and shook his head sadly. "Jimmy, Jimmy, Jimmy. I can't believe I'm hearin' this… Buddy, what you gotta realize here is Shelly's more than just my agent. She discovered me. She believed in me when no one else did. And she never lost faith."

An exaggeration.

"Even helped me out a coupla times when the unemployment checks stopped comin' in."

An out and out lie.

"I understand all that. Really I do," Jimmy began. "All I'm sayin' is it would be nice if I could get her to return a phone call once in awhile... Now don't get me wrong here, Cody. You're a real pal and I love bein' on the Show with you. It's just that... I'd like to be doin' more."

Cody understood the sentiment. Knew what it was to crave the attention of someone who had no interest in whether you lived or died.

"I'll talk to her. See what I can do."
Jimmy brightened.

"You could tell her there's a role in a low-budget feature that I know I'm dead on for. It's Vampire Cowboy 2. Maybe if it comes from you she'll make a phone call."

Cody put a hand on Jimmy's shoulder. "Consider it done, Jimmy-Bo."

Later, when Jimmy had left him unattended for a time, Cody picked up the letters from the table, rifled through them. When he came to a letter with a particularly floral scroll, he froze. The familiarity of the handwriting made his left eye twitch. The return address was in Texas, and the name on the return address was, indeed, Ms. Bobbi Clifton. Cody's chest felt tight as he tore open the envelope.

The letter was in the same fancy scroll and had a faint odor of jasmine. As Cody read it the muscles in his jaw tensed.

Dear Cody,
I know it's been a long time, but that is all water under the bridge (as they say). I thought you'd like to know I never miss Chuck Dallas, and that I am your number one fan. I always knew you'd be a success. I am so proud of you. I'm planning a trip to Los Angeles soon and I was hoping we could get together. There's someone I'd like you to

meet. It would be so nice to get caught up. You can reach me at (713)714-7157.

> With Much Love,
> Bobbi

Cody reread the letter several times before methodically tearing it into small pieces, which he then deposited in an ashtray. Lighting a match, he tossed it into the ashtray and watched the pieces ignite. When only ashes remained, he deposited them in the garbage can and then headed out of the trailer.

19

After thirty days went by with no more dead prostitutes littering up the hillsides, the Police Chief decided the fiscally prudent thing to do was to scale back the Coyote Murders Task force. Task Forces were damned expensive, and there were more worthwhile ways to utilize the city's dwindling police resources, what with the War On Drugs and all.

So the investigation continued with a skeleton crew of four. Calderas and London were the Lead detectives, with the youngsters, Smith and McCallister, rounding out the unit. It had been nearly four months since the last victim had been discovered and they weren't any closer to catching the killer than they had been on Day One.

For the better part of the last several weeks, Calderas and London had spent their time chasing down paper trails. They'd made enquiries at the Bureau Of Prisons and searched the lists of recent inductees. On several occasions they'd made excursions to various penal institutions and conducted interviews. When Max had voiced her displeasure at being relied upon to conduct said interviews, London had grinned.

"Aw c'mon, Max. You know you get more information out of those degenerates in two minutes then I could get in two days."

Max had chuckled. "When I was twenty-something I might've found this sort of thing amusing. But now, at fifty-something, I recognize it for what it is."

"And what's that, Max?" London enquired.

"Just basic anthropology."

London made a face.

"The study of lower primates. Unfortunately, it's not getting us any closer to our killer."

"It's procedure."

"It's a waste of time," Max insisted. "The Coyote is either dead, or he's moved out of the area. And in either case, he's not our problem any more."

London shook his head.

"You know I didn't mean that. I want this bastard as much as anyone."

"Do you want to know what I think?"

Max nodded.

"I think if the Coyote is still suckin' air, he'll be coming to the surface any minute. Psych profiles don't lie. This fucker kills hookers because he likes it. It's what gets him off. And then on the other hand, maybe we got lucky and one of the victims's pimps knew the guy, took care of the problem for us."

"Now there's a warming thought," Max replied.

But they both knew this was just wishful thinking. The Coyote was still out there. And there was no question in anyone's mind that he would kill again. He had a taste for it.

*****

At twenty-nine, Detective Seana McCallister was the youngest of the three female detectives, so she had been 'volunteered' for the special assignment.

She dressed herself up in a tight, red mini and pulled sheer nylons over her long, muscular legs. Then she slipped into a silk halter top that left tan midriff exposed. Next, a pair of slinky stiletto heels that would make chasing down a perp impossible.

To complete the ensemble, she tucked the Walther PPK back-up piece into a tiny beaded purse. It fired .380's, which had a lot less stopping power then her .40 caliber Glock, but Seanna had staggered the Walther's magazine with Glazer and Hydroshox rounds, and made certain one was in the pipe. It would be sufficient firepower, especially at the distance it was apt to be deployed.

She showed up at the Division HQ at eight, and was exhibiting her wares on the street less than an hour later.

Her partner, Detective Francine Smith, along with Detectives Calderas and London, covered her from a nondescript panel van located a couple hundred yards down the block.

This routine continued for the next three weeks. Detective McCallister stood on various street corners and the three detectives rested on their hemorrhoids in the van.

If the idea had been to harass johns, then the undercover operation had been a smashing success. But as for catching The Coyote, not so much. It was beginning to seem as if he'd stepped off into another dimension. Or never existed in the first place.

Except Max knew he existed, had personally witnessed his handiwork.

The Nightmare returned with stunning clarity right after she'd finished her seventh shift observing the young detective on Hooker Masquerade Patrol. She'd awakened on a cold, wet pillow with a racing heart. And for a minute, she'd been completely disoriented.

Then she'd remembered.

The Nightmare was the same one that had terrorized her as a child, in the weeks and months following her sister's disappearance. Bernie had gone to a high school dance on the evening of April 3,1984. It had been the last time anybody would ever see her. Max had been twelve at the time. The police investigation, though thorough, had turned up zip, and Bernice Calderas ended up as a photograph on a milk carton. She had simply vanished off the face of the Earth.

The scenario in Max's nightmare had never deviated. It was late at night and she was walking on streets that were unfamiliar. And when she looked at the faces of the people passing by on their way to God knows where, she couldn't see any detail at all. Even a child being pushed in a stroller by its mother lacked all distinguishing facial features.

But when Max glanced at the toddler as it rolled by, making its happy morning-dove noises, she was repulsed by what she saw. Upon closer examination, the infant was nothing more than a pustulant, bubbling mass, surrounded by a veneer of milky skin.

Max sprinted away from the grotesque apparition, feeling the urge to vomit. And as she ran the night grew darker, and the buildings began to shape-shift into trees. Before her very eyes they changed and grew, into oaks and cedars, with trunks as big around as oil storage tanks.

And as the city morphed into forest, Max could hear the voices of desperate Spirits as they whispered and screeched in the branches above her. She could smell the earthy scent of loam and molds in the air as well as the oily perfume of fear that exuded from her pores.

And as she ran with the wind whipping through her hair, she became keenly aware that she was being pursued. She'd catch an occasional glimpse of a large, hooded figure, stalking her from the shadows. Its nature was pure malevolence.

In the decades that had passed since Bernie's disappearance, there had been only one significant alteration to the pattern of the dream. Now, at the very end, Max would reach back to the spot above her right hip where her Smith normally rested, and she'd come back with an empty hand. Her weapon was missing! And then she'd feel the panic rise like a bird, from her belly into her throat. The Beast would hover there and beat its wings, choking the breath out of her with angry feathers. But on each and every occasion, Max'd wake up before the ultimate confrontation with her pursuer could transpire.

When she was a kid, she'd been in therapy for two years following Bernie's abduction. That was the word Max had kept hearing people whisper. And at the time she'd felt there had been no escape.

But two years later, the ever-recurring nightmare inexplicably retreated to the ether from which it had materialized. And Max had stopped seeing her therapist soon thereafter.

She had gone several decades unmolested in her dreamscape, which made it all the more difficult to cope with the macabre dream's return.

After a month of sleep deprivation Max's nerves were pretty frayed. And things didn't get any better when the undercover op was shut down. Still, she couldn't bring herself to seek out help. Last thing her career needed was a negative psych evaluation in her personnel file. So onward she soldiered, making a conscious effort not to tear Greg a new asshole every time he opened up his sexist yap.

"Few of us can stand prosperity.
Another man's I mean."

-Mark Twain

20

Sylvia Fox finished applying the lipstick and stepped back from the mirror, checking her pout. Her lips glistened glossy pink. Men loved pink. Made 'em think about pussy. And whenever they were thinking about pussy they were at their most vulnerable. At the ripe old age of twenty, Sylvia was already an expert at exploiting a man's vulnerabilities. It came with the territory. Ms. Fox was a girl with extremely high aspirations. Working as a receptionist in a talent agency was pretty boring, but it gave Sylvia a chance to meet a lot of important people. She had absolutely no intentions of remaining on the phones for long, and had already taken steps to that end.

Satisfied that her lips were perfect, she checked her watch. She'd been gone twenty minutes. Raymond would be apoplectic by now. Sylvia smiled at the thought and began touching up her mascara.

*****

"Monroe Talent, this is Raymond. Who may I ask is calling?"

The unctuous voice belonged to Raymond Allen Sinclair, Shelly's new Man Friday.

"I'm sorry, Carlos. Shelly's in a meeting right now." Standard Agency Lie Number One.

"No, Irv's not available," Raymond continued, his speech taking on the pitiless clipped tone reserved for third-tier clients. As he listened, his perfectly manicured fingers carefully logged the caller's name and number onto the message sheet, as well as the fact that it was the fourth time the client had called in today. Raymond found such neediness boring. He had to convince Shelly to send that one a Release Letter.

Raymond disconnected the line and removed the headset. He adjusted a mirror on his desk and smoothed his plush brown hair. Perfect. He glanced at the time and felt a flash of irritation.

"Where is that girl already?" He mumbled under his breath, wondering what had become of Sylvia.

Line three rang and Raymond replaced the headset and punched a button on the console.

"Monroe Talent Group. Raymond speaking... Oh, hello Felice. Shelly's been trying to reach you all day. Hang on a second."

Raymond pressed another blinking light on the console and cursed Sylvia under his breath.

"Monroe Talent group. Hold please."

And three more lines lit up.

"This is too much," Raymond hissed. "Where is that little   bitch?"

Two seconds later the door opened and Sylvia drifted in, honey blonde ponytail swaying. She was dressed conservatively in black jeans and a white blouse, but the girl oozed youthful sensuality.

Raymond wasn't fazed at all by her sexuality. He preferred mustaches. Neatly trimmed.

"It'd be nice if you'd take care of your personal business on your personal time," Raymond snapped.

Sylvia looked at him innocently. "Sorry, Ray, but when a girl's gotta go," She left the remainder unsaid as she accepted the headset.

Another button lit up on the console and Shelly's voice boomed through the Intercom.

"Raymond, did you locate Felice Snow for me?"

"Ms. Monroe, she's on line three."

"Thank you."

Shelly sat back in the luxury of her high-back leather Executive's Chair and propped her feet on the balcony's railing. She clicked a button on the hand-piece.

"Felice, darling, how are you?... I'm so glad... Got a pencil handy? Good. Four-fifteen tomorrow. Warners, building twenty-one, room C... Yeah, that's going to be on the bottom floor. Knock 'em dead, sweetheart. And don't forget to check in afterwards... And don't you ever go off M.I.A. on me again, okay?... Good! Ciao for now, darling."

"Ms. Monroe, Bill Hacker's office, line five."

"Thank you, Sylvia," she replied, clicking the hand-piece. "Afternoon, Bill. What can I do for you today?"

*****

Shelly was sitting outside on the balcony hypnotized by the traffic backing up on San Vicente. She imagined herself a Queen reviewing the vastness of her empire. Ah yes, for the first time in her life, Shelly Ilene Monroe was truly happy. Deliriously happy. And there was absolutely nothing that could spoil her mood.

In the five months since Cody Clifton had started filming Chuck Dallas, and she and Irv had moved into their
gorgeous new offices, the phones simply hadn't stopped
ringing. Casting directors who wouldn't return her phone
calls six months ago, were putting other agents on hold
when Shelly rang.

And as her power base extended, so, too, did the
quality of the clientele the Monroe Talent Group attracted. Now, A-List people were contacting the agency,
and Shelly was getting taken out to four-hundred dollar lunches by upper-echelon managers. All courtesy of
Cody Clifton, her personal Golden Goose.

Another wonderful aspect of success was, it tended
to attract even more success. One fabulous client would
bring over several of her friends, who'd bring over several of his fiends, ad infinitum. Shelly simply vibrated with
joy whenever she gazed upon the names on her client
list. The growth the agency had experienced in the last
ninety days had been truly phenomenal.

But in Show Business, Phenomenons occurred daily.
As did Miracles...

Falling into the latter category, even that lox, Jimmy
Bodine, had scored! Shelly had just signed him to do the
third lead in a low-budget horror flick with the unfortunate
title: Vampire Cowboy 2. It would probably go straight
to DVD, but so what? A commission was a commission
after all. And the best part was Jimmy would be out of
her hair for three-and-a-half glorious weeks, on location
in Phoenix, with filming scheduled to begin on or about
May 3rd.

Halle-Fuckin'-Looyahhh!

Ah yes. Shelly was right where she'd always expected she'd end up. Sitting on top of the world looking down at the peasants.

Life was outstanding.

*****

When the Official Word came down from the Network that Cody's show had been picked up for the back nine episodes, Irv's blood pressure finally began to level off. As the agency started signing a virtual parade of top-notch talent, his hair loss visibly decreased. And when these new clients started hitting, and the money started rolling in, his morning erections had returned. Ah, yes, the future was certainly looking rosy for Irving Birnbaum.

Shelly had worked on him for weeks to unload his nineties Nissan Z. She'd told him that he was her representative, and asked him what kind of message he thought his automobile sent. Irv had finally acquiesced and leased a five-hundred series BMW convertible. Unlike Boss Lady, He'd opted for a sedate silver.

Shelly had said that he should go for the seven-hundred series. But Irv didn't concur. Besides the ridiculous monthly payments and the insane insurance premiums, Irv was petrified of getting carjacked.

Besides, the Baby Beemer had been doing just fine for his sex life, thank you very much. For the first time since college Irv was getting laid. And he seemed quite intent on making up for lost time. But who could blame him?

No business like Show Business!

*****

It was close to six when the call came in from Berlin Productions. A casting director by the name of Eddie Matthias was making inquiries as to Cody Clifton's availability.

"Eddie! So good to hear your voice. How the hell are you?"

Shelly knew the answer. Eddie Matthias's quandary had been in the Trades for weeks. Berlin productions was having difficulty casting the male lead for their next feature; the hotly anticipated Ballistic, scheduled to begin shooting on or about July 15th.

"Great Shelly, just great... Listen, we'd like to bring Cody in to meet for one of the leads in Ballistic."

"Sorry Eddie. I'm afraid Cody's tied up for the next couple of weeks. His schedule should lighten up after Chuck Dallas wraps."

"And when exactly is that?"

"July 2nd," she replied, thinking back to Cody's expression the day she told him he was going to have to put his vacation plans on hold.

"We could arrange a meeting on Saturday. No reading, you understand. Mister O'Brian is quite a fan of the show."

Eddie Matthias was referring to Zachary O'Brian, flamboyant kid director, and Hollywood's current Flavor-Of-The-Month.

Shelly replied matter-of-factly: "Let me get your number. I'll get back to you after I check with the production office on Cody's schedule. I'm sure we can work something out."

Shelly wasn't at all sure she could work something out, but decades of casual exaggeration made it sound convincing. She already had a pretty good idea what Cody's reaction was likely to be. He'd been a very unhappy camper when she'd broken the news about the Network wanting another nine episodes in the can before the company went on break.

"But you told me I was getting' a coupla months off, Shell. I was lookin' forward to it," he'd protested.

Shelly had stifled the impulse to bitch-slap some sense into him. Instead, she'd put on her most soothing maternal voice, and attempted reason.

"Relax, darlin'. Everything's going to be just fine... I saw the schedule. Company's down from the Fourth of July holiday to the end of August," she'd told him.

But Cody hadn't been mollified and his expression had darkened.

Shelly shifted gears. A hint of steel crept into her voice. "Now listen to me," she'd lectured. "I know you're tired. Anyone would be under these conditions. But you'd better stop right now and think about how lucky you are. Do you have any idea how many actors in this town would sell their souls, or sacrifice their first-born, to be in your position? Got any idea? Ask your pal, Jimmy Bodine."

As Shelly's logic had started seeping through, Cody's expression had shifted from brooding to sheepish.

Shelly had concluded with: "Trust me, Cody. This is a good thing, It means the Network is fully committed to Chuck Dallas."

And Cody had nodded his head. And that had put an end to the episode.

But Shelly had glimpsed the future. Her darling, Cody, was going to take a firm hand from here on out. But that was okay. Because whatever it took, Shelly planned to deliver. She had no intention of standing by and watching her Cash Bull commit acts of self-sabotage.

Now the mission was to persuade him into meeting with the folks at Berlin Productions. It shouldn't prove too difficult. He'd have to be a complete moron to turn down the opportunity to work with the hottest director in town.

As far as Shelly was concerned, an actor should work whenever work was available. And that applied especially to any actor she could sell for upwards of a hundred grand a week.

In the mercurial world that defined Hollywood, Heat could vanish as suddenly as it appeared. Cody Clifton could sleep when he was dead.

"What we remember from childhood we remember forever –permanent ghosts, stamped, imprinted, eternally seen."
-Cynthia Ozik

21

Cody hadn't slept well the last couple of weeks and it was taking a serious toll on his disposition. He was prickly on set and spent the endless hours between shots isolated in his trailer. No more playing Frisbee with the crew.

Jimmy Bodine had departed a couple of weeks back, to shoot a flick in Arizona, and wasn't due back until the end of May. Cody missed the camaraderie and looked forward to his friend's return. He genuinely liked Jimmy. He thought of him as the brother he never had. And beyond that, Cody trusted him. And trust wasn't something he gave up easily.

Cody had learned at a very tender age that everybody had an angle. And now that he was a Celebrity, the rule applied even more. Everyone he came in contact with, without exception, wanted a selfie taken with him, or worse, had a screenplay they wanted him to take a look at. On one particularly bizarre occasion, a gas station attendant who'd filled up the tank on Cody's new Suburban had handed him a manuscript, along with the credit card receipt. Cody had smiled and nodded his head at the pump jockey and then shit-canned the pages as soon as he got home.

And then, of course, there was the paparazzi. Fucking parasites. Even out walking old Blue, Cody could never completely relax, knowing there was a good chance he was under observation –Bright lights attract many elements, and Cody was burning oh so brightly.

And then he thought about Bobbi and her recent letter, and felt a swirl of emotions: anger, resentment, curiosity and dread. Cody knew there wasn't a sentimental bone in his mother's body. And he wanted no part of her real agenda –whatever it may be.

With Jimmy gone and nobody around he felt comfortable talking to, Cody locked the door of the Airstream and pulled the blinds, retreated to comforting darkness. But he was restless in his aluminum sanctuary. He may have even felt some regret about prodding Shelly on Jimmy-Bo's behalf though he'd certainly never admit it to himself.

Cody was lonely and bored, and anxious, all at the same time. So he cracked a bottle of Absolut and knocked back a couple of shots. It didn't have much effect, calming or otherwise, so he drank several more. After the seventh go-round he finally stopped feeling like he was going to jump out of his skin.

Truth was, there was no escaping one's DNA. No point in even trying.

*****

Cody had never known his father, had no memory of the man, whatsoever. All he had were the stories Bobbi had told him, and she was more than a little biased in the telling.

Liar. Drunk. Thief. Felon. Womanizer. Loser. –The last adjective, spoken in her soft purr, was by far the most damning.

And whenever she was angry with her only child, which had been a great deal of the time, Bobbi would say things like: "Cody, you're just like your daddy. Yah got a pretty face and pretty teeth, but you're no goddamn good! You're never gonna amount to nothin'."

After listening to those sentiments, and much worse, for his first eleven years, it had been no surprise to anyone when Cody started drinking. Alcohol had always been easy enough to come by.

Bobbi's preferences had leaned toward vodka and gin, whichever happened to be on sale. And there had always been several bottles in the cabinet just in case 'Company' came by.   And in all the dozens of cities they'd lived in together, in all the many trailer courts and rundown apartment buildings they'd inhabited, Cody remembered Bobbi entertaining Company almost every night... So he'd started pilfering her vodka, replacing it with water. It had been remarkably easy, and she'd never caught on.

The vivacious beauty, Roberta Jean Clifton, known to one and all as 'Bobbi', had turned sweet sixteen a scant three weeks before giving birth to her first and only child, Cody Lee Clifton. On the birth certificate, in the space reserved for 'father', the word 'Unknown' had been handprinted.

For as long as he could remember, Cody had referred to his mother as Bobbi, or Aunt Bobbi. She had insisted on it, often introducing him to Company as her young nephew. He'd made the mistake once, of contradicting her. He had vivid memories of the occasion. He'd been seven or eight at the time and had called her a liar. He'd told everyone in the room that Bobbi was his mother, not his aunt. He remembered her smile, and the chill it had sent up his spine, from his puckered little asshole all the way to the tiny blonde hairs on his neck.

If nothing else, Bobbi had been smooth, a master of the poker face. You could hit her with a brick and it wouldn't rustle a feather. Not so as anyone would notice, anyways. She'd simply laughed at him and dismissed him to his room. But later that night, after Company had departed, Bobbi had crept into her son's bedroom. She'd shaken him from a sound sleep and then proceeded to beat him senseless with a leather belt.

Cody remembered whimpering and begging her to stop. But as the violence continued unabated, Cody had realized she wouldn't stop, couldn't stop, until exhaustion had replaced anger.

That had been the first time he'd seen the rage in her smoky eyes, and that recognition had caused him more pain than any beating ever would. But Cody had learned a valuable lesson that night. A lesson he'd carry with him for the rest of his life: That Love and Pain are connected.

And after that night Cody never referred to his mother by anything other than Bobbi.

*****

Tonight, when they'd wrapped for the week, Cody had put another check mark on his special calendar, and felt completely spent.

Twenty down, two to go.

He packed up what he was going to need for his fifty-seven hours off and dragged his ass the twenty paces to the town car. Felix opened the rear door and Blue jumped into the backseat. Cody slid in beside the hound.

As Felix silently navigated, Cody stared out the tinted glass. The windows in the stores and restaurants were filled with lights that blurred and flowed into one another, like hallucinogenic watercolors. Cody saw shadowy motion trails on the street that vaguely disturbed him and quickened his pulse. But all he was looking at were the neighborhood people going about their lives. The images that were forming in Cody's mind were the result of chronic sleep deprivation compounded by too much caffeine.

*****

It was almost ten when Cody collapsed beside Blue and switched on the Samsung Plasma big screen. The fucker took up an entire wall of his living room and the color saturation would make your eyes bleed. Cody hadn't had the time or inclination to face changing residences, but he'd certainly found opportunity to upgrade his surroundings.

He'd donated his entire collection of garage-sale furnishings to Good Jill. Then he'd visited an upscale furniture store in West Hollywood, called Exotica Leather Importers, that Shelly had turned him on to. There, he'd purchased a complete living room set. The ensemble had run a little over eighteen grand, and Cody hadn't blinked an eye.

Next, he'd gone across the street to Electronix City, and paid cash for the massive Sammy big screen, as well as a seven-speaker THX surround sound system. By the time he'd left the store, Cody had dropped another eight grand. But that had included free delivery and setup. The best part was, according to Shelly, the entire home theatre was deductible!

So here he was at ten o'clock on a Friday night, watching a DVD of Pulp Fiction, with his old pal, Blue, at his side. If he'd given it a thought, he could've picked up the phone, and any one of a dozen ladies would have gladly dropped whatever they were doing, and responded to his invitation.

But he wasn't in the mood. He seldom was.

But even so Cody had slept with so many women in the last several months that he'd lost count. Most of the time it had been a nice lingering blowjob on the couch in his Airstream, or in some host's closet or Jacuzzi. Occasionally, it was a lunch-time quickie with Shelly's receptionist, Sylvia, who was really quite amazing.

But despite all the attention, Cody just couldn't shake off the sense of isolation. It was at the very center of his psyche. Isolation; the Kevlar chain mail that surrounded him, protected him from those who would do him harm. And they were always around, lurking in the shadows, waiting to catch him off guard. To catch him weak and wanting.

The women who had sought Cody out were all Show Biz Beautiful, and full of lust and agenda. They pleasured him in every conceivable manner with orifice and tongue. But none ever touched him. None made contact. Cody merely accepted what they offered, for to do otherwise would raise questions. And that was the last thing Cody Clifton wanted. From anyone.

So he continued to draw inward, and concentrate on the day Chuck Dallas would wrap for the season, and the night he'd be set free. And the Glory his release would be! But between now and then, Cody's sleep would be anything but restful. His dreamscape teemed with images of violence and perversion.

… And those were the good nights.

On the not-so-good nights, Bobbi would be there to torment and tantalize him. Just as she had done for his first fourteen years.

*****

It was the summer of '88, and the landscape tore by at seventy-five miles an hour, in a miasma of oranges, reds, greens and blues. Cody observed through the passenger window of the battered Eldorado as the colors swirled and flowed. The air was humid, and thick with Bobbi's perfume; a jasmine scent that made him feel light-headed and vaguely nauseous.

They were on Interstate 55, somewhere between Memphis and Jackson, Mississippi. The Cadillac's windows were rolled down and Fleetwood Mac blasted from the radio. The air zipping from the AC vents had turned tepid well before noon. The hours tumbled into one another as Cody sweated profusely. His mood grew dark. He grumbled under his breath.

"Knock it off, Cody! You're startin' to piss me off."

Cody silently cursed her as the sweat rolled down his neck and accumulated in rivulets around his collar. Outside, the heat ascended from the asphalt in a rippling liquid mirage.

Bobbi ran slender fingers through her fiery mane, lit up a Kool, and carelessly flicked the match out the window. Her cheeks hollowed as she sucked on the filter, lost in her thoughts.

"Why couldn't we wait just another day?" Cody griped.

Bobbi turned in his direction and narrowed her eyelids. "Excuse me?"

"Frank said he coulda fixed it in a couple of hours," Cody protested.

Bobbi laughed. "You still going on about the busted air conditioner?"

"Frank said…"

"Goddamnit Cody, enough already!"

"I liked it in Saint Louis. Why did we have to leave? It's not fair."

Bobbi exhaled a plume of gray smoke and quoted one of her favorite sayings: *"Who ever promised you fair, kid?"*

Cody fumed. He closed his eyes tight and wished for something to happen to the car. Nothing fatal. Just something so they'd be forced stop somewhere. Stop and stay. And not just over night, either, but Forever. And Cody knew Forever hadda be longer than six months, which had been the most time they'd stayed anywhere.

Cody had fuzzy memories of huge, moist cities, with names like Savannah and Atlanta, and smaller ones, with names like Hopkinsville and Kerry's Harbor. All the trailer courts and shabby apartments, all the cities and towns were interchangeable to him. Cody had never felt at home anywhere. He had never stayed any place long enough to know what it was like to have friends. Always an Outsider…

…And now there was something strange in the wind, something sinister. Through the miles of silence an undercurrent flowed between them, a tension existed.

Cody studied his mother from his peripheral eyesight. And as he examined with his appraising eye, he learned lessons that would stick a lifetime.

Whenever she graced him with a smile, the sun would come out. She was so lovely that it hurt his eyes when he looked too long. But Bobbi's beauty was as hard and cold as steel. It was her power over men, and she wielded that power like a bludgeon, without mercy, and without conscience. And just beneath her lustrous surface there lay an unfathomable darkness. Something poisonous, built on a foundation of insatiable Want.

Yes, his mother was beautiful. She drew men to her like moths to flame. But when they flew too close to her radiance, their little wings would combust, and they'd die screaming.

And how she loved to watch them suffer!

Ah yes, so beautiful.

But the time had come when she could no longer manipulate her own son so easily, and it made her feel old at thirty. Cody had committed the ultimate sin of seeing her for who she was, and that was something Bobbi couldn't forgive. His knowledge made him dangerous. He knew too many of her secrets. And what's more, he'd begun to challenge her authority.

So, they were on their way to New Orleans where Bobbi planned to look up an old friend. That had been the routine for as long as Cody could remember. Whenever she'd gotten bored, or wore out her welcome in one place, she'd invariably move on under the auspice of 'looking up an old friend.'

Cody had figured it out by the time he was seven, that Bobbi wasn't to be trusted. And yet, she was his mother, his whole family, and he needed to trust someone, to love someone, and to have someone love him. It would become a defining characteristic of the person Cody would grow into. A wound covered with scar tissue. Something that festered over time.

On and on they traveled. And through the numbing hours Cody felt sweat burn his eyes and humidity sear his lungs. He remembered the names of the towns they passed through, but not the towns themselves. They had good 'cracker' names like Scoby and Winona, Goodman and Canton, McComb and Magnolia. Fly specks on a map. Homogenous in the ways that mattered. Small Southern Towns.

Eventually they reached the outskirts of New Orleans and checked into a flea-bag motel just off the Interstate.

The first thing Cody did once the door was closed was switch on the air conditioning. It was an ancient window unit with push-buttons and a dial thermostat. When he turned it on the vibrations rattled the room, but the air that blasted from the vents became frigid almost immediately. The frosty air dried the salt and dirt on Cody's face and hair, and he began to feel better.

"Honey, help me with this," Bobbi said, turning her back to him and holding her hair away from the zipper.

Cody unzipped the back of the dress and Bobbi let it fall to the floor. She stood there, shamelessly, in her bra and panties, and lifted her purse from the bed. She retrieved a twenty-dollar bill and handed it to her son.

"Here. Go and get us a coupla cheeseburgers at that place across the street. Extra pickles on mine... And you might as well get us a coupla orders of fries, too."

"Shakes?"

"Sure. Why not? Make mine strawberry."

"Be right back," Cody replied, a smile spreading across his face.

"Take your time," she replied, unfastening the bra, and letting the garment drop to the ground beside the crumpled dress. Next, she stepped out of her panties and strolled into the bathroom. Cody heard the faucet switched on, the splash of water against porcelain.

He returned half an hour later with three greasy white bags that contained their dinner. Bobbi was just finishing in the bathroom, and as usual, had soaked every single towel.

*They ate in silence, and then Cody hiked down to the
office to see about getting more towels. By the time he
returned to the room, she was gone. He didn't think much
of it. Bobbi had pulled the vanishing act on so many prior
occasions it no longer had any effect on him.*

*So, as any curious teenager might, he set out on foot
on a reconnaissance of the area. It was the middle of July
and the night was balmy, lit by a pregnant moon. A billion
insects buzzed and dipped in the moisture, and a bullfrog
chorus sang in the background.*

*It was late when he got back to the hotel, and he saw
that Bobbi's beat-to-shit Cadillac wasn't in the parking
lot. He surmised that his mother probably ran into an 'old
friend', or more likely, made a new one.*

*Cody pulled out a deck of cards and switched on the
TV. He practiced his one-handed shuffle and watched a
rerun of 'The Mechanic'. It was the story of an aging hitman.*

*He awoke the next morning to the sound of the TV.
A squat man with a red face and the bushiest sideburns
Cody hadever seen, was hawking used cars.*

*"Cmon down to Smilin' Sam's! Bad credit? We don't
care! New to the area? We don't care. We got somethin'
down here to suit any budget! So do yerself a favor, and
c'mon down! Don't wait! Do it today!"*

*Cody rolled over and rubbed his eyes. He glanced at
the clock beside the bed, saw that it was after ten and
that there was still no sign of his wayward mother.*

*She'd always tell him not to worry about her, that she
could damn well take care of herself. But her words did
little to alleviate the unease he suddenly felt. Sometimes
she'd be gone for days at a time, and there were inher-
ent risks associated with her chosen profession. Cody*

*couldn't help thinking that her luck might run out some-
day. As it was, he could remember some pretty close
calls. Towns they barely escaped. Threatening, angry,
red-faced men who'd been bilked, cheated, and manipu-
lated by one of the best.*

Caveat emptor, baby. Let the buyer beware.

*And now that he was almost fourteen, Cody's grasp
of his mother's sexual machinations only served to con-
fuse and frustrate him. The thought of her with other men
made him angry.*

And lately, Cody was angry a lot.

*He sat up in bed and pondered what his next move
should be. When he drew a blank he decided it was time
to get up. He called the front desk and asked what time
checkout was. The manager informed him that checkout
time was eleven a.m., unless otherwise agreed upon.*

*When Cody asked if he could get a late checkout, the
manager had told him no problem, asked Cody if one
p.m. would suit him.*

Cody replied that it would suit him fine.

*And then the manager said something that caught
Cody completely by surprise.*

*"Okay, son. We'll see yah tomorrow at one. And by the
way, we got a letter here for you."*

"Huh?"

"Your name Cody Clifton?"

"Yeah."

"Well, there's a letter here with your name on it."

"Thanks," Cody replied, stunned.

*Before the handset hit the cradle Cody felt panic begin
to rise. His mother made it a hard and fast rule whenever
they were traveling never to pay for more than a single
night's stay.*

"Can't ever tell when you're gonna have to leave some place in a hurry," she'd lectured him.

And then there was the letter.

Cody slipped on a shirt and sprinted to the manager's office. He retrieved the letter from the front desk and stuffed it in his back pocket, thanked the manager.

He proceeded at a casual pace back to the room. Once there, he sequestered himself and removed the envelope from his jeans. He tore a corner and inserted an index finger, pulled down hard. He reached inside and withdrew the note. When he unfolded the yellow-lined paper two bills fell on the bed. They'd been rolled up into straws and pressed flat, secreted within the letter:

Dear Cody,
First off I want you to know I love you more than anything in the Universe. Don't ever forget that you hear??!! But you're a big boy now and it's time you made your own way in the world. Whatever you decide to do with your life I know you'll knock 'em dead. You are tired of traveling with me. New Orleans is a great town to set up shop. A`smart boy like you will have it wired in no time.I left you two-hundred dollars to get you going. That's two-hundred dollars more than anybody ever gave me.

My Love Always,
Bobbi

Cody crumpled the letter into a ball and threw it at the trash can, wiped angry tears from his eyes. He snatched the bills from the bedspread and quickly unfolded them. Ben Franklins, sure as hell. The humor of the situation momentarily overcame his hurt and anger, and he shook his head and laughed.

What was wrong with his Street Sense anyway? He shoulda known something was up last night when Bobbi didn't pounce on him for the change from the burgers. He had almost eight dollars left in his pocket. Shoulda known right then!

*****

It was after one when Cody rolled over and glanced at the clock.

"Jesus, Blue, why didn't you wake me up?"

Blue looked at him with smiling hound dog eyes.

Cody rose to his full height, arms over his head, and stretched. He turned his head slowly from side to side and heard crackles as his spine realigned with the forces of gravity. Then he padded toward the bathroom, scratching at a mosquito bite on his hip.

When he entered the kitchen in search of sustenance, he spied the flashing red LED on the answering machine. He felt an immediate sense of trepidation, and seriously considered ignoring the damned thing. Really wasn't anybody he cared to talk to.

But the annoying little light continued to flicker as he prepared his meal. This exercise in futility lasted approximately a minute and a half.

Cody depressed the button on the blinking grey box. A moment later he heard Shelly's voice:

"Cody, darling, I've got really exciting news! Call me as soon as you hear this. I'm at home. 818-766-7667. Ciao for now."

Cody rubbed his head. What could be so important that it wouldn't wait until Monday? He could only hazard one guess and it made his sphincter pucker up. He picked up the phone and dialed her number.

Shelly snatched the handset from its cradle on the first ring.

"That you, Cody?"

"How'd you do that?" Cody asked, a little put off by her precognitive powers.

"It's a secret-agent thing," she teased.

"Uh-huh... So what's the exciting news you gotta tell me?"

"First, you have to promise me you'll hear me out, and I mean without interruptions."

That piqued his curiosity, alright. "Okay Shelly. You got my attention."

"I got a call last night from Eddie Matthias. He's casting 'Ballistic'. You know, Zachary O'Brian's next picture. You've heard of him, haven't you?"

Cody answered reflexively. "Sure I've heard of him."

"He wants to meet with you, this afternoon if possible."

"You gotta be kiddin' me."

"You don't have to read for him. It's just a meeting."

Cody paused, reflected for a moment. "What's the role?"

"Second lead, opposite Rebecca Grant... Now listen up 'cause I'm not through talking yet. Cody, they're ready to offer you the part, pending your meeting, of course!"

Cody felt his chest constrict. "Jesus, Shelly, what was I just tellin' you the other day? I'm burned out. Toast. I can't fucking think straight."

Shelly's voice took on a sterner tone. "I thought you agreed to hear me out!"

Silence on the other end of the line.

"This is a fabulous role, Cody, truly fabulous! Worthy of an actor of your caliber. It could make you an International Star!"

Shelly glanced at the breakdown pages on the desk and quoted: "Cole Riley is a misunderstood stranger who wanders into the wrong town at the wrong time. He's accused of a crime he didn't commit, and in the end must take on corrupt forces in the town, to save himself and those he loves."

Shelly paused to take in some oxygen. On the other end of the line there was still silence.

Cody?... Cody, are you listening?"

"How much?"

Shelly could hardly contain herself. "They want to pay you a million bucks for four weeks work!"

Complete and total silence on the other end. Not even breath sounds.

"Cody? Cody, did you hear what I just said?"

"Jesus, Shelly. That's a shitload of money!"

Ah, so the redneck wasn't completely brain dead after all.

"So what do you want me to tell them?"

"Cody?"

"I'm thinkin'."

"Christ Cody, what's there to think about? Brad-Fucking-Pitt lobbied for this part, but Zachary O'Brian wants you! And a million bucks for four weeks work! That should set you up for one hell of a vacation, wouldn't you say?"

"Is there a stop date?"

"Absolutely. They get you for four weeks, period."

"C'mon Cody, don't be stupid. This kind of opportunity doesn't come around every day."

"What time do they wanna see me?"

Thank God! Shelly inwardly breathed a sigh of relief.

"The man's words were 'at Cody's convenience'. What works for you?"

"How's six?"

"Should be fine. I'll call you back in a couple of minutes to confirm... And Cody?"

"Yeah, Shell?"

"This is a smart move. 'Ballistic' is already generating heat and they haven't even started shooting yet." Shelly thought to herself: And let's not forget the money, honey. Ten Percent of which belongs to Yours truly... Ten Percent of a Mil equals a cool hundred grand! Was that an orgasm I just had?

"Yeah, Shell, I'm sure you're right."

There was a sadness in his tone, but Shelly wrote it off to simple sleep deprivation. A million bucks could buy a whole lot of anti-depressants. Pick your flavor.

*"A celebrity is one who is known to
many persons he is glad he doesn't know."*
-H. L. Mencken

22

(Six Days Later)

Jimmy Bodine loathed Phoenix. The town had all the congestion and filth of Los Angeles with absolutely none of the redeeming qualities. It was a city completely devoid of charm.

Jimmy's morning had started out lousy and the day had gone progressively downhill from there. In a scramble for his good-morning jolt, he'd spilled nearly a gram and a half of Peruvian Monkey Powder on the hotel room carpet. He'd cursed his clumsiness and then gave his upper lip a severe rug burn reclaiming what he could from the fibers and dust. It would have to hold him until he got back to his apartment this afternoon.

The last three and a half weeks had been the longest, hottest and dirtiest Jimmy had ever experienced. The company had worked six days a week, fourteen, fifteen hours a day, sometimes more. There had been a lot of night time exteriors, and not a great deal of sleep. The worst part had been the heat; It was barelyJune, but the thermometer had hovered in the triple digits the entire shoot. Jimmy couldn't wait to catch the next big bird heading west. People hadda be insane to live out here.

His bags were packed, and he was anxious to get moving. But after an arduous drive from hotel to airport, he was informed at the gate that his flight had been delayed, some kind of problem on the ground in El Paso. At least that's what the perky co-ed behind the ticket counter had told him.

Jimmy nodded his head as his blood pressure rocketed. He adjourned to the Skyway Bar, ordered up a double shot of Cuervo with a beer back, the first of many.

The airplane that had been scheduled to depart Phoenix at eleven-ten a.m. received clearance for takeoff at four-forty pm. It was a packed flight full of surly passengers. The flight attendants pretended not to notice.

By six-fifteen, Jimmy was de-planed and standing in front of carousel number four at LAX, wondering where the fuck his bags were. At five minutes before seven he crossed from the 'Lost Luggage Office', stepped from the terminal and hailed a taxi.

"Hey mahn, I know you!" the man behind the wheel exclaimed in a thick Jamaican accent. "You're Chuck Dallas! I watch your show every week."

Jimmy wiped a palm across his face.

The first couple of times this had happened, Jimmy had thought it was hilarious. But by the fifth or sixth time the novelty had worn off. Now the attention was just one more irritant, like a piece of sand floating on one's cornea.

"Nah, I ain't him," Jimmy replied stone-faced.

The driver tilted his head. "You sure?"

"You gonna drive, or are you gonna ask stupid questions?" Jimmy snarled. He slid into the backseat longing for silence and a couple of lines of toot.

Forty minutes later the cabbie deposited him in front of his building. When the cowboy paid the fare with exact change, the cabbie mumbled an ancient Voodoo curse and accelerated away from the curb.

Jimmy scratched his head and sauntered into the building. Damn, but it was good to be home. He pressed the 'up' button and the elevator doors slid open. He stepped inside and pressed another button, this one marked 'nine'.

The apartment was stuffy, so Jimmy opened up the French doors in the bedroom and then plugged in his now dead cell phone. Then he headed for the kitchen, retrieved a bottle of Bass ale from the fridge, and popped its cap. He took a long swig, rubbed the icy brown glass against his forehead. The flickering red light on the answering machine caught his eye. He reached across the counter and slapped the top of the machine, then noticed an envelope tucked beside it.

As the answering machine recycled, Jimmy tore open the corner of the envelope and extracted the note from within. It was from good old Irv, House-Sitter Extraordinaire. He'd sent his regards and wanted Jimmy to know that he'd stopped by the apartment to feed the fish on Tuesday. Jimmy figured they must be getting pretty hungry by now.

The answering machine beeped once and began playing.

"Hey Jimmy-Bo! It's me, Cody! Pick up if you're there.... So where the hell are yah? Tried your cell and just got your voice mail. Shelly told me you was supposed to be home early Friday afternoon... Anyways, I arranged a little welcome home party for you, tonight. It's gonna be at that club on Santa Monica you're so partial to. You know the one I mean. Party starts at eight."

Jimmy glanced at the time and shook his head. It was already after eight and he wasn't much in the mood for a party. But there really was no graceful way out. He finished the beer and crossed resignedly into the master bath, shedding clothes along the way.

*****

As usual, 'Mystique' was standing room only. A queue of would-be patrons lined the sidewalk in front of the building, forever hopeful of receiving their turn at rubbing elbows with the glitterati within. Two steroid-enhanced bouncers guarded the door, ruthlessly checking the ID's of only the creamiest lasses. Low-paid muscle getting their rocks off on a Friday night.

The club's interior was twenty-first century plush. All polished oak and leather cushions. Celebrants were packed three deep, and they jostled one another in competition for the bartenders's attentions.

Jimmy Bodine was sitting in a booth at the very back of the club. He was flanked on one side by the vivacious brunette, Maggie Sepulveda, and on the other by the lovely redhead, Megan McKinnon. Megan had brought along a couple of friends from Trevor's class.

Paula was a platinum blonde with the nicest rack Jimmy had ever laid eyes on. And Lisa, the doe-eyed piranha who was sitting beside her, had just polished off her third pint of ale. An empty pitcher sat on the table beside an untouched bowl of pretzel mix.

Jimmy's evening was definitely looking up. A charming smile graced his face, and at this point, he didn't even care that Cody was two hours late to an event Cody had personally arranged. Fuck 'im.

And just as that thought entered his mind a sudden commotion arose at the front of the club. A murmuring ensued and traveled in a human vocal wave throughout the establishment. Jimmy immediately knew the source. His superstar buddy must've arrived.

A few minutes later Cody emerged from a crush of people. And the man was dressed to kill. Tailored white Levis, grey shirt, and a white Stetson. But it was the boots that set off the outfit and received the most commentary.

It was obvious that they were custom made and extraordinarily expensive. Cut from the single skin of an albino python, the boots were completely hand-worked. The leather possessed the texture of a favorite baseball glove, soft and supple. The boot heels were laminated and three inches high, slightly cut-in. Absolutely no detail was overlooked, and no cost spared. The final touch was pure Redneck ostentation, or perhaps Kansas City pimp; hand-crafted, eighteen carat gold, toe and heel guards.

"Jesus, Cody! Where'd you get those fancy shitkickers?" There was a slight slurring to Jimmy's words and a touch of awe in his voice.

"And a howdy-do to you, too, pal," Cody retorted. He removed his hat and graced the table with his most debonair smile. "Good evening, ladies."

"Hi Cody," they mutually bubbled in reply.

Then Cody gently pulled at his pants leg revealing the tops of the hand-tooled leather. "Pretty slick, huh Jimmy-Bo?"

"Never seen anything like 'em."

"Probably 'cause they're one-of-a-kind," Cody kidded. "What size you wear?"

"Eleven," Jimmy answered without hesitation.

Cody chuckled. "Shoulda figured."

He pulled up a chair along side the booth, tugged off the cowboy boots and handed them over to Jimmy. Not one of the ladies at the table so much as blinked.

"You gotta try 'em on."

Jimmy slipped off his well broken-in Dan Post's and replaced them with the pimp boots. Paula excused herself to visit the ladies room and Jimmy exited the booth behind her. He strutted across the room, did an about-face and returned with a huge smile spread across his face.

"Jesus Cody, these are sweet. They actually feel as good as they look. Where'd you get 'em?"

Cody's smile was sly. "I know a guy..."

Jimmy laughed. "I'd like to know him, too."

He gave Cody back his python boots and slipped into the Dan Post's.

"So what's a guy gotta do to get a drink around here, anyway?" Cody asked.

"I was wonderin' the same thing," Megan chimed in.

"I'll take care of it."

Jimmy snatched the pitcher from the table, stood up and crossed toward the bar. He hadn't traveled thirty paces when he saw a woman carrying a tray full of drinks. She stopped at her table, smiled brightly at the flawlessly attired men, and began to offload the cocktails. Jimmy caught up to her as she was setting the last drink down. He put the empty pitcher on her tray, glanced down at her nametag.

"Hey, Julie."

The server was perhaps thirty, with stringy dark brown hair that hung past her shoulders, and a longish face. She looked at Jimmy with a blank expression.

"See those folks sittin' at that table over there?" Jimmy asked, pointing to the location. "Every one of 'em is real thirsty. Hungry, too."

"I'll be with you as soon as I can," Julie replied politely. "We're kinda short-handed tonight."

"Right."

Jimmy's smile sent a cold chill up the server's spine. "Just bring a couple more pitchers of your best ale, an extra mug, and three, no, make that four orders of Kobe sliders, okay?"

Jimmy didn't bother to wait for a reply. He returned to the table and slid in beside Megan. She placed a hand on his thigh and gave a little squeeze.

"So how'd it go in Phoenix?" Cody asked, just as soon as Jimmy's ass had hit cushion.

"Buddy, let me tell yah... I used to think August in Tennessee was about as close to Hell as you were likely to find," Jimmy began. "I was wrong."

"Yeah, but it was a dry heat," Cody quickly put in.

That got the table snickering.

"Thing amazes me is some folks actually seem to like it out there. Can you imagine?"

"One of my girlfriend's moved to Tempe a couple of years ago," Megan added. "One summer was enough. Told me she didn't want to end up having lizard skin by the time she hit thirty."

"Takes all kind I guess," Cody replied.

At that moment Julie approached the group with two pitchers of brew balanced on her serving tray. She set the pitchers on the table.

"Food order'll be up in a couple of minutes," she said, her face expressionless. She turned and disappeared among the throng of people.

Cody shook his head and reached for one of the pitchers. He proceeded to refill all the mugs on the table. "Guess I'm playin' hostess tonight."

"And doin' a damn fine job of it," Jimmy commented. Cody continued the interrogation: "Tell us about the shoot."

"All 'n' all it was great. Lotta overtime. And the place we were holed up in was pretty swank. Pool, gym, cold AC, thank God, and pretty decent room service."

"A man could get used to that, huh?" Cody kidded.

"Not in Phoenix," Jimmy replied.

Cody chuckled. "Nice thing is you got a real choice credit on your resume now. Lead in a film."

"Let's see how it does in the theaters, first."

"It doesn't matter, pal. Fact is, you had a starring role in a feature film. And now Shelly's got tape to show on you. That's all yah need to get a little heat generated."

Judging by the nodding heads at the table, the ladies all concurred with Cody's assessment.

Moments later, Julie turned a corner with her serving tray piled high with Kobe sliders. She paused by the table and unloaded the dishes from the tray.

Cody reached over and snatched a slider, took a bite. His expression soured instantly, and he spat the half-chewed meat onto the plate.

Jimmy almost fell on the floor laughing.

Cody reached for the mug of brew and knocked back several swallows. "Damn cow musta died of old age! Take this shit back to the kitchen!"

Julie was stunned. She didn't know what to make of the ranting cowboy. "That's the first complaint I've ever heard about it," she stammered.

Cody notched up the decibels. "Listen, sweetheart, I was born and raised in Missouri, and I damn sure know what sliders supposed tah taste like. And let me tell yah, this isn't even close!"

"I'm sorry, sir," she apologized, replacing the orders onto her tray. "Is there something else I can get you from the kitchen."

"Forget about it!"

"Another pitcher would be nice," Jimmy chimed in.

The waitress retreated to the kitchen.

"This place used to be first class," Cody complained. "I dunno what happened. The service sucks and so does the food. I don't know why you like this place so much, Jimmy."

23

The park near division headquarters was a restful place to spend an afternoon, an oasis in the middle of the urban sprawl. On one end of the acreage there was an Olympic-size swimming pool, a popular destination during the hellish summers. Across from the pool, there stood a red brick building that housed a gymnasium and several utility rooms. A short distance from the front of the building, designed especially for the younger set, there was a sand-filled play area, complete with swings and monkey bars. There were benches set up around the play area where the mommies and various nannies could sit and gossip. At the opposite end of the acreage there was a dirt jogging track that abutted a fenced archery range.

The June sun felt good on Max's shoulders. She stood erect, feet apart and firmly placed. She inhaled deeply, smelled fresh mown grass and eucalyptus trees. She focused her energy on the paper bull's eye sixty feet to the east and pulled back the string. The bow flexed as the pulleys and cables strained. Max held the position, her arms and shoulders a mass of ligatures and sinew. As she exhaled she let the string slip from the fingertips of her right hand. It slapped the leather forearm guard with a hollow 'thwop'. The arrow took flight, penetrating paper an inch above, and three-quarters of an inch to the right of center. It nestled beside five of its siblings in a pattern no larger than a grapefruit.

Max removed another arrow and notched it to the string. She set her stance and concentrated on her breathing, counting to ten during each inhalation and exhalation. The traffic and the yelling children faded into the background. She drew the string back and held, focused on the center of the target. At the end of an exhalation she let the arrow fly. The sun flashed off the aluminum shaft as it flew its course, punching through paper dead center. Max felt a rush of pure satisfaction.

She was feeling better. Being out in the sun had that effect on her. Her mother always told people that Maxine was a solar-powered child. She never could sit still on rainy days. Some things never change.

It had been a hard couple of months and Max was just starting to feel like her old self again. The recurring nightmare had abated and her disposition had improved. The Coyote appeared to have gone to ground, and no more strangled girls had turned up. Things were slowly returning to normal.

Max credited her emotional shift to her return to basics. She hadn't had the bow out in several years, and when she'd removed it from its case in the closet, it had been dusty, and all the pulleys had been in need of lubrication. She'd spent an entire day on it, disassembling and cleaning, lubricating and polishing. And when she'd finished she'd stood back and felt pride in what she had accomplished.

And then she'd started practicing again. She made a ritual of it. And she found that the more time she spent alone, concentrating on the arrow's flight, the better she felt. It was the healing power of meditation.

As she notched another arrow to the bow, her concentration was suddenly interrupted by her phone.

*****

Max showed up at division headquarters half an hour later. London was waiting for her at his desk, an open case file in his lap.

"What's the word?"

London frowned, handed her several sheets of paper from the top of the case file. "We got a hit off our Serial Killer Alert. This came in about an hour ago off the Fed's National Crime Data Exchange... thought you might find it interesting reading."

Max took the sheets and scanned them. By the third page her facial muscles had tightened appreciably.

London raised an eyebrow. "What do you think?"

Max looked her partner in the eye. "M.O.'s the same. Young woman with possible bite wounds, raped and strangled, dumped in the desert by the Salt River... I'd say it's possible the Coyote's been visiting his relatives in the desert southwest."

"I rang up Phoenix P.D. According to the locals the vic was a co-ed from good family. No criminal record. Our guy does prostitutes."

Max arched an eyebrow. "Maybe Phoenix was a gifted amateur, decided to turn pro with the wrong guy."

"Maybe. I guess anything's possible."

*"Half the people in Hollywood are dying to be discovered.
The other half are afraid they will be."*
-Lionel Barrymore

24

The company was halfway through the last episode of the Season, and there was an excitement in the air. But it wasn't the good kind.

The past three days had been particularly hard on cast and crew alike. There'd been a host of technical difficulties, a ton of overtime, as well as a near-fatal accident involving a background player and a jet-engine sized Ritter Fan.

Fortunately, the fan hadn't been damaged.

This morning had started out well, with the first two shots going off flawlessly. Even Cody had cracked a smile when Reed Sloane had called out from Video Village, "Check the gate, new setup," after the second shot.

While the company was busy setting up for the next sequence, the Line Producer headed back to the production office.

Pam Downey was as tough as she was smart. Fifty-three, a single mother raising two teenagers, she was as adept at conflict resolution as she was at balancing numbers. She'd replaced Arnie Kellogg three weeks back when he'd fled to Florida for a three-month run on a feature. Ms. Downey was already counting off the days until blessed hiatus. She sat down at her desk and sighed.

Wayne, a narrow-shouldered P.A., dashed into the production office. He handed the line producer a large manila envelope.

Wayne muttered: "Sherry said you should get a look at these ASAP."

As the line producer tore open the envelope from the Accounting office, the P.A. scurried off.

Pam scanned the 'Hot Costs' and grimaced. The numbers on the sheet, up to date to the hour of the day, painted a bleak picture. The disparity between budgeted and actual costs for this, the last episode of the Season, was a tremendous chasm of deep red. Some of the costs were 'approved studio overages', but others were going to necessitate yet another unpleasant conversation with the studio brass. On the other hand, Chuck Dallas was a hit, and as long as its ratings remained golden, the studio would forgive these financial transgressions.

*****

The curtains in Cody's Airstream were pulled down and the interior felt stuffy. Jimmy Bodine shifted in the chair, holding the pages in one hand.

"Relax, pal. It's gonna be alright."

The script for 'Ballistic' was open in Cody's lap, and a half-full tumbler of Cuervo Gold rested on a table nearby.

"The fuck it's gonna be alright!" Cody replied, his upper lip curled into a snarl. He reached for the tumbler, downed several swallows.

"We'll keep runnin' it 'til you feel comfortable," Jimmy offered.

His words did nothing to console Cody.

"I just can't seem to get a handle on this!"

"You'll get it. Just need some time, is all."

"That's the problem!" Cody roared. "There isn't enough time."

*****

The third sequence scheduled was an interior, with Chuck Dallas and his executive secretary, Cassie Helms. The office set was assembled in the front quarter of Stage 18.

The lack of a ceiling and the 'wild' walls was standard stagecraft. The design allowed the actors to be lit correctly and gave the director choices in how he wanted the shot to look. Showbiz Rule #4: Gotta give the director choices. That's why he's the director.

Mike Brennan, Cody's regular stand-in, was seated in the executive chair with his elbows resting on the desk.

"Hey, you're leaving grease prints on the props!" commented Sue Evans, the beefy-shouldered boom operator.

Mike smiled and broke into an off-key rendition of an old Cat Stevens tune, complete with an updated lyric. "Oh, I'm being followed by a boom shadow. Boom shadow-boom shadow."

Sue Evans extended a central digit salute.

Sean Sennett, the trusty camera operator, was fiddling around with a 'Hot-Head' remote camera mount, off of a 'Techno-Crane'.

Ron, his assistant and shifty-eyed son-in-law, stretched a tape measure from the front of the lens to the tip of Mike Brennan's nose. Then he adjusted the focus on the camera.

Jack Pinion, the silver-haired sound mixer sat at the controls of a Nagra, checking the audio input feed.

In a quiet corner of the stage, tucked in behind some roll-around backdrops, the Fluff brigade exchanged gossip over croissants and coffee.

At Video Village, Sterling Carpenter keyed the walkie. "Cindy, me darlin'. I believe we're ready for number one."

Cynthia Abbott was a D.G.A. trainee working her way up the ladder in the Assistant Director's Program. She was full of energy and ambition, the two personality traits essential to the job. That, and the ability to withstand a shit storm without the aid of an umbrella. She was seated on the curb outside the stage, smoking a Marlboro and perusing The Hollywood Reporter.

"On our way, chief," she replied cheerily.

She stood up and ground out the butt.

Ten minutes later, Cindy, Cody and Jimmy Bodine came through the stage door, approached the group at Video Village.

Cody's expression was sullen, tight. He'd received a fresh coat of makeup, and there were tissue papers in a ring around his shirt collar. He carried a sport coat draped over one arm.

"So are we ready to shoot this scene?" he asked no one in particular.

"Ready when you are, Cody, my man," Reed replied evenly.

Cody's response was cold. "Yah know what, Reed? My call was at seven in the a of m, I've been ready since then."

Reed exchanged a look with Pam Downey, who had rejoined him at Video Village. "Well let's get to it then, shall we? Places everybody."

And with that said, Cody slipped on the sport coat, crossed from Video Village and took his position behind the desk.

Ron held the slate in front of Cody's face and Sean Sennett focused in. At the same time Jack Pinion started recording sound, waited for a sync tone.

"Chuck Dallas, episode twenty, scene twelve, take one…. Mark!" Ron clapped the slate and stepped out of frame.

"And action," Reed commanded.

The director was seated in the center of a herd of high-back canvas chairs, positioned in front of twin, twenty-seven inch monitors. One monitor showed camera A's POV, the other showed camera B's.

Tina Jacoby, the effervescent blonde who recurred as Cassie, stepped into frame, and the camera pulled back to a lopsided two-shot.

"Detective Tarlick just called. He said to…"

"Cut. Let's try it again," Reed said.

"Sorry," Tina apologized. "I'll hit my mark next time. Promise."

"Christ," Cody mumbled under his breath. Tina glided to her off-camera position and Ron stepped up with the slate.

"Resetting back to one," Sterling called out.

"Chuck Dallas, P.I., episode twenty, scene twelve, take two… Mark!" Slap went the slate.

"And action," Reed demanded regally.

Tina/Cassie stepped into frame and hit her mark perfectly. Just as she was about to deliver her line, someone's cell phone began playing the William Tell Overture.

"Cut!" Reed cried, snapping his head in the direction of the noise.

All eyes followed a thoroughly embarrassed extra who attempted to slink away unnoticed. Lotsa luck, pal!

"Can we please get this fucking shot in the can?" Cody pleaded.

Reed took a deep breath.

"Places everybody. One mo' time," Sterling said.

And the slate procedure was repeated yet again.

"And action..."

Tina/Cassie entered the shot, hit her mark dead-on.

"Detective Tarlick called. He said to tell you to stay put, that he was on his way over here, to ask you some questions."

Cody looked up at her and raised an eyebrow. "I don't know what he expects to accomplish questioning me. Even if I knew something that could help him out, I couldn't tell him. I'd be violatin' client confidentiality, and yah know what..."

Cody's speech was rudely interrupted by a high-pitch whining that was emanating from the Hot-Head camera mount. Sean Sennett struggled valiantly with the remote control, cursing in whispers. His effort was answered by spastic camera motions atop the Techno-Crane.

"Cut," Reed sighed, glancing Heavenward.

The camera operator affected a superior Scottish brogue. "I can't hold her Captain. She's breaking up!"

"Alright everybody, let's take five," Pam Downey wisely suggested.

"Yah know what?" Cody seethed. "I don't need this! Call me when y'all get your shit together! Comprende? I'll be in my trailer."

Cody stormed off the set. As the door sealed shut behind him, the murmuring began.

"He didn't mean it," Jimmy Bodine insisted, turning towards the shocked faces seated in Video Village. "He's just got a lot on his mind. I'll talk to him."

"That'd be nice," Pam resounded. "That'd be real nice."

Jimmy walked off feeling deeply embarrassed for his friend.   As soon as he was out of earshot the commentary began.

"God, what happened to him?" Cindy asked, genuinely bewildered. "He used to be such a nice guy."

"They all start out nice guys," Wayne responded.

Reed Sloane huddled with Pam Downey. "I'm beginning to suspect our dear Mister Clifton has a 'lifestyle problem'," he commented in a conspiratorial tone

"That'd certainly explain some things," Sterling chimed in, nodding his head. "You know he's been late to his makeup call three times this week."

Pam Downey lifted an eyebrow at the news.
*****

Cody burst into the trailer red-faced and cursing. He slammed the Airstream's door, startling the sleeping Blue, who commenced barking at Cody.

"What the fuck's wrong with you? Shut the fuck up!" Cody screamed.

He kicked the coffee table, shattering glassware and sending a spray of Doctor Pepper across the room. Blue dove for cover.

Cody crossed to the kitchen, opened a cabinet and retrieved an open bottle of Cuervo Gold. He poured several fingers worth into a tumbler and knocked it back. He set the glass down and refilled it. Just as he finished the second helping someone knocked on the trailer's door.

"It's me. Open up, buddy."

Cody knocked back a third belt and curled his upper lip. "You alone?"

"Yeah," Jimmy replied.

"Door's open. C'mon in."

The door opened a crack and Jimmy cautiously peered in. He entered the trailer and closed the door behind him.

"Can I get yah somethin' to drink?" Cody asked, motioning to the half-empty bottle of tequila.

Jimmy shook his head.

"Aw c'mon, Jimmy-Bo, be a pal," Cody insisted. "Yah know I hate drinkin' alone."

Jimmy nodded acquiescence and Cody poured him a glass.

"Lime?"

"Jesus, Cody. What's the matter with you?"

"I guess that's a no to the lime," Cody continued, unrelenting.

"I don't get it," Jimmy said, accepting the glass and swallowing the amber liquid in a gulp. "All those folks've been working their asses off, doing their best to make this show a success. Your Show, Cody. Hear what I'm sayin'? ...And you go and talk to 'em like that? What's wrong with you?"

Cody took a pull from the bottle, swished the liquid cheek to cheek, like one-hundred-twenty-proof mouthwash. He righted the coffee table, set the bottle down, and collapsed on the sofa. He placed his forehead into his hands.

"Fucked up pretty good back there, didn't I?"
Jimmy nodded his head.

"Pressure's getting to me, I guess. Haven't been sleepin' much."

"All you need's some time off, pal."

Cody laughed. "Try tellin' that to Shelly."

Jimmy shrugged his shoulders and smiled. "A lot of folks'd kill to be in your position. And buddy, I'm not too proud to admit I'm one of 'em."

"It's not all it's cracked up to be," Cody began. "It's like all of a sudden my privacy vanished. Poof! I'm livin' in a goddamn fish bowl and everybody's watchin' me. If I go out for groceries, people are takin' notes on what I put in my cart. I tell yah, Jimmy-Bo, I feel like I gotta put on a disguise just to walk my goddamn dog."

"Like I said before Cody. Lotta people'd kill to have your problems."

"I suppose you're right."

Cody stood up and straightened the wrinkles out of his slacks. "Guess I owe everyone an apology... Think they'll forgive me?"

Jimmy didn't hesitate to answer. "They're all good folks, Cody. They know the pressure you've been under."

*"Conscience: The inner voice which
warns us someone may be looking."*

H. L. Mencken

25

The last three days of principal photography for the season went by in a blur. The company ran like a finely tuned machine, flowing from set-up to set-up. On the last day, the final shot was actually in the can before five, a miracle in and of itself. By five minutes after five the entire company was in party mode.

The caterers had been at work since before breakfast. Angel and his nieces, referred to by one and all as 'The Sisters of Mercy', had prepared a celebration spread to beat all. Six linen-covered tables were lined up in a crescent behind the Chuck Dallas set. It was time to celebrate.

Within half an hour everyone was in good spirits, tensions lifted. The conversation turned to upcoming gigs, in town and outta state. A commotion by the stage door caused heads to turn.

Cody strutted in, flanked by Jimmy Bodine on one side, and Wayne the P.A. on the other. Jimmy was carrying a bluetooth speaker as big as a carry-on. Cody's theme song, George Thorogood's 'Bad To The Bone', howled from the dual ten inch speakers. Wayne sweated profusely as he lugged a dolly stacked with cases of Dom Perignon. As the trio came into view the entire company started to cheer and whistle. Cody nodded and smiled, accepted the accolades with grace.

"Thank you. Thank you one and all," he began.

The applause quieted.

"Y'all are the best folks I've ever had the privilege to work with... I'd like each of you to take one of these bottles home with you tonight. Share it with someone you love and try and have a kind thought for old Cody Clifton."

Cody lowered his head and continued. "I know at times I've been... aw, how should I put this?"

"Difficult?" Pam Downey suggested amid titters of laughter.

"Thank you Pam. I'll use that," Cody replied with a charming grin. "I know at times I've been difficult, and probably a whole lot more. But y'all've been there for me every step of the way, and I just want you to know how much I appreciate that... For those of you who can't make it to the wrap party next week at Club Brazen, y'all have a great vacation. Hope to see y'all back for season two."

As he finished speaking, cast and crew crowded around, collected their gift bottles, and thanked him with kisses, handshakes, or a friendly slap on the back.

Giving expensive gifts to his friends and co-workers made Cody feel worthwhile and alleviated some of the lingering guilt. And besides making him feel good, Shelly had told him it was all tax deductible.

God bless that Shelly.

When all the bottles were spoken for, Cody waved at the company and exited with Jimmy. They crossed through the lot headed toward their respective vehicles.

Cody pressed a button on his keychain that disarmed the alarm and unlocked the doors on the Suburban. He opened the rear hatch and removed a large rectangular box, handed it to Jimmy.

"What's this?"

What's it look like, buddy? It's a present."

"You didn't have to do that."

"I know," Cody replied. "That's why I did."

Jimmy opened the box. "Damn!" he exclaimed.

"They're genuine Python skin, just like mine. Hand made toe 'n' heel guards and everything. I got you black ones figurin' you'd get more use out of 'em."

Jimmy rubbed an appreciative palm over the hand worked leather. "Thanks, Cody. That was a real nice thing yah did."

Cody reached over and gave Jimmy a bear hug. "Nothin' one brother wouldn't do for another brother. Give me a call next week and we'll get together for a coupla beers."

Cody climbed into the lumbering four-by-four, fired up the beast and waved goodbye to Jimmy.

PART 3

TEN PERCENT

*"Whoever said, 'It's not whether you
win or lose that counts', probably lost."*
-Martina Navratilova

26

Sylvia sat at the reception desk with a headset telephone draped around her honey locks, and a copy of Cosmo opened on her desk. She ran an Emory board around her fingernails while she carried on a conversation with her girlfriend in South Carolina.

"... Like duh, what did she expect? No, I'm totally serious..."

And line three lit up.

"Hang on a sec." Click.

"Monroe Talent Group, this is Sylvia. Who's this?"

The voice on the other end of the line sounded young, cocky. "Ricky Ramirez here. Shell around?"

Not recognizing the name or the voice, Sylvia slipped into call-screen mode. "And what is this regarding?"

"Oh, she'll know."

Sylvia's eyes narrowed to slits. "Can I put you on a hold for a second?" Sylvia enquired innocently, and then quickly stuck the button that sent Ricky between the circuits.

Sylvia clicked another button and returned to her conversation. "Sorry Keri. So where were we?"

Two lines lit up simultaneously.

"Shit! Gotta go girl. I'll call you back."

Sylvia disconnected line one and picked up line two. "Monroe Talent, hold please."

She slapped the hold button and picked up line four. "Monroe Talent, Sylvia speaking. Who may I ask is calling?"

"Hi Sylvia. It's Erin with the David Bloom Company."

"Good morning, Erin," Sylvia replied cordially. "Hang on a second and I'll put you through to Ms. Monroe."

Shelly was stretched out on the leather chaise with her feet propped up. Just last week she'd taken the liberty of having a sixty-four inch flat screen installed in her private office. At the moment, A Hollywood E! Special on Nicole Kidman was winding down.

A chirp, and then Sylvia's voice over the Intercom: "Ms. Monroe, you have David Bloom's office on line four."

Shelly sat up, muted the TV and snatched the headset phone off the carpet, pressed a button on the handset. "Good morning," she said. "This is Shelly."

"One moment for Mister Bloom," replied the voice on the other end of the line.

Five seconds later, an older smoother voice: "Good morning, Shelly. David Bloom here."

"Good morning David," she cooed. "To what do I owe the pleasure?"

"I wanted you to be the first to know. The official word just came down from the Network. Chuck Dallas got picked up for season two –A full order –Twenty-two episodes."

"That's terrific! Cody'll be thrilled!"

"It's been good news all around today," the executive producer said. "You'll be getting the official letter later this week... I'll let you get back to what you were doing."

"Thanks for the call, David. And congratulations!" Shelly disconnected the line, removed the headset telephone and let it fall to the carpet. She unwrapped another piece of Nicotine gum, popped it in her mouth, and crossed to the balcony. She chewed rapidly and gazed out at the horizon. Before long a triumphant smile began spreading across her face.

They were all wrong! The naysayers, the cynics, everyone who had ever said Shelly Monroe would never amount to anything. The Fuckers were all wrong! And she was right! The moment felt so good that, in a rare display of emotion, Shelly actually had to dab a hand against leaky eyes. She wiped it off on the back of her Armani jacket, and laughed at the show of sentimentality.

Shelly turned and faced into the office and let out a blood-curdling victory cry. "Yeeeeee-Haaaaaaa!!!!!!"

Thirty seconds later Irv poked his head into Shelly's office, eyes magnified comically behind thick prescription lenses. "Jesus, Shelly! You alright?" he asked with genuine concern.

"Couldn't be better," she replied, wiping at her eyes with the back of her sleeve.

In all the years he'd known her, Irv couldn't remember a single instance when she'd gotten emotional.

"That was David Bloom's office on the line. The Network picked up Chuck Dallas for a full order for Season Two!"

Irv's expression was stunned. He blinked rapidly, unable to speak, attempting to process her words.

"Irv?... You with me, Irv?"

Irv took off his glasses and polished them on his Dior shirt, tried not to hyperventilate.

"Uh, Irv?"

"Incredible," he croaked.

Shelly's smile was huge, but there was something about it that caused Irv's nut sack to seek immediate shelter up his asshole.

"No, Irv. Let me tell you about incredible. For the past several weeks I've been quietly negotiating an endorsement deal for our dear Mister Clifton with Ford Motor Company. 'Incredible' is how much Cody's price just went up!"

Irv adjusted his glasses and looked at Shelly with a combination of awe and fear. Sure glad we're playing on the same team.

"Success is a public affair. Failure is a private funeral."
                                                        -Rosalind Russell

27

It was the first weekday morning Cody had slept in since the beginning of January. It was a luxury he wouldn't get a chance to become accustomed to. Today was Thursday, and he was due on the set of 'Ballistic' this coming Tuesday, at seven a.m. sharp. No rest for the weary.

In Cody's mind this translated into one-hundred and twenty hours of freedom, a commodity that had been in rather short supply the past seven months.

He awoke a little after nine and popped out of bed like a piece of toast, anxious to make the most of his short holiday. No way was he gonna spend his time catching up on lost sleep. Too many things needed doin'.
Blue trotted into the bedroom, tail wagging mightily.

"Good mornin', Blue dog," Cody said, bending down to scratch the hound's ears. "Yah feel like goin' for a run this mornin?"

Blue looked up at his master and woofed an affirmative response.

Cody chuckled.

"Glad to hear it... Just give me time to get a quick shower and slam down some biscuits 'n' coffee. Okay?"

Blue woofed again and Cody padded across the carpet to the bathroom.

*****

The black Cadillac SUV turned past the 'For Sale' sign and lumbered up the drive, coming to a stop across from a flagstone entry.

Gloria Elrod, Realtor-To-The-Stars, stepped from the vehicle and brushed the wrinkles from her skirt. She was in her early-thirties, with thoughtful brown eyes and a salesman's hungry heart.

"So what do you think so far?"

"Nice neighborhood," Shelly commented, slamming the passenger door.

"Best in the West," Gloria gushed. "And at one-point-five-mil I don't expect this property to be on the market long."

"Mmmmm," Shelly responded noncommittally.

The two women crossed through the courtyard landscaped with bright red bougainvillea and Mexican sage. A small pond and waterfall took up one corner of the courtyard, adding a calming ambience.

"The owners spent eight grand having the place Feng-Shui-ed by C. Lee Ishi. Can you believe that?"

Shelly didn't believe much that spewed from the realtor's mouth, but then again, anything was possible in El Lay.

The realtor unlocked a massive Cherry wood door that led into the main residence and the two women stepped inside.

"I really think you're going to like this one, Ms. Monroe," Gloria encouraged. "It has three bedrooms, three-and-one-half baths, a formal dining room, an office, a gourmet kitchen, and an entertainer's backyard with pool and spa."

"Mmm," Shelly replied.

"Of course at this price it's bound to need some work."

"Oh, of course," Shelly agreed, mentally rolling her eyes.

*****

"This is our Top of the line model, Mister Birnbaum," Jeff, the Jacuzzi salesman said. "It's called the Macho Royale."

He motioned to the enormous redwood-wrapped tub. "That puppy has three separate lounges, twenty-four different jet configurations, and a shell made out of space-age polymers. It comes in your choice of sixteen metal flake colors. Drives the Babes wild! Care to take it for a spin?"

Hollywood Irv stuck a furry forearm into the frothing liquid and grinned. He was clad in orange swimming trunks and beige flip-flops. Gold chains dangled from his chicken neck, and eighteen carat Versace framed glasses shielded his eyes.

"This the one that comes with the built-in DVD?"

*****

As he swung the Suburban into the lot at Cahuenga Park, Cody's eye was drawn to the singular figure poised on the archery field. The woman was dressed in cutoff jean shorts and a white sports-bra that contrasted nicely against smoked honey colored skin. Her chestnut brown hair was streaked with silver and tied back in a lush ponytail. In his mind's eye, Cody painted the Stranger as a Fairy Tale Indian Princess.

He nosed the seven-thousand pounds of American steel into a space reserved for compacts, switched off the ignition, opened the door and stepped from the rig. Blue crossed to the driver's seat and paused for a moment as if measuring the distance between soft leather and hard ground.

"Aw c'mon Blue. You're embarrassing me."

When it became apparent Blue had no intention of risking life and limb in a free-fall from the hopped-up Chevy, Cody snatched him off the seat and set him on the ground. Then he closed the door and chirped the alarm.

"C'mon, yah big pussy," Cody chided as he trotted off toward the running track.

There were about a dozen people scattered around the track, a pretty typical crowd for a weekday morning. As Cody began his warm-up stretches, some of those passing by recognized him and waved.

"Haven't seen you around here in quite a while," one runner called out. He was a bald-headed guy with a red, white and blue sweatband stretched across his formidable forehead.

"My work schedule's kept me kinda busy," Cody replied honestly.

Two more runners recognized him and stopped to chat. They were both fit young women in their late-twenties, and Cody was more than happy to play along.

"Love your show Cody," oozed one of the young women.

"I think you're the sexiest man on TV," chimed her friend.

Cody's smile was George Clooney suave. "Thank you, ladies."

When he'd completed his stretching routine Cody loped off, with Blue at his heels and the two women flanking him, chattering away in a continual stereo stream. The consummate actor, he tuned them out but kept right on smiling, nodding occasionally for effect.

And in short order, Cody found himself running in the middle of a pack.

Ah, the price of Fame.

*****

Max felt a sudden tingle and the baby-fine hairs at the base of her neck stood erect. But she held her position, left arm straight, hand lightly grasping the bow, right arm bent at the elbow. She exhaled slowly, controlling her breath, and released the string.

The arrow's flight was too fast to follow. The eye simply witnessed an acceleration of reflected light that crossed a slight parabolic arc. And then the brain registered the 'thwock' of tip punching through paper.

Sight and sound. Cause and Effect. Random neurons. Max glanced over her shoulder at the dirt track and unconsciously flexed her nostrils, tasting the air like a predator. Nothing was out of place, not a soul within a hundred yards of where she stood. She dismissed the sensation as a fluke response to internal stimuli and returned to her workout.

But when that tingle flashed across the nerves of her cervical vertebrae for the second time in less than five minutes, Max once again turned instinctively in the direction of the running track. As she did, a pack of about a dozen runners jogged past the chain link fence that separated the two fields.

The man running in the center of the group caught her eye. He was remarkably good looking, and she was sure she'd seen him somewhere before. She just couldn't quite put her finger on where. And when he made eye contact with her for that brief moment, his smile was pure warmth and charm.

Where did she know him from?

*****

Arriving home, Cody shaved and showered, then stepped from the bathroom suddenly overcome with exhaustion. Probably should have eased into the workout instead of going balls out. But then that just wouldn't have been Cody.

By the time he and Blue had finished lunch it was nearing two-thirty. By quarter 'til three Cody was nodded out on the sofa, in front of the bigscreen. A half-consumed bottle of Redtail Ale sat alone on the coffee table, perspiring impolitely, and leeching into the grain of the Koa, a brand new circular sibling added to the family.

And as he slept, Cody began to dream.

And as the dream came to his master in clips and snippets, something made Blue stir from his catnap and exit the room.

*****

… Two-hundred, eight dollars, and some change, a deck of cards, and the clothes he was wearing. That was Cody's net worth in July, 1988. It was fortunate he had a sharp mind and more street sense than any fourteen year old had a right to possess. Summer in "The Big Easy" would put his survival skills to the test.

He managed to go unnoticed by the local authorities for almost a month, mostly by keeping his antennae up at all times. Even though summer vacation was in full swing and there were young people everywhere, Cody got nervous every time he saw a police cruiser.

His life had become a rather bumpy adventure ride, but at least he was free to come and go as he pleased… In mid-August it all came crashing down around his ears.

Over the course of a single weekend there had been a crime wave in the park. Nine tourists had been robbed, and one had been beaten severely enough to require hospitalization. Very bad for business. The victims had described the assailants as a mixed-race gang of teenage thugs. This resulted in a series of high-profile police sweeps that netted more than one-hundred arrests, mostly for loitering and public intoxication.

Cody had been picked up on the very first sweep. He'd been in the park enjoying the summer evening with a group of friends. They'd been sharing a gallon jug of 'Red Mountain' Burgundy and playing cards when a police helicopter appeared overhead. It hovered like a dragonfly for a few moments and then unleashed about ten billion candle power into the faces of the congregated youths.

In an instant, midnight became high noon.

Cody bolted for cover just as a contingent of dark blue uniforms advanced from the tree line. The cops were outfitted in full riot gear; helmets with face-plates, clear plexiglass shields, and shiny black billys. They swarmed the teenagers and met little in the way of resistance.

Cody ran for all he was worth, headed for the relative safety of the underbrush. He knew if he could get out of the open and beneath some trees, he just might have a chance. He put out a final burst of speed, sprinting the last hundred yards. But just as he was about to dive for cover, something clobbered him from his blind side and compressed the air from his lungs.

When he came to, he was in a hospital bed. His very first thought was escape. But as his senses cleared, Cody became aware that his clothes were gone. In their place was a flimsy, mint green hospital gown, the kind that ties in back. He sure as hell couldn't get very far wearing this getup.

And then he noticed the IV line plugged into a vein in his left hand. He stared at the battered tissue surrounding the insertion point of the needle. There were shades of blue all the way to deep purple, with tinges of pale yellow. A virtual kaleidoscope of bruising. He felt nauseous, closed his eyes to make the room stop spinning. It didn't help.

Two days later, Cody was deemed recovered enough from his concussion to be discharged, and was placed in the protective custody of the State Child Welfare Office. The Kiddie Klink. Three days after that he was sent to live in a foster home that housed nearly a dozen other kids.

All in all, it hadn't been a bad place to wind up. There was a roof over his head, a clean bed to sleep in, and three squares a day. And as luck would have it, Cody was the second oldest kid in the place.

The woman who was in charge of the group home was a matronly woman in her fifties, referred to as 'Aunt Becky'. She was a pleasant sort, with lively blue eyes and sand-gray hair. She was a real 'live-and-let-live' kind of person whose approach to 'child management' was strictly hands-off. Aunt Becky's real genius was in knowing how to take advantage of the System. She'd been working the Foster Home gig for more than a decade.

On the First and Fifteenth of each and every month, a brown envelope would arrive in the mail. Inside, there'd be a green government check, made out to Rebecca Tidwell. The sum would vary month to month based solely on the number of foster children currently in her care. And each month Aunt Rebecca redistributed nearly two-thirds of those funds for her own personal use. This was managed by feeding the kids a diet of macaroni and cheese, peanut butter and jelly sandwiches, and creamed corn.

Funny thing was, nobody ever complained. Because as long as nobody rocked the boat, Aunt Becky left the kids to their own devices. Basically, the inmates were in charge of the asylum. And a pleasant asylum it was.

Cody's new home was a rambling old farm house with a wrap-around veranda, situated on twenty, green, semi-rural acres. The residence consisted of six bedrooms and four baths, a large dining room, and an even larger kitchen. Currently, the place buzzed with the energy of twelve urchins, half under the age of ten. There was a continual turnover of children, constant chatter and a definite feeling of warmth.

Cody arrived at the facility mid-afternoon, and Aunt Becky met him at the van. She introduced herself and escorted him, past a dozen chickens along the walk, into the residence.

"Everybody, this here's Cody. Cody, this is everybody." Aunt Becky smiled and crossed to the kitchen.

Four of the older children approached Cody, curious about the new kid.

"So Cody, how long yah in for?" the pretty girl with the strawberry-blonde hair asked.

Caught off-guard, Cody blinked. "Huh?"

The girl giggled. "I'm just kiddin'. My name's Holly." She offered a delicate, freckled hand.

Cody hesitated, took her hand awkwardly. "Uh… nice to meet'cha, Holly." He looked her over, was charmed by the freckles across her nose and her warm brown eyes. He became aware that his heart was pounding in his chest, and he thought: *God she's pretty!*

"And this is my friend, Chrissy," Holly continued, introducing a girl of thirteen with dark hair and even darker eyes.

"Hi," Chrissy said with a quick wave.

"Hey."

Then two boys stepped up.

"Hey Cody. I'm Leon, and this is my little bro', Mikey."

Leon was big for thirteen, but his 'little' brother, Mikey, was already a head taller than Leon, and he'd just turned twelve. Both boys were blue-eyed towheads with mullet haircuts. Future quarterback-eaters.

"Nice to meet y'all."

"So Cody, do yah play poker?" Holly asked, a mischievous smile spreading across her face.

"A little," Cody replied. He thought: "Damn, I think I'm in love."

It was the third week of August and they had three more weeks until school started. Three more weeks of freedom.

*****

As it turned out, Holly was a lot more than just a pretty face. She was a fuckin' criminal mastermind as well as a natural born leader. She hadn't been at the facility more than a week before she'd organized the older kids into a crew of skilled delinquents.

They'd take the bus into town and indulge in a little light shoplifting, at the mall. Or they'd fan out and case neighborhoods in search of soft targets to burgle, meaning empty houses, sans dogs or bars on the windows. Afterwards, they'd return to the facility and examine the day's booty.

Holly knew an older boy from town who'd give her cash for the stolen loot. His name was Eddie, and he had a jacked-up gold Firebird. Holly would split the proceeds amongst her crew, taking an extra share for herself. She was their Leader after all.

And when they weren't out stealing, or attending to the few chores Aunt Becky required of them, they would often spend their days outdoors, hiking and fishing and enjoying Nature. And then at night, they'd stay up late, playing poker and listening to music. All this would pretty much end once school began.

Cody fell right in with the crew and proved himself a valuable asset the first time out. He scouted a house in a quiet upscale neighborhood, complete with a hedge that obscured the front door. He checked around back to make sure that no one was home and then picked the lock. Holly and her crew entered, fanned out, and spent a total of ten minutes inside the residence. They left with several thousand dollars worth of jewelry that Chrissy had located in the refrigerator, of all places. The crew was jubilant!

But later that day, when Holly stopped by Eddie's double-wide, he took one look at the rings and gold chains and shook his head.

"That shit ain't worth nothin', Holly," He lied. "Here, you can see what I'm talkin' 'bout. Take a look."

Eddie handed Holly a magnifying glass and stepped closer to her, an arm brushed against her breasts.

"See that color shift in the light? That means the stone's a fake."

Knowing nothing of such things and trusting Eddie's veracity, Holly looked disappointed. "Stuff sure is pretty. Guess I'll just hang on to it."

Eddie put a consoling arm around Holly's shoulder. "Tell yah what I'm gonna do. Because I like you, and because you usually bring me nothin' but primo shit, I'll give you two-hundred bucks for the lot. How's that sound?"

It sounded like robbery, but Holly gratefully accepted the cash. When she returned home and produced the money Eddie had given her, Cody became livid.

"You gotta be kiddin' me! That stuff hadda be worth close to ten grand!"

"Eddie said the stones were fake…"

"How the fuck would Eddie know? He a jeweler? No, he's just Eddie, the full o' shit asshole, who just fucked all of us!"

Holly was flustered. *"Cody, I really don't know why you're so upset. I've been doin' business with Eddie for a long time and…"*

"He's probably been fuckin' y'all all that time, too."

"What makes you so damn sure?" she insisted, with a note of anger to her tone. Holly didn't like being challenged.

"I know about these sorta things, Holly," Cody explained. *"'Cause when I was little, my momma taught me about jewelry, how to tell real stuff from 'paste'. Said it fell under the category of 'things worth knowin'."*

Holly paused to digest that little tidbit.

"Was it your momma taught you how to pick a lock, too?" Holly mused, suddenly less agitated.

Cody nodded his head.

Holly's expression clouded as the realization struck home. She turned from the crew and marched purposefully toward the door.

"Hey, where're you goin?" Cody asked.

"Gonna get our stuff back from Eddie."

"Hold on a second. I'll go with you."

"I don't need your help."

"I know. But I'm comin' along, anyway."

Because if Eddie became too big a problem, Cody knew how to make a body disappear. He'd done it before. It was another skill that had been passed down from mother to son.

*****

The sun was setting as Cody and Holly stepped from the tree line and approached Eddie's double-wide. Eddie was nowhere in sight, but his gold Firebird was parked out front, and the pair could hear music emanating from within the dilapidated aluminum box.

"Wait here," Holly instructed in a whisper.

"I don't think so," Cody argued.

Holly shoved him with both hands. "Eddie lied to me and I believed him. So this is my problem. And I intend to fix it, myself. Okay, Cody?"

Holly was so angry she was trembling.

Cody relented. "Have it your way."

As Holly ascended the steps to Eddie's front door, Cody took up a position a few yards from the trailer's rear entrance. He could smell the sweet aroma of marijuana wafting through the open windows. He leaned in so he could hear better what was going on inside.

Holly turned the knob on the front door, stepped inside, and closed the door behind her.

Eddie was perched on the sofa in the living room, hovering over the coffee table, and a small mountain of marijuana trim. A dozen joints were fanned out in one corner of the table, and Eddie was in the process of rolling lucky number thirteen. He looked up from what he was doing, saw Holly, and flashed a gapped-toothed grin.

"Goddamn girl! Ya know, I was just thinking 'bout you." Eddie couldn't believe his good fortune.

Holly's expression was all business as she pulled the wad of cash from her pocket, placed it on the coffee table in front of Eddie. "There's your money, Eddie. I want my stuff back."

"Really?" Eddie tugged at his scrawny blonde goatee.

"Yeah, really," Holly insisted.

"Well sorry, darlin'. A deal's a deal."

"You fuckin' lied to me, yah prick!..."

"Oooh, I just love it when yah talk dirty," Eddie said, rising from the couch.

"I want my shit back!"

Eddie stepped in front of the enraged girl, an amused smile mocking her.

"Not gonna happen, darlin'. But let me tell yah what is gonna happen."

Eddie grabbed Holly, pulled her towards him, kissed her.

Holly struggled, but Eddie was much larger, much stronger. He reached around and grabbed her ass with both hands, pulled her onto his erection.

Holly threw a wicked knee and pulled away.

Eddie bent over in agony. "Fuckin' bitch!"

He straightened, and back-handed her across the face, sending her sprawling.

"Now your sweet little ass is mine!"

He jumped on her, started to pull her pants down.

"Get off me!" Holly screamed, twisting and throwing elbows.

Hearing the commotion, Cody crashed through the back door. He ran straight at Eddie, head down, smashing into his chest. They tumbled together into the coffee table, sending weed and shards of glass across the trailer.

Cody glanced over his shoulder and reached for the first thing he saw that could be used as a weapon. It turned out to be a heavy glass ashtray. Cody swung it with authority and accuracy. A three-inch gash opened above Eddie's right eye and he crumpled to the floor, bleeding profusely. Cody stood up and kicked him a couple of times, for good measure, as did Holly.

Five minutes later, the pair left Eddie's double-wide and headed for the tree line. Cody carried a pillow case that contained their jewelry and some various odds and ends the couple had liberated from Eddie... for all the trouble. There was a real nice car stereo, some silverware, and a little over seven hundred dollars in cash.

*****

Over the course of the next three weeks, Cody and Holly spent a lot of time together. There was a mutual attraction that would not be denied.

After dinner, on one particularly warm, early September evening, Holly took Cody's hand. She bent over and whispered in his ear, "Meet me out back in fifteen minutes, by the chicken house."

Before Cody could say a word in response, Holly kissed him gently on the ear and quickly stepped away. Cody felt a pleasant tingle shoot down his spine and his heart begin to pound.

It was twilight as they ran, hand in hand, down the rutted path towards the swimming hole. They were serenaded, along the way, by a bullfrog chorus, and cicadas singing in the trees.

Holly led Cody to the edge of the water. Both of them were breathing hard from the run. Then, without a word, Holly slipped off her clothes and dove into the pond.

It didn't take Cody more than a micro-second to shed his clothes and join her in the water.

Holly splashed him and giggled.

Cody swam up to her and they embraced. And as they kissed, Cody felt a strange warmth in his chest. It was something he had never experienced before, and as such, it was a bit unnerving. Cody didn't like feeling vulnerable, but he certainly liked the way he felt whenever he was with Holly.

They made love under a rising moon.

"Tell me again, Cody. How's it gonna be?" she teased.

"It's gonna be great, Holly! You and me together, forever. And when we're eighteen, we can go wherever we want."

"And where yah gonna take me?"

"Darlin', I'm gonna take you anywhere you wanna go."

"I wanna go to Hollywood and be a star!"

"Baby, you are a star."

*****

A week later, school began, and everything began to change.

Cody had never liked school, and Lyndon Johnson High was destined to be no exception.

The building itself was depressingly ugly. A two-story, red brick, block house, with what looked like guard towers on each corner. The students entered through a central double-gate that was monitored at all times during school hours. There would be no unauthorized comings or goings at this institution.

Cody had always managed to get by in school by doing the minimal work necessary, and by keeping a low profile. That would be difficult now, if not impossible, because Cody could no longer concentrate. The only thing Cody could think about was Holly, and how much he enjoyed making love to her. The fact they didn't have a single class together, and only saw each other during lunch, served to further exacerbate the issue.

Holly was the other side of the coin. She loved school, excelled in anything she had an interest in, with Drama being first and foremost.

And Holly had real acting talent.

Mister Alan Bond, the handsome young drama teacher, had said so himself, on more than one occasion.

*****

By early October, Cody's mood had noticeably deteriorated. He was doing alright in his classes, but he definitely wasn't happy. He felt stifled and bound. All he wanted was to be with Holly. Nothing else mattered.

Five days a week they rode together on the bus to school. They would hold hands and plan their shiny future. Then they wouldn't see one another again until lunch break. At school, they never had a private moment.

And the week nights at the Group Home were even worse.

Holly would be in her bed on the other side of the wall from where Cody tossed and turned. No matter how hard he tried, he couldn't get the images of her out of his head. Moist, vivid images.

There was no privacy for them anywhere there, either.

The only time they had together was on the weekends.

Cody felt like he was on fire. And at one point a thought occurred to him. Perhaps this is what it felt like when someone was losing their mind.
*****

It was a Friday, late in October, when things began to disintegrate.

It had started out as a normal enough day. The kids from the facility had ridden to school together on the bus. Cody and Holly had sat together in the last row, holding hands and talking. Nothing had seemed out of the ordinary.

But when lunch time rolled around, Holly was a no-show.

She'd been late before, on several occasions, but always had a quick explanation, usually involving a rehearsal for the school play. Then, it had only been ten or fifteen minutes. Today was different.

When Holly hadn't turned up after twenty minutes, Cody started getting anxious. After half an hour had elapsed, he stood up and headed across the quad, towards the auditorium.

As he approached, Cody had a bad feeling, but he shook it off and proceeded. He opened the door and stepped inside the auditorium. The stage was set like the interior of a house, with two brown couches, a coffee table, and assorted paraphernalia scattered around. Not a soul was about.

Cody went up the wing steps, walked silently across the stage. He stepped behind the curtain, heard faint sounds at the back of auditorium. He followed the sounds to where an office and some dressing rooms were located.

*He poked his head into the office, saw that it was emp-
ty, and withdrew. Next, he crossed to one of the dressing
rooms.*

*As he got closer, Cody heard voices from behind the
door. Without thinking, he nudged the dressing room door
open. His heart was racing.*

*On the other side of the door, he saw Holly and Mister
Bond. They were snuggling together on a couch, kissing
and fondling one another. It took a moment before they
even noticed that they were no longer alone.*

"Who's there?" Mister Bond called out.

*A hundred thoughts flooded Cody's mind as he fled the
scene. He stepped from the auditorium into the Louisiana
sunlight, crossed quickly through the quad. There were
people moving in waves all around him, but Cody was
completely unaware. He was numb and no longer thinking. Cody was past thinking, moving now on adrenaline
and survival instinct alone.*

*He headed for the bungalows at the back of the school,
continued to the chain link fence at the perimeter. He
checked over his shoulder, saw it was clear, then scaled
the fence in an instant.*

*Cody hit the pavement on the other side of the fence
with both feet and took off running.*

*****

*At three-fifteen, Cody, Holly, and the rest of the kids
boarded the bus back to the Group Home. Everything
back to normal.*

*"Sorry I missed you today at lunch," Holly apologized.
"Rehearsal ran late again."*

*"It's okay, darlin'," Cody lied. "It's Friday! We have the
whole weekend."*

Holly kept a poker face and thought: "That pretty much depends on whether I hear from Alan."
*****

Cody lay awake most of Friday night, thinking and planning. Despite his hurt and anger, he had convinced himself that he could fix this problem. Convinced himself that he was in love with Holly, and that she was worthy of that love.

By dawn he had concocted a plan. At breakfast, he sat down next to Holly.

"Good mornin', darlin'," he said cheerfully.

"Back at'cha," Holly replied.

"We still on today?" Cody asked.

"I don't know, Cody," Holly began. "I got a paper due Monday. I really oughta stay home and study."

"Aw, C'mon Holly. You can study tonight. Today I got somethin' real special to show yah."

"Yeah? What is it?"

"I can't tell yah, darlin'. I gotta show yah. It's a place I stumbled on, on one of those little islands. There's a secret cabin. It looks like it's been there since pirate times. Holly, you gotta see it."

Originally, Holly had other intentions for her Saturday, but Cody had her intrigued. A secret cabin could be something very useful.

"Okay, Cody. Let's see your secret cabin."
*****

About a mile beyond the swimming pond, a finger of the Great Mississippi touched the land. A scruffy rowboat bobbed on the dark water, with a length of rope securing it to a post on the shore.

"C'mon," Cody said, climbing into the row boat. He disconnected the rope from the boat, tossed it on shore.

Holly stepped in the boat, and moments later, Cody cast off.

"It's not far," Cody assured. "Just around that bend."

Half an hour later Holly and Cody beached the boat.

"It's this way," Cody said, starting off at a lope.

Holly paced him, step for step.

About a hundred yards from the river's edge, Holly could make out the corner of Cody's secret cabin. It was tucked neatly between two cypress trees and mostly obscured by overgrown bushes.

"Pretty cool, Cody," Holly said, stepping through the overgrowth, and finally reaching the front door.

Cody pushed the front door open and stepped inside. Holly was right behind him.

The cabin consisted of one large room, with an old iron stove at its center. In one corner, there was an old ice box and some counters, with storage shelves above. On the opposite corner, there was a bed and night stand. The cabin seemed to have been abandoned some time ago, but had remained remarkably intact.

"Check it out," Cody said, taking Holly's hand. "It ain't fancy, but we could fix it up. It's everything we need."

Holly withdrew her hand, looked confused. "What're you talkin' about, Cody?"

"I'm talkin' about you and me buildin' a life together," Cody began. "We can make this place our own. There's nothin' can stop us."

"You're sweet," Holly said, unbuttoning her blouse and crossing to the bed.

Later, when they lay naked in each others arms, Cody asked, "What do you think about my plan?"

"Plan?"

"Yah know, what I was sayin' before. About us livin' together."

"Cody, this cabin's a real neat place to spend a week-end, camping, but I sure wouldn't want to live here... I like takin' hot baths. And gettin' chomped by mosquitos, and possibly eaten by gators, just isn't my idea of a good time."

Cody looked into her eyes and then asked the question that had been tormenting him for months.

"Holly, do you love me?"

"I'm not wearing any clothes, am I?"

Cody paused, took a breath.

"I'm serious, Holly. I gotta know."

"Of course I love you," Holly said quickly, wanting to put an end to the conversation.

From the tone of her answer, Cody doubted Holly's sincerity.

"Am I the only one?"

Holly sat up in bed.

"Why would you ask me a question like that?"

"Holly, you're it for me. Am I it for you?"

Holly laid her head on Cody's chest.

"Yes, Cody. I love you, and you're the only one."

Cody tensed. "You're lying, Holly."

Holly sat up, eyes wide, cheeks flushed with anger.

"I know you're lying," Cody continued. "'Cause I saw you with him yesterday."

Holly was furious. She jumped out of bed and got dressed.

"You spyin' on me now, Cody?"

"Yah didn't show up for lunch. I was worried, so I came lookin' for yah," Cody tried explaining.

"You don't need to worry about me, Cody. I can take care of myself."

"Was that what you was doin' with Mister Bond then, takin' care of yourself?"

"You're such a boy, Cody," Holly said. And she said it with such a mocking tone that Cody felt his hands ball into fists.

Holly was unrelenting. "You don't own me, Cody. I can fuck anybody I choose to! I woulda thought your momma would've taught you better."

At that very instant, something inside Cody snapped.

He grabbed Holly and threw her down on the bed, fell on top of her. She opened her mouth to scream, but Cody clamped both hands around her windpipe.

Holly twisted and turned, desperately struggled to lever Cody's fingers from her throat. "Cody! Please! Stop!" she rasped, eyes wide with fright.

But Cody didn't hear her. Holly was no longer there. She had transformed into this creature beneath him; the physical manifestation of every hurt, every wrong, every betrayal that had ever been inflicted upon him.

Holly was dead a full ten minutes before Cody returned from the trance and released his grip. He looked down at her corpse and felt completely empty.

Despite what had just transpired, Cody felt calm. He knew everything would be alright.

In time, he would be questioned by the police, as would the rest of the kids at the facility. Eventually, the authorities would hear rumors, and they would grill Holly's drama teacher, a Mister Alan Bond, whose career would wind up going down in flames.

And in the end, the missing person's case would be closed, and everyone would assume that Holly simply ran off with some local lothario.

Holly's body would never be found. There were a lot of critters in the 'Glades that preferred meat.

*"This is a town that doesn't just want you to fail,
it wants you to die."*

-David Geffen

28

Cody woke up with a start, his heart thumping triple-time, a sticky patina of perspiration clinging to his face. He blinked as his pupils tried to compensate for the darkness. The only light in the room emanated from the blinking LEDs on the DVR, and Cody realized there must have been a blackout while he was asleep.

The demons were stirring.

He rolled off the sofa, stood up and smashed his shin on the coffee table, heard glass shatter, and smelled the unmistakable odor of stale beer, as it splashed on the floor.

"Sonofabitch!"

He bent down and rubbed his shin, hobbled in the direction of the wall switch, and flipped it.

Ah, let there be light.

Moments later, Blue appeared, checking to see what all the commotion was about. Cody passed him on the way to the bathroom. A couple of minutes later, the sound of cascading water pelting tile issued forth, and then an off-key rendition of 'Bad To The Bone'.

Cody showered away the remnants of his bad dream and prepared himself for the night. He chose a pair of well broken-in jeans, black in color, and a sea-green cotton shirt. He slipped a hand-tooled, leather belt around his

waist, cinched it. Then he strode to the closet and perused his cowboy boot collection. He selected a pair of
black python skins, with eighteen carat gold toe and heel
guards. He slid them on. Next, he checked his reflection
in the mirror, pulled his lips back and inspected his teeth.

On the way to the front door he glanced at the clock,
noted the time as nine-fifteen, and shook his head drea-
rily. He couldn't believe he'd slept the entire day.

Blue cocked his head and woofed when Cody's hand
made contact with the doorknob.

"Sorry, pal. Tonight's for the big dog. I'll see yah in
awhile."

Cody stepped into the night, locked and dead-bolted
the front door, and crossed to the rear of the property.
He removed a key from a pocket and inserted it into the
padlock on the garage door. The hasp opened with a
'snick' and Cody lifted the garage door, stepped into the
black.

He climbed behind the wheel of the old Chevy
pickup and cranked the ignition. The starter churned
for a few seconds before the engine caught, and Cody
made a mental note to fire up the old girl more often.
He switched on the headlights, dropped the tranny into
reverse, and backed the truck from the garage. He
slammed the gearshift into park and leaped from the
cab, closed and locked the garage door. He returned
to his rumbling ride and backed it down the driveway.
Once in the street, he shifted into drive and smiled at
his jacked-up Suburban, parked along the curb. God,
how he loved driving that monster around town. Riding

around high off the ground made him feel important, bigger and badder than your average work-a-day citizen. But tonight Cody had special plans. Plans that required discretion. And that big-ass Cowboy Cadillac was anything but discrete.

Cody slipped a disc into the player, Tim McGraw, and dialed up the volume. He drove north to Sunset and turned east, headed for the heart of the city. At stoplights he gazed out the window at the street circus and ached with anticipation.

Soon. His release was coming soon.

An hour later, he was cruising a rundown section of southeast El Lay. Now that he was far enough from home, he relaxed and began the search in earnest. Only the lowliest of animals would soil the area where it had to sleep.

Cody pulled up to a red light and glanced toward the street. A young woman, dressed in cobalt blue Spandex and stiletto heels, signaled and approached the passenger side window. Cody leaned over and pushed the door open, and the woman poked her head inside.

"Lookin' for a date, honey?"

The woman's body was tight, but her face was hard, a virtual road map of excess. Too much alcohol, too much nicotine, and far too many miles. But tonight, she'd suffice for Cody's purposes.

"Sure am," he replied sweetly. "What's your name, darlin?""

It was at that moment he noticed the billboard directly behind Many Miles. A giant full-color advertisement for Chuck Dallas, Private Investigator, with Cody's smiling mug encompassing ninety percent of the ad.

"My friends call me Divinity..." She hesitated, took a longer look. "Hey, don't I know you from somewhere?..."

Cody started to shake his head.

"Yeah! I know you," she repeated, excitement growing. "You're the guy on that new show about the private dick, aren't you?"

This was the last thing Cody needed. A random neuron fired in his brain, and a fleeting image of Hugh Grant appeared in a heads-up display on his windshield. Cody skillfully segued into improvisation mode.

"I get that all the time," he replied, disguising his voice with a nasal twang. "Actually, I'm a lot better lookin' than that guy."

Divinity cocked her head and squinted her eyes. "Well, you sure do look alike. So what's it gonna be?"

"I think I'm gonna shop around a little," Cody responded. "Thanks just the same."

He pulled the door closed and as he accelerated through the intersection, Divinity tossed him a single-digit salute.

Cody took a series of turns that put him back on a westward course, and he popped a new CD into the player. Garth Brooks sang about love gone wrong. Cody drove aimlessly for several miles, and then on a whim, decided to head back toward Hollywood. Maybe tomorrow night would yield better results.

When he reached the freeway on-ramp, he noticed a young woman standing on the curb with her thumb stuck out. He pulled over to offer her a ride.

"Where yah headed?" Cody drawled, flashing his best heartbreaker smile.

"Hollywood," she replied brightly. "You going that far?" Cody nodded, and the woman climbed into the cab.

"My name's Melanie," she offered casually, as the Chevy approached cruising speed.

Cody nodded his head in response and then shot her an appraising glance. She was twenty, maybe, and would have been beautiful if she combed out the blonde dreds, and lost some of the facial jewelry. She was dressed in an Indian print skirt, and a shear white cotton blouse. Sixties retro chic. Her breasts were lush and bounced enticingly with every lurch of the Chevy's ancient suspension.

After several miles of silence, she did a cat-stretch and said, "I hitched down here from the Bay area, last week. Ever spend any time there?"

"Sure," Cody replied. "Been there a coupla times."

"I love it up north. It's just so pretty… but there's a lot more action down here."

"Yeah, I know what you mean," Cody agreed. Melanie looked him over and smiled. "You interested in some action, mister?"

This caught Cody off guard. But then he glanced once again at her swaying breasts, saw the nipples standing erect against the diaphanous blouse, and felt his cock stiffen.

"What've you got in mind, darlin'?"

"C'mon. You're a big boy," she teased, her eyelids narrowing to slits.

"I just thought you needed a ride."

Melanie's smile was mercenary. "Need some money, too."

"Ah-hah," Cody chuckled. "And what are you offerin' for my hard-earned dollars?"

She lifted her skirt, slowly, revealing strong tan thighs. And when Cody arched an eyebrow she lifted the skirt further, reached into white cotton panties, and stroked golden pubic hair.   "See anything that interests you?"

Cody smiled and shifted his eyes back to the road. "Yah know, you remind me of someone."

*****

The pickup was parked well of the road, concealed amid scrub Oak and juniper. The windows were fogged, and the sound of a woman moaning issued forth, and escalated in intensity.

Inside the cab, Melanie was on her back with her legs up in the air. Her white Reeboks smacked the metal roof in rhythm to Cody's thrusts. All the while, Melanie was thinking about the crisp fifty dollar bill the cowboy had peeled from the top of a two-inch wad, and the quarter-ounce of red-haired Buddha Bud that it would purchase.

In a trance-like state, Cody continued pummeling. Deeper. Harder. Faster. And as he started to climax, he lowered his hands to the young woman's throat, completely encircling it. As his ejaculate began to fill the condom, Cody's eyes rolled back in his head, and he pressed his thumbs against her windpipe.

Melanie gagged trying to scream and fought to wriggle free. But the big cowboy was too strong. He had her pinned.

As the oxygen levels in her brain diminished, Melanie's survival circuitry kicked into action. Adrenaline flooded her bloodstream, and for one fleeting instant she possessed superhuman strength.

She twisted and turned onto her belly, brought her elbow back, hard, connected with Cody's solar plexus.

She grasped for the handle on the driver's side and pushed the door open.

Cody was stunned by an explosion of pain in his chest. For several moments he was unable to inhale or exhale. The girl pulled away from him and tumbled out the door. She rolled in the dirt, scraping both shins bloody, scrambled to her feet, and fled into the brush. Cody was left red-faced and gasping.

Melanie ran up a hillock and disappeared behind a rise. A waxing moon hung above the horizon, washing the scrubby hillside in a pale sickly light, and creating a patchwork of deep shadows in the creviced ground.

Melanie sprinted for the shadows and crawled on her belly beneath some brush, where she curled herself into a fetal ball. And as she lay there, bleeding and crying, and trembling with fear, she began to pray. "Help me, please God! Don't let him find me! I promise I'll be good! I swear! I'll never do this again, ever! Please, God, I don't want to die!"

When he was once again able to breathe, Cody yanked his jeans up and set off after the girl. And as he ran up the loose-packed dirt slope spreading clouds of debris, Cody was praying to God, as well.

"Please, God, don't let her get away! I promise I'll be good. I won't ever do this again, I swear! Just don't let this one get away!"

Cody came trotting over the rise, head turning to and fro, searching. He paused near the beginning of a trail that led into Nichols Canyon and sniffed the air.

The girl saw him clear the rise and watched as he came within ten yards of her hiding place. She could hear the blood pumping through the veins in her ears, felt her entire head pulse in rhythm to her heartbeat. And she trembled uncontrollably, a rabbit hoping to elude a coyote.

Cody couldn't see her, but he could sense her presence, knew she was close by, and knew she was watching him. He stood perfectly still and pulled the air in through his nostrils, sampling, tasting. He shifted his weight onto his back foot and peered over his shoulder, saw a flash of color that didn't belong, and proceeded in that direction. He hadn't taken five steps in her direction when Melanie erupted from behind some bushes, and streaked toward the highway, shrieking for all she was worth.

Cody took off after her, running her to ground inside of a hundred yards.

"No, please!" she begged, wild-eyed with fright.

Cody fell on her, dragged her behind some bushes, and finished what he'd started in the truck. She managed one last gurgling scream before Cody's hands closed around her trachea and cut off her oxygen.

When he was finished with her, Cody felt a deep sense of relief, like some great burden had been lifted from his shoulders. He paused beside the corpse and ran a palm over still-warm breasts. Then he stood up, dusted himself off and hiked back to the truck.

"You gotta know when to hold 'em, know when to fold 'em, know when to walk away, know when to run."
-Kenny Rogers

29

Cody's sleep was dreamless, and he awoke in the afternoon feeling refreshed. He rolled out of bed, Stretched toward the ceiling, and padded naked toward the bathroom, humming an old Willie Nelson tune.

'On the Road Again. Oh I can't wait to be on the Road again'

Moments later, the sound of urine hitting water issued forth, followed by the throaty gargle of a flushing toilet. Cody exited the bathroom, stepped into a pair of Levis, and crossed to the kitchen.

"Hey Blue! Where the hell are yah?" he called out. He opened the pantry door and removed a can of 'Super-Dog', liver and bacon flavor.

A minute went by before Blue poked his head through the doggie door and barked a greeting.

"Well hey there, buddy. You 'bout ready for some lunch?" Cody inquired while he scooped the contents of the can into the hound's bowl.

Blue trotted towards Cody, with his toenails clicking a rhythm on the linoleum.

Cody knelt beside the hound, placed the bowl under his nose, and for good measure, scratched him behind the ears. Then he crossed to the refrigerator, removed a carton of orange juice and took a long swig. He clutched the OJ carton as he padded back toward the master suite.

The clothes he'd worn the previous night lay in a heap at the foot of the bed. Cody stepped past the dirty laundry headed for the closet when something caught his eye. He squatted, pushed the dusty black jeans away from the python skin boots, and stared down in utter amazement.

The toe guard from the right boot was missing!

Time contorted, and the sound of his rapidly escalating heartbeat magnified a thousand-fold. Cody could hear the fluids coursing through the blood vessels in his inner-ear. And his peripheral vision was flickering, fading to black. An oblong tunnel appeared before his eyes, with the damaged boot at the far end. He picked the boot up and examined it, touched a finger to the toe to verify what his eyes had already told him. He stood there holding the boot as a feeling of dread crept over him.

When the phone rang, Cody jumped at the unexpected noise. He turned and faced it with apprehension. On the second ring, he crossed quickly from the bedroom into the kitchen. The machine picked up and Cody listened in.

"Hey buddy, it's me. Pick up if you're around."

Cody snatched the handset from the cradle. "Jimmy?"

"How yah doin', Cody?"

"I'm... good," Cody said. "What's up?"

"Feel like knockin' back a couple of pitchers?"

Cody's mind was racing so fast he missed the question.

"Cody?"

"Huh?"

"Well, whadda ya say?"

"I- uh, I'll have to get back to you, Jimmy."

"Everything okay, pal? You don't sound so hot."

Cody took a deep breath and thought for a moment. Everything was definitely not okay, but there really wasn't anything his friend could do to help matters. As much as he wanted to let Jimmy in on this nightmarish turn of events, he knew it was best not to get him involved.

"I'm fine, Jimmy. Really. Everything's great.`I've been working on my lines for 'Ballistic'," Cody lied convincingly.

"Well, if you change your mind, give me a holler," Jimmy replied.

"Will do, brother. Thanks for the call."

Cody hung up the phone and spent the next two hours in a frenzied and fruitless search of the duplex. He looked everywhere he thought the toe guard could be, his chest tightening with each consecutive failure. When he was finally convinced it wasn't in the residence, he loped barefoot to the garage and tore through the pickup. Once again, he came up empty.

He returned to the duplex with his shoulders hunched over, and his head throbbing in rhythm with his undulating heart. One phrase kept repeating over and over inside his head: "I'm so fucked."

*****

Detectives Calderas and London received the call at the division house at four P.M., and an hour later they were picking their way through underbrush at another crime scene off Mulholland Highway. By the time they arrived there were already three black and whites on site as well as a channel six news van.

Two patrolmen were busy corralling Beverly Crescent and her crew while two other teams conducted an evidence search of the area.

The detectives stepped from their unmarked unit and crossed toward the news van.

"London!" the newscaster yelled. "Glad you're here. Maybe now I can get this sequence shot."

"Oh, really?" London responded.

One of the officers standing by the news van spoke up. He was about twenty-three, with a blonde buzz-cut. His name tag identified him as Larsen.

"I was just informing Ms. Crescent that she couldn't shoot any footage until the investigators were finished gathering evidence."

"And I was attempting to educate Skippy here about First Amendment issues," Beverly snapped in response. "I always thought you boys had to pass a written test on Constitutional guarantees before you could graduate from the Academy."

London winked at Larsen. "Sorry Bev. They eliminated that requirement some time ago. It was replaced by a twelve hour course on advanced media harassment techniques."

The detectives walked away while Beverly fumed. "Your superiors will hear about this," she called after the pair.

"Just make sure you spell my name right," Calderas commented under her breath.

When they'd picked their way through the underbrush to where the victim was located, Max bent down and pulled the blanket back. The woman was on her back, dark eyes open, staring blankly into space. The vitreous showed signs of petechial hemorrhage, and there was severe bruising surrounding the neck. The victim's blouse was shredded, and Max saw the tell-tale bite marks on her breasts, neck and stomach. The degree of savagery had markedly increased.

Max replaced the blanket, stood up and faced her partner. "Looks like the Coyote's back in town," London commented, stating the obvious.

"But why now?" Calderas asked, a haunted expression clouding her face. "I mean, it just doesn't make any sense. Is he working off some weird astrological shit, or what?"

"Tell you what, Max. As soon as we catch this deranged motherfucker, you can ask him."

Just then, one of the uniforms conducting the evidence search shouted and waved his arms. "Hey, I think I found something!"

Calderas and London trotted to where the officer was crouched. He pointed to an object that was partially obscured by rocks and dust. It glimmered golden, reflecting the late afternoon sun.

London knelt beside the officer, produced a pen from a shirt pocket, and proceeded to unearth the object. After a minute or so of scraping rock and dust, London cocked his head.

"What the fuck is it?" he queried, precariously balancing the chunk of polished metal on the pen.

"Looks like toe-guard off a fancy pair of cowboy boots," Max interjected, after examining the piece.

London raised an eyebrow, an unasked question.

Max smiled slyly. "I have four brothers, you know."

*****

The thought process of 'why is this happening to me?' to 'how the fuck am I gonna get outta this jam?', took Cody all of two minutes. His first thought, as cliché as it was, was to return to the scene of the crime and search for the missing toe-guard. A tempting, but truly bad idea. His survival instinct wisely dismissed the notion as simply too dangerous. First thing they teach 'em at Cop School is 'the killer always returns to the scene of the crime.'

Cody's next thought was that maybe the toe-guard didn't pop off last night at all. Perhaps he'd lost it last week, or the week before. Classic, text book Denial. Completely delusional.

Though he tried to ease his mind with the possibility that it could be true, the Inner-Cody wasn't buying it, not for a second. And that was the voice currently screaming inside his head.

"You just hadda ignore me last night, didn't you? I warned you that little bitch was Bad Mojo! And I told you to head for home. But you couldn't wait, could you?!?! And now look what you did. Yah went and left evidence behind. Yah fucked up BIG time!"

Cody's mind was in melt-down mode, neurons firing in endless circles. All his life he'd managed to take care of problems in a private sort of way; quietly, no muss, no fuss. And he always did it personally.   Just the mere thought of needing to ask for assistance made his stomach acids churn.

Cody realized that his survival now depended on thinking outside the box. He took a few deep steadying breaths.

Bobbi had always told him, "Cody, don't ever get locked into one way of doin' things. Yah gotta be flexible in this life. And yah gotta be able to adapt to the Game while it's in play."

Words of wisdom

Cody analyzed the situation from every conceivable angle and came to the painful realization that his monumental fuck-up the previous night was simply too much for him to fix alone. FACT: The stakes were too high, and he was holding a losing hand. Like it or not, he needed help.

But who?

Who could be trusted to share such a burden? Who stood to lose as well if Cody's problem could not be resolved?

The answer came to him in a sudden flash of white light, as if handed down by the Gods, themselves.

"When the going gets weird, the weird turn pro."
                                        -Hunter S. Thompson

30

Cody's Suburban was too tall to park in the under-ground lot, so he pulled alongside the curb in front of the office building. He descended from the vehicle, fed the meter a handful of quarters, and disappeared behind smoke-tinted glass doors.

The elevator deposited him on the seventh floor. And he walked across multi-colored, industrial carpeting to the agency's door.

There were nine people in the reception area, and not a single one so much as lifted their head from their phones to acknowledge Cody's existence. Cody smiled inwardly -actors were all so self-involved.

Cody approached the reception window, opaque rip-pled glass. He tappity-tapped, and several moments later a shadow appeared and the partition slid open.

"Oh, hi, Cody," Sylvia bubbled. "I didn't know you were coming by today. I've got a bunch of messages for you." Cody was all business. "Is Shell around?"

"Uh-huh," Sylvia replied. "Hang on a sec and I'll take you back... Gotta give Jimmy Bodine this interview first."

The partition slid closed.

One of the actors in the waiting room lifted his head. He was an old guy with fluffy white hair and bushy eyebrows framing steel-blue eyes. He grimaced at the thought of someone coming in off the street and usurping his place in the queue.

A minute later the door to the Sanctum sanctorum swung open and Sylvia appeared in the doorway. "C'mon back, Cody."

He followed the plush young woman to Shelly's private office, and as usual, Shelly was on the horn. She signaled him with an index finger. I'll just be a minute.

"... I'm afraid that won't be possible, Bruce... Yeah, I know. She wants to do the role, believe me. She absolutely raved about the script..."

Cody nodded an acknowledgement and began an impromptu inspection of the facilities. He spotted something of interest on a teak bookcase, beside the big screen, and drifted over in that direction for a closer examination.

It was a spiral hunk of crystal mounted on a cube of obsidian. A silver plate was affixed to the base, with an inscription that read: American Cancer Society Meritorious Service Award. Beneath that was Shelly's name. Perched beside the spiral crystal sculpture were half a dozen wood and brass award plaques commemorating good deeds allegedly perpetrated by Shelly.

Cody's eyes wandered from the awards to a series of photographs artfully displayed on the wall. The one that caught his attention was an eleven by fourteen of Shelly and him on the set of Chuck Dallas. In the shot, she was sitting on Chuck's desk, smiling ear to ear, and Cody was frozen mid-laugh. He had autographed the print for her in white ink.

"Well Bruce, I'm afraid I've done all I can do," Shelly explained. "The money's just gotta come up-up-up... See what you can do and get back to me... You're the best! Ciao for now, honey."

Shelly clicked the Intercom. Button on the handset.
"Sylvia dear, please hold my calls."

She shed the headset, stood up and approached Cody,
gave him a bear hug.

"Place is lookin' real good, Shell." Nervous small talk.

"I'm glad you think so," she kidded. "Considering you're
paying for most of it."

That elicited Cody's first chuckle of the day. "Long way
from Hollywood Boulevard," Cody commented.

"This is how the proverbial 'other half' live. And I'm
definitely getting used to it... So, what's up with my superstar?"

Cody's eyes darted back and forth. He'd rehearsed his
speech on the way over, but for some reason the words
weren't coming.

Shelly could tell he was tense. "Are you feeling alright,
Cody?" she asked with genuine concern. "You look pale."

She placed the back of one doughy hand against his
forehead. Doctor Monroe. "You don't seem to be running a
temperature, but you feel kind of clammy."

Cody's heart hammered as he searched for a vocal
response. "I've got a problem Shell, and I don't know how
to fix it."

Shelly flopped on the couch and patted the space
beside her. "Come, come dear. Have a seat and tell Shelly
all about it. After all, your problems are my problems."

He collapsed beside her and put his head in his hands.
"I don't know where to begin," he stated in all honesty.
Shelly the Nurturer responded. "That's easy, dear. Begin
at the beginning." She noticed a nervous twitch in his left
eyelid.

215

"I'm in trouble, Shelly. Serious trouble."

She tried to put him at ease. "Oh, come on Cody," Shelly began. "Don't be so melodramatic. You know there's nothing that can't get fixed."

Cody rolled his eyes. "It's bad Shell."

Shelly laughed, held up one hand, and reached for her iphone. "Don't say another word. I've gotcha covered. It's a marvelous little rehab place up in Santa Barbara. Trees, ocean air, all very discreet. You'll love it."

Cody shook his head. "It's nothin' like that."

Shelly tapped and slashed at the screen, flipping through her digital rolodex. "Okay. I get it... You knocked someone up. Not to worry. I got you covered there as well. Doctor Hadad in Beverly Hills is the best. Also, very discreet.'

Cody continued to shake his head.

"Gambling?"

"Jesus, Cody, you're not into underage boys, are you?"

Cody cocked his head, narrowed his eyes. "Huh?"

"Never mind."

She could see he was in pain. "C'mon Cody, take it easy... I mean how bad could it possibly be? It's not like you killed somebody."

Cody's eyes widened. His mouth suddenly felt dry.

"Cody?"

Time slowed and Shelly ticked off her life in milliseconds, felt the entire office start to sway. It was an eternity, or at least half of one, before Cody broke the silence.

"That's just it, Shell. I think I might have."

Shelly swallowed hard. "What do you mean, you might have? Don't you know?"

Cody's eyes brimmed as he began to relate the story of the previous night.

"I went out last night... I'd been drinking... a lot. I was just drivin' around, mindin' my own business, and I saw this girl hitch-hikin'. I thought to myself, hey Cody, you oughta give this girl a ride, before some perv picks her up."

"That was very chivalrous of you," Shelly commented, feeling a sudden tightening in the pit of her stomach.

"Yeah, well that's kinda what I thought, too..."

"So what happened?"

Cody hesitated, searching for the right words. "Well, Shelly, what can I tell yah? She came on to me, hot and heavy, and we ended up out on Mulholland. We did it in the truck, and then right afterwards she started getting nasty. Told me she knew who I was, and that she was gonna tell her story to the National Inquisitor if I didn't give her money."

Shelly's mind was traveling at the speed of light. Measuring, calculating. "How much did she want?"

"Little bitch told me she'd keep her mouth shut if I gave her five thousand dollars! Can you imagine that? I told her I didn't have that kinda money to throw around, what with all the lawyers and publicists ridin' my coat tails... She thought it was funny, laughed in my face."

"And what happened next?" Shelly prodded.

"I was pissed, so I told her to get her little ass outta my truck... she says..." He mimics her speech: "How am I supposed to get out of here? I told her she shoulda thought about that before she tried to shake me down." Cody's smile was grim. "That's when she started hitting me."

And then Shelly knew. She'd been around liars all her life, made a living out of being one, herself.

"I swear, Shell. All I was tryin' to do was keep her off me. Cody was wide-eyed, working it for all it was worth. "I guess I got carried away."

Cody paused, summoned an acting class exercise, and wiped away tears with a shirt sleeve.

Shelly's smile was all warmth and understanding even though, underneath, she was shaken to the core. Deep inside, she could hear a quiet voice off in the distance saying goodbye to next season. And she saw an image of millions of birds taking flight, each with a huge dollar sign emblazoned in red along its feathered ass. She wanted to cry, or scream, or commit acts of wanton destruction. Instead, she steadied herself and focused. She was a far better actor than Cody.

"Go on, dear. Tell me the rest."

"Anyways, when it was all over, she wasn't moving... I musta panicked. I shoved her out the truck and drove away."

Shelly knew there was a great deal more to this story that Cody was holding back, but that wasn't her concern at the moment. Shelly was thinking triage. Handle the worst trauma first and then move on down the line. Gunshot wounds receive priority over simple fractures, and this was definitely a GSW. Multiple holes in the victim's torso and lot's of leaking bodily fluids.

She placed her hands on Cody's shoulders and looked into his eyes. "Now this is important, Cody. I want you to think very carefully before you answer me... Did anybody see this girl get into your truck? Were there any traffic cameras in view?"

Cody paused for effect, counted to ten. "I don't think so, Shell. It was gettin' pretty late."

"Are you sure?"

"Sure as I can be," he replied.

Cody was in deep shit and that was a fact. But Shelly had come too far to turn back now. She had no intention of sitting idly by while her golden goose went to the chopping block.

"I'm not going to lie to you, Cody. This is bad! But you made the right decision coming here today and telling me about it."

Cody was beside himself with angst. "There's more, Shelly. It gets worse."

"How could it possibly get any worse?" she inquired, not really wanting to know.

"Yah remember those cowboy boots I had custom made? The ones with the gold toe and heel guards..."

Shelly had a picture of them in her head. Gaudy animal skin Pimp boots with tasteless gold accent pieces. How could she forget? "Sure. What about them?"

"I was wearing a pair last night. And when I got up this mornin', I noticed one of the toe guards was missin'. I tore the house apart and couldn't find the goddamn thing any-where."

Shelly felt a wave of nausea. A voice in her head howled, "I slaved away all these years, hand-holding, nose-wiping, ass-kissing. And just when things are finally going good, what happens? An idiot child comes along and fucks it all up. Why is this happening to me?"

"How about the truck, Cody? You searched there too, didn't you?"

Cody was morose. "I think I lost it somewhere up on Mulholland last night. I don't know what to do, Shell. Should I ditch the boots somewhere, or what?"

Shelly's mind was sifting through a dozen potential scenarios, none of them very pleasant. A three-dimensional chess game of the highest order. Winner takes all.

"No, Cody. That would be way too dangerous."

"Well, what should I do?"

The poor dumb redneck was in way over his head and he was beginning to come unraveled. All the signs were there. Shelly stood up and crossed to her desk, reached in a drawer and produced a small orange-brown bottle. She snapped off the cap and spilled several small blue pills onto the desk. Valium, ten milligram tablets. Breakfast of champions.

"Here," she said, taking Cody's arm and pressing two pills into his palm. Then she crossed to the mini-fridge, removed a can of Doctor Pepper, and handed that over as well. "Swallow those. They'll help you relax."

Cody popped the tablets into his mouth and washed them down with the cold soda. Didn't hurt at all.

"Now listen to me. There's nothing you can do to help right now, so I want you to go home and try to get some rest. I need a little time to formulate a plan."

Cody's expression was heartsick.

Shelly put her arm around him consolingly. "Don't worry. We can fix this," she assured him. "But I need a little time, okay?"

He looked at her, his eyes pleading.

"Have I ever let you down before?"

He thought about it for a moment and his lips curled into a half-smile. "No, Shell. You've always come through for me. Only one who ever has."

"And I'll come through for you this time, too. You're my superstar, Cody. Just go home, try to relax, and don't talk to anyone until you hear from me. Don't worry, Shelly's on the job."

31

The next day, detectives Calderas and London made contact with Barry "Duke" Horowitz, the owner and proprietor of Duke's Booteteria, in Van Nuys –Largest selection of cowboy boots and accessories for over thirty years, if you believed the Yellow Page ad.

Duke was a round-faced gentleman in his fifties, with a beer belly and a fringe of salt and pepper hair peeking from a tan Stetson.

"Good afternoon," he called out from behind the cash register. "What can I interest you folks in today? We've got a terrific special going on this weekend. Buy one pair of boots and get the second pair at a third off."

London flashed his badge. "I'm detective London. We talked earlier on the phone."

"Of course, of course…"

"And this is my partner, detective Calderas."

Duke stepped from behind the counter, eyed Calderas appreciatively. "Pleased to meet you," he replied, offering up his hand. "How can I be of service?"

Max produced a plastic evidence baggie from her blazer, handed it to the proprietor. "We were hoping you might be able to help us with this."

Duke accepted the package and smiled at Max, exhibited crooked, nicotine-stained teeth. "Helluva nice piece," he said, examining the contents of the bag, as well as detective Calderas.

Max ignored the innuendo. It was nothing she hadn't heard a thousand times before.

The proprietor's eyes returned to the heavy gold decoration in the bag. "Looks like Roy Healey's work."

"You sound pretty sure about that," Max suggested.

"Oh, I'm more than pretty sure, lovely lady," he replied, moving close enough to Max to point out what he was talking about. "There're only a handful of goldsmiths in the whole damn country that turn out this caliber of work... Just look at the detail. Yup, Healey's your man, alright. He's not in any sort of trouble, is he?"

"No, it's nothing like that," London piped in, examining a woven leather belt off of one of the racks. "Do you have any idea how we can get a hold of him?"

"I'm sure I have his number on file somewhere around here. You want me to see if I can find it?"

"That'd sure save us some time, Mister Horowitz," Max answered with a friendly smile.

The old man winced. "Mister Horowitz was my daddy. Please, call me Duke."

"Duke."

The old man grinned, did an about-face, and stepped behind the counter. He bent over with a grunt and began rummaging around underneath. A minute later he produced a cardboard shoe box, set it on the counter, and started picking through its contents.

"Ah-hah!" he blurted, pulling a business card from the dusty box. "I knew I had it around here somewhere."

He wrote the number down on a piece of paper and handed it to detective Calderas. "Roy's got a place out in the desert."

"Thanks for your help, Duke," she said, folding and pocketing the note.

"Any time. Glad to be of service."

London flipped the price tag over on the belt, blinked twice and swallowed. Then he returned it to the rack. Very gently.

As the two detectives departed the establishment, Duke's eyes never strayed from Calderas's shapely posterior.

*****

When they were comfortably ensconced in their unmarked unit, Max removed the slip of paper from her pocket. She punched the sequence of numbers into her cel, held the device to her ear.

After the third ring a machine picked up, and a pleasant male voice informed any, and all, concerned that 'Goldy' wasn't going to be around this weekend, so sorry. Due back in town Monday though, best to try after three, thank you, oh so very much... punctuated by a long warbling beep tone.

"Mister Healey, my name is Maxine Calderas. I'm a detective with the Hollywood Division of the El Lay P.D. I need to speak with you as soon as possible. You can reach me at area code three-one-zero, four-nine-nine, eighty-one hundred, night or day. Thanks."

Max clicked off, folded the cel and tucked it away.

"Message on the answering machine said Goldy was gone 'til Monday."

London frowned.

"Maybe we can get a line on him before then," Calderas suggested. "We're getting close. Can't you feel it?"

Greg paused, lifted his head, nostrils flared dramatically. "I feel something, Max..."

Another pregnant pause followed by: The trumpet of flatulence. An entire herd of low-flying ducks, only partially absorbed by worn naugahyde.

"Jesus, Greg," Max protested, stubbing her knuckles in a scramble for the power-window button. "I'd see a specialist about that, if I was you."

"Reality is something you rise above."
                                    Liza Minnelli

32

Shelly gave Cody very explicit instructions and sent him home with the entire bottle of Valium. It was a little before five and she made an executive decision to call it a week.

She rose from the couch, crossed to a collection of photographs on the wall beside the big screen. She nudged a copper-framed eleven by fourteen print, stepped back and checked the alignment.

The photo was the cover for 'American Entertainment Weekly' and depicted Hollywood's Dozen: The Twelve Most Influential Women In Showbiz. Shelly was the short round one on the far right.

She touched the frame once again and sighed, her chest feeling tight. She adjusted her bra and took several cleansing breaths. Then she swung around and returned to her desk, clicked the Intercom button.

"Irv, can I see you in my office for a moment, please?" A minute later, the door opened a crack and Irv poked his head through. Shelly was in the process of gathering her belongings.

"What's going on, Shell?"

"Something's come up. I gotta go."

"What about your appointments?" he protested, knowing full well what she intended.

"C'mon, you're always bitching about feeling less than equal. Now's your chance to do something about it." She looked at him beseechingly. "I need you."

Irv was stunned. "What did you say?"

Shelly placed her hands on her hips and snorted. "Don't push it, Irv. I know you heard me."

Irv's smile was full of self-assurance. "No problem, Shell. I gotcha covered."

Shelly could swear her intestines were tying themselves in square knots, but there was no way she was going to let Irv know it. As far as she was concerned, the son of a bitch had already gained himself an unwelcome upper hand.

"Thanks, Irv. I appreciate you taking care of business."

Irv beamed a smile and withdrew to his office.

Shelly knew exactly how to push his buttons.

By this point, Shelly's blood pressure was elevated to a number just slightly below her cholesterol level. Definitely time for a drink, or three, before she even attempted to formulate a plan.

*****

Shelly pulled into the lot behind the Coconut Cantina and stepped from the glistening Mercedes. She made a mental note to give Esteban-down-at-the-carwash a bigger tip next week. The little hustler had a real touch with that polishing cloth.

The Coconut Cantina was a popular West Side watering hole that serviced an eclectic mix of humanity. Everything from the ubiquitous button-down Agency types, conspicuous in their uniformity, to a growing contingent of the arty crowd; gallery owners, antique shoppers, tech developers, hipsters and the like.

227

Shelly shouldered her way to the front of the bar and then made herself comfortable on a padded stool that had just been vacated. She tuned out the crowd and grabbed a fistful of pretzel mix.

"What can I getcha?" the bartender asked as she whipped up a pair of Stoli Bloody Marys.

She was maybe twenty-five, green-eyed, and dressed in skin tight jeans and a man's muscle tee, the kind often referred to as 'Wife-Beater Underwear'. On her the Look actually worked.

Shelly checked out her sinewy, nut brown forearms, admired the muscle tone. This girl spent a lot of time at the gym. Probably didn't even eat red meat, if she stooped to eating flesh at all. An actress? No doubt. Shelly contemplated offering her a business card. The girl certainly was impressive. She probably made a fortune in tips with that fabulous rack.

"Double shot of Glen Livet, straight up, and a pint of your best ale."

Green Eyes placed a couple of napkins on the bar, refilled the munchie bowl from a plastic gallon container, and slid it towards Shelly.

Shelly nodded her appreciation and shoveled another fistful of pretzel mix into her mouth. A minute later the drinks arrived.

"Jeez, what took you so long?" Shelly teases. Reaching for the first of the heavy shot glasses.

"Shall I keep the ticket open?" Green Eyes inquired.

Shelly sucked back the first shot in one gulp, snatched the second glass from the bar and downed it as well, nodded at the bartender.

"Excellent idea," she said, exhaling high octane fumes. "And when you get around to it, hit me with another double dose of Glenn."

"Yes Ma'am."

Shelly felt the liquid fire penetrate, felt herself relax, just a little, And she desperately needed to relax, so she could think straight and formulate a successful plan. And whatever she came up with had better work. There wouldn't be any second chances.

She took a couple of deep cleansing breaths and followed it up with a long swallow from the frosty mug of Bass Ale.

Alright Shelly, think! How're we gonna pull Cody's ass outta the fire? There's gotta be a way to salvage this. Has to. Too goddamn much at stake for it to be any other way.

Sometime later, Green Eyes returned with two more shot glasses filled well past the line with twenty year old single malt. She placed them on fresh napkins beside Shelly, who nodded an acknowledgement.

Shelly's mind was elsewhere, and she was lost in napkin doodling. Flashes of the not-so-distant-enough past sang across her mind, a jolting off-key chorus. Her old, seedy offices, and the smell of urine in the stairwells. Unsecured parking and crack-heads loitering in the alley. Car alarms, honking horns and sirens. Howling fucking dogs in every yard for miles in all directions. Welcome back to Hell! We missed yah!

Shelly's dream of a better life was suspended by gossamer threads, and she could feel them unraveling around her. All the effort she'd expended for all these many years. And for what? To watch it turn to ash because of one savant's idiocy? Shelly felt her anger rising. She placed her pen on the bar, picked up another shot glass, tossed the single malt straight back and returned the empty to the bar, bottoms up.

No matter what kind of plan she might come up with, Shelly knew she was going to need help to pull it off. And not just any help, either. Help she could trust. Long term.

The line of thought was making her nauseous because she had a pretty good idea what dear Irv's participation could cost her.

As the haze slowly crept over her foul mood, she became acutely aware of the humanity that swarmed around her. Bleached hair and bleached teeth. She suspected some bleached assholes as well, now that that was becoming a thing. Bad rhinoplasty aplenty and lots of Tupperware breast implants. Every solitary soul the center of their own dysfunctional universe.

Before she was even aware of it, Shelly was noticing men's footwear and making mental notes. You could tell a lot about someone by what they chose to cover their feet with. And then for some reason, her mind free-associated to a popular Urban Legend: The one that postulated a connection between shoe size and dick length…

And then a random neuron fired in Shelly's frontal lobe and she felt a glimmer of an idea that just might save their collective asses.

"Sonofabitch," she muttered, reaching for the wallet in her purse. She removed a pair of Benjamins, slapped them on the bar.

"Need change?" Green Eyes asked.

Shelly shook her head and vacated the barstool, picked her way through the crowd, and exited the establishment.

*****

230

It was a little past eight when Shelly unlocked the deadbolt on the agency door and stepped inside. As she had anticipated, the rats had long since deserted the ship. Conditions were perfect.

It was a miracle that Shelly managed to negotiate the walk to the end of the hallway without gravity intervening. She turned the corner and stepped into 'The Tombs'.

She could find the information she needed right here without having to switch on a computer. Shelly loathed the New Technology, much preferred to deal with entities that possessed tactile interplay.

It took her less than ten minutes to locate the files she was seeking, and then five minutes more to find the specific details.

Shelly tilted her head and smiled at the ceiling. "Thank you, thank you, thank you!"

She returned the manila folders to their rightful cabinet drawers, and then exited The Tombs.

"If you can keep your head when all about
you are losing theirs, it's just possible
you haven't grasped the situation."
                        -Jean Kerr

33

Just as soon as they'd settled in at the new offices, Irv bailed from his rent-controlled, bachelor apartment, and moved into a small house in Brentwood. It was a two-bedroom bungalow at the end of a quiet, tree-lined street, less than a mile from where OJ's house used to be. The place was a bargain at six grand a month, including garbage and gardener.

Irv reclined on his favorite chair, burgundy silk robe tied at the waist, hairy-knuckled feet propped up on the ottoman. A half-smoked joint of 'Purple Thunderfuck' rested in a marble ashtray beside him. Irv was pleasantly stoned.

On the opposite side of the room, a giant screen Samsung provided a flickering ambience. The ten o'clock news was about to begin. Irv depressed a button on the remote and the audio portion of the program burst to life. A pale-skinned, peroxide-blonde stood amidst a backdrop of bushes and trees.

"Good evening. I'm Beverly Crescent," The Barbie clone began. "Late this afternoon, El Lay P. D. homicide detectives discovered the body of a young woman dumped in underbrush off Mulholland Highway. Cause of death has yet to be determined, and the victim's name is being withheld, pending notification of the family. Police have refused to speculate as to whether this is the latest victim of 'The Coyote', an elusive serial killer who has remained at large, and frustrated authorities since November of last year. The last known victim of The Coyote was Kathleen Becker, found in rugged terrain off Laurel Canyon, on December 21st. Anyone with information about these crimes is encouraged to call the We-Tip Hotline. You could be eligible for the reward, which currently stands at fifty thousand dollars. Back to you in the studio."

Irv muted the newscast, reached for the stubbed joint and a book of matches. He fired up the hooter, took a long drag, and closed his eyes. The doorbell surprised him, and he expelled a blue-gray plume of THC-laden smoke, suddenly coughing uncontrollably.

The doorbell rang again.

Irv frowned, re-stubbed the joint, rose from his position of comfort, and stomped towards the door. "Who is it?" Irv demanded, long before he reached the peep-hole.

"It's Shelly," came the reply. "Open up!"

Irv was agog. In all the years he'd known her, Shelly had never set foot inside his residence. He jammed an eye up to the spy lens just to verify, unsnicked the dead-bolt, turned the knob.

"What's up, Shelly? Everything alright?"

"Everything's excellent," Shelly replied, quite obviously buzzed. "I brought you a present," she continued. Then she produced a half-empty bottle of Glenn Livet from be-hind her back. "Well, I brought us a present anyway."

Irv's attire finally registered with Shelly. The possibility he might have company over had never occurred to her. It was an unexpected complication.

"Jesus, Irv. Did I catch you at a bad time?"

"Not especially," he replied.

Shelly brightened. "Well, are you gonna invite me in, or what?" Shelly asked, listing slightly to starboard.

Irv stepped away from the entrance, blinking rapidly. Shelly weaved past him into the living room.

"You know, you look like some kinda poor man's Hugh Hefner in that getup. Got any women stashed in the closet?" She opened the closet door and poked her head in to check.

Irv's expression soured.

Shelly crossed to Irv's chair and sat down. She picked the roach from the ashtray, lit it, and took a long, whis-tling hit, before handing it to Irv.

"Mmmm, tasty shit, Irv!"

"Thanks."

"You catch the news tonight?" Shelly asked.

"I was just watching it when you rang the bell..."

"So you heard about the Coyote," Shelly continued. Irv nodded solemnly and took another hit. "It's horrible. Cops found another body this afternoon. Fucker really has 'em chasing their tails."

A thought struck Irv and he giggled. "I bet there's a Cable Movie-of-the-Week in there somewhere. What do you think?"

Shelly shook her head. "What do I think? I think I need another drink. How about you?"

Irv shrugged in agreement and crossed to a liquor cabinet, retrieved two short tumblers.

Shelly snatched the spotted containers from him, filled each with three fingers of twenty year old single malt. "Here yah go," Shelly said, handing Irv one of the tumblers. "Salud!"

Shelly raised her glass to Irv and then polished off the alcohol in a single gulp.

Irv took a tentative sip and his ears visibly reddened. "So what brings you out and about, Shell?"

Shelly studied Irv and laughed. "Well Irv, I'll tell yah. It's a good news, bad news kind of deal. What do you want to hear first?"

Irv's expression was guarded, suspicious. "And this is some kinda I.Q. test?"

"Why do you always have to be so contrary? Just answer the question, Irv. Good news or bad?" Shelly demanded.

Irv felt a sudden chill and decided it might be best to humor her. "Alright, I'll play along. Go ahead and hit me with the good news."

Before she drove over, Shelly had played all the moves repeatedly in her mind. She'd examined the board from every angle and figured each possibility. If I do this, then he'll do this. Shelly only put her money on sure things. Gambling was for morons. Just visit Las Vegas some time.

Shelly had finally figured out a solution to their wicked little conundrum, and it was actually quite simple. And as such, quite likely to succeed. The plan required but one thing; plausible deniability. But obtaining it was going to require Irv's participation. There just wasn't another suitable choice.

Shelly was betting Irv could be had for a price. And in her heart of hearts, she knew what Irv's asking price was going to be, what it had to be. A full partnership. And so she prepared herself for the ultimate sacrifice. It was simple arithmetic. Five percent of something was better than ten percent of nothing.

Now the carrot.

"I know this is something you've wanted for a long, long time," she began, priming the pump. "And after deep and careful consideration, I've decided to offer you a full fifty percent partnership in the agency. Congratulations, Irv. You earned it."

There. She said it. And her lips didn't jump off her face after all. Amazing!

Irv blinked trying to assimilate her words. His mouth moved wordlessly, much like a suffocating sturgeon.

Before Cody hit the Hollywood Jackpot, Irv's life was rich only in his fantasies. Reality had been a rent-controlled 'bachelor' apartment, a glorified closet really, and staring at the dark side of forty with absolutely nothing to show for it. No wife, no kids, no girlfriend, no prospects. No real friends of any sort. Not even a pet.

While Irv loved his work, he barely made enough money to cover his nut each month. No retirement benefits, either. Irv was strictly a gun-for-hire. A balding mercenary. But he aspired to be so much more.

"I-uh, I don't know what to say," he replied, still in shock. "Thanks."

Shelly slapped him on the back. "You're welcome, partner."

There. She said it again.

"You won't be sorry, Shell. I promise," he babbled.

Shelly held up her hand. "Irv, aren't you the least bit curious as to what the bad news is?"

He swigged the remaining single malt from the tumbler, coughed once and grinned. "After good news like that, Shelly, there's nothing could bring me down right now. So go ahead, shoot. What's the bad news?"

Shelly poured him a refill, placed one hand on each of his narrow shoulders, and locked eyeballs with him. Boa constrictor to mouse. "Well partner, here it is straight up... We, meaning you and I, represent The Coyote."

The grin vanished from Irv's face. "What?"

"The serial killer, known affectionately by the media as The Coyote, is none other than our, again Irv, meaning yours and mine, prize meal ticket, the charming, talented, and oh-so-hot Golden Goose, Cody-fuckin' Clifton."

As Shelly's words sank in, the color seeped from Irv's face. "I've got to sit down," he croaked, his skin ashen. "This isn't some hideous practical joke, is it Shell? Because that would be seriously fucked up!"

"No joke," she continued, all business. "Right before I took off this afternoon, Cody dropped by. He confessed everything, and I told him I'd fix it."

Irv felt his rosy little world collapsing around him. "Why would he confess?"

"How the fuck do I know, Irv? Maybe he thinks I'm the reincarnated Virgin Mary, and I'm going to absolve him of all his sins."

Irv fixed Shelly with his fish-eyed stare. "Are you insane?"

"I'm perfectly lucid, partner. How about you?"

"Partner huh? I should have known." Irv was dismayed.

"Nothing's free, sweetheart. Gotta pay if you wanna play. You do wanna play, don't you Irv?"

Irv began to pace. "You have any idea what you're asking?"

Shelly coolly poured herself another drink. "I haven't asked anything yet."

"Having knowledge of a crime and not reporting it, that's a felony right there," Irv babbled. "But what you're thinking about, that's becoming an accessory after the fact in a homicide, Shelly! No, change that to multiple homicides."

Shelly argued for her star. "Cody told me he was defending himself, and that things just got out of hand. He's real sorry, Irv. He's just sick about it."

"Let me see if I have this right," Irv replied, his timbre much higher that it was five minutes ago. He took a long pull from the tumbler, nearly got it down without flinching. "Cody accidentally strangled six young women after chewing on various portions of their anatomy! Please, Shelly, tell me you don't seriously believe that! The only thing he's sick about is the possibility of getting caught."

Shelly switched tactics and in her most commanding Marine Corps drill sergeant voice, hammered him. "It doesn't matter what I believe. The only thing that matters is fixing this! So are you in or out?"

Irv was appalled. "You can't just spring something like this on me and expect an answer in two seconds! I need time to think, okay?"

"Sure, fine. Be like that, Irv," she replied, making no attempt to mask her annoyance. "You've got until noon tomorrow to make a decision. And partner, just so you're aware, our star client left evidence behind. So time is definitely of the essence. Tick-fuckin'-tock."

"Everybody's negotiable."
                    -Muhammad Ali

34

Max was up before seven, refreshed and eager to begin her day. She showered and ate a quick breakfast, leaving the dishes in the sink. She exited the apartment building dressed in red and white jogging shorts and a white sports bra. Her Walther .380 was tucked inside a fanny pack.

The park across the street from the North Hollywood library was a three block jog from Max's apartment. The grounds were little more than a tree-shaded triangle of grass, about a block long, running adjacent to the Hollywood Freeway. It served the community as a running path as well as a tranquil place to relax in the company of a good book.

On Saturday morning the regulars would gather there to practice Tai-Chi. The group consisted of a cross-section of humanity; young and old, advantaged and disadvantaged. When her schedule allowed, Max would join them. It was ritual and ritual was good.

The hunt was also ritual. And in order to be successful in the hunt, the Huntress must prepare herself.

*****

It was the longest, most tortuous night Shelly Monroe could remember enduring. Thank God for her good buddy, Glenn Livet. He was always there when she needed him. And Boris, too. Sweet creature.

240

Waves of uncertainty and doubt kept her mind reeling most of the night. The big what if?

What if she'd been wrong about Irv? What if he told her to fuck off? What if he went to the police? Her stomach churning, she reached for the industrial sized bottle of Maalox in the medicine cabinet.

What if?

By sunrise Shelly had once again examined all the angles and made the decision. She was going to fix this Cody situation with or without Irv's assistance. And if the little weasel turned on her, God help him. Because if that turned out to be the case, she'd resolved to do whatever was necessary there, too.

*****

The telephone rang at Shelly's house at nine-fifteen, and Boris flattened his ears at the sound.

"That you Irv?" Shelly asked, exercising her extraordinary powers of precognition.

"It's me, and I'm in," came the reply from the other end of the line. "But I want that Partnership deal in writing." Shelly silently praised the Gods. "Of course, Irv. Wouldn't have it any other way."

It had been a long, sleepless night for Irv as well. He'd smoked through his stash of Purple Thunderfuck trying to numb the shock of Shelly's revelation. Then he spent the night drifting in and out of mental scenarios, all leading to the same conclusion.

Cody's success had changed Irv's life. Over night, Irv's money worries had evaporated, and his once-empty dance card was now full. Irv had been transformed. He was a Somebody, a Star Maker.

Around three in the morning he came to the conclusion that it was far too late to turn back now. His mind was made up. Partners it was.

"Got any lunch plans?" Shelly enquired, prepared with the logistics.

"Sounds like I'm having lunch with you, Irv responded. "What do you have in mind?"

"How about Rudy's on San Vicente? Say around twoish?"

"Twoish it is," Irv repeated, feeling his life slip out of his control.

Shelly disconnected Irv and a wave of relief washed over her.

"Alright, Boris. Onward to Stage Two."

And then she froze as an ominous thought materialized. Another What if? What if Cody had freaked out and done something stupid last night while she was dealing with Irv?

Shelly pressed a button that speed-dialed Cody. After the second ring she had a moment of heart palpitations. What if her Golden Goose had panicked and flown the coop? Visions of channel six newscasts flashed through her mind.

On the fourth ring, Cody croaked into the receiver. "Yeah?"

"It's me," Shelly replied cheerfully, her heart hammering against her ribs. "How're you feelin' this morning?"

"Like I been run over by a bus," Cody said, his mouth tasting like the interior of a desert hiking boot.

"Well honey, this is your wake-up call... Time to get cleaned up and get some java in you. Irv's gonna be dropping by later, and I want you to do exactly like he says. Understand? We're gonna fix this."

Cody sat bolt upright in bed. "Jesus, Shelly, why'd yah hafta bring Irv into this??!" There was a distinctly hard edge to his voice.

Shelly had anticipated this reaction.

"Don't worry about it, Cody. Irv's your agent, too. And an agent is just like a priest. It's a Holy trust." She paused. "You trust me, don't you Cody?"

Cody sighed. "Of course I do. You're about the only person I do trust." He thought: You and Jimmy Bodine, in that order.

"Good. That's what I needed to hear..."
"Shelly?"

"Don't you worry, Cody. Everything's gonna be just fine. Shelly's on the job."
*****

The hip and trendy Rudy's Coffee Shop, on San Vicente, was clogged with the usual Saturday brunch traffic. Ostentatious and chaotic, conversations were carried on in twenty-four distinct languages. The Melting Pot boiled over and permanently annealed to the stove.

As in most of El Lay, the servers were largely actress/ model wannabes, who were working part time while they awaited their big Hollywood break.

Shelly and Irv sat in the back corner booth, blending in with the parade of humanity. They talked over Chinese Chicken Salads and lattes. They nodded and laughed. At one point, an envelope passed discreetly between them, and soon thereafter a request was made for the check.
*****

It was ten of nine when the silver BMW convertible pulled alongside the curb in front of the duplex. Irv

243

stepped from the interior, smoothing wrinkles from his trousers. He walked casually to Cody's front door and rapped gingerly. Less than a minute later he heard toe-nails stampeding across hardwood floors, followed imme-diately by a vicious watchdog roar.

"Aw, Blue, shut the fuck up, yah beast! Came the shout from the other side of the door. Then the knob turned, and Cody stood in the doorway, massaging his temples. "Hey Irv. C'mon in," Cody said, brows furrowed.

Irv stepped inside and Cody closed the door.

"Nice place you got here," Irv said reflexively, head pivoting. He silently estimated the value of Cody's fur-nishings and electronics.

Blue began sniffing at Irv's ass.

"Nice doggie," Irv said, attempting to make friends.

Blue wasn't interested in making new friends. He had something of a more intimate nature in mind. Blue grasped one of Irv's scrawny thighs with both paws and commenced humping for all he was worth.

"Goddamnit Blue! Knock that off!" Cody yelled, taking a soft back-handed swipe at the grinning hound.

Blue squealed like he'd been stuck with a hot poker and slunk off towards the kitchen.

"Sorry about that," Cody apologized. "Can I get yah something to drink?"

Irv stood there blinking, not knowing what to say.

I'm standing in the Coyote's living room, and he just offered me a beverage. What should I do? I certainly don't want to offend him.

"Uh, thanks anyway," Irv replied nervously. "Is that package ready for me?"

"Yeah. Got it right here," Cody responded, handing him a large cardboard box.

Irv frowned. "Do you have any grocery bags?"

"I thought this'd be better."

And this is why you're not paid to think, Cody. Best leave it to the professionals.

"Grocery bag's more discrete," Irv responded matter-of-factly, as if he'd been doing this all his life. Irv Birnbaum, Criminal Mastermind.

Cody nodded and strolled to the kitchen, returning a minute later with several brown grocery bags.

"Take your pick."

Irv produced a pair of latex gloves from a pocket, stretched them over his bony fingers. Opening the box Cody had provided, he removed the boots and carefully wiped them down with a cloth. Satisfied they were finger-print-free, Irv carefully placed them in a paper bag.

Cody stood there with his arms folded across his chest, wearing an amused expression. He found Irv's elaborate precautions extremely humorous. But when he started thinking about what those cowboy boots represented, he was suddenly overcome with apprehension.

"What're you gonna do with those?"

Irv removed the gloves, retrieved an envelope from an inside coat pocket and presented it to Cody.

"It's from Shelly," Irv stammered. "She said to tell you this would answer all your questions."

Cody took the envelope, started to tear it open.

"You're not supposed to open it until later. After I'm gone," Irv insisted.

"Why's that?" Cody snarled, Valium hangover irritable.

"Like I'm supposed to know what makes that woman's mind work? Please. I'm just a simple messenger boy."

Irv nearly suffered a coronary when Cody's telephone suddenly rang.

"Hang on a second."

Nerves shredded, Irv stood trembling while Cody crossed into the kitchen. He could smell the sour odor of his own fear-sweat, and wanted nothing more than to flee the monster's lair. And yet he stood there paralyzed, unable to command his limbs.

The one-sided conversation being carried out on the phone in the kitchen, was spilling into the living room. Irv began to hyperventilate. The final straw came when Blue trotted back into the living room, eyeballing Irv with lascivious intent.

"Hey Cody!" Irv called out. "I gotta go."

Cody poked his head from around the corner, held up one finger.

"... Honey, I'm kinda in the middle of somethin' right now... No baby, it's nothin' like that, I swear... I'll call yah back in a couple of minutes."

Cody hung up the phone and returned to the living room.

"What's the hurry, Irv?"

Irv blinked rapidly.

"Did Shelly have anything else to say, or is this it?" Cody asked, holding up the envelope.

"She said you should burn that when you finish reading it."

Cody smiled and nodded his head. "Thanks, Irv. I don't know what I'd do without you guys."

Irv thought: *"Does the phrase 'lethal injection' ring any bells for you?"*

Irv grimaced, tucked the grocery bag under one arm and exited.

Cody stood in the living room and stared at the envelope, heart pounding. He opened it, removed a single sheet of alabaster writing paper, unfolded it and began to read.

Two minutes later, Cody lit a match and held it to the paper, waited for it to catch. He let the flaming sheet fall from his fingers into an ashtray on the mantel. Beside the ashtray was a framed eight by ten inch photo of Cody and Jimmy Bodine, on set, laughing, brothers in arms.

Cody watched the carbon curl. And as he stared into the dying embers, tears of profound sorrow stained his cheeks.

Sensing his master's suffering, Blue dog put his head on Cody's knee. Cody scratched Blue's ears and thought about the genius of Shelly's Master Plan. His sadness would wane over time, but not his admiration for Shelly, which had grown a thousand-fold over the last days.

Yes, he would make the sacrifice she demanded of him. He would do whatever was necessary to remain free. And if Shelly needed an Academy Award performance out of him, then that was what he planned to deliver. She could count on him. Cody was on the job.

35

Max was floating upward in warmth and darkness, and she could hear voices fading in and out. Sirens far off in the distance? She couldn't make out was being said, and it frustrated her. When she commanded her eyelids to open, she was amazed that her vision penetrated the darkness. She felt the skin on her back make contact with something hard, cold and smooth. Wall? Or floor? Or?

She stared down at the pale form stretched on the stainless steel table and felt a rush of sadness wash over her. Thick dark hair and lovely young skin, an athlete's body, but she couldn't make out the face.

An overhead light was switched on and the antiseptic space flooded with tungsten light. Max felt the room warp and ripple, a rude introduction to the elasticity of time.

She attempted to speak, discovered her voice box inoperable, and felt a momentary surge of anger. A silvery flash of light caught her attention. It was the reflection from a scalpel as it sliced a long vertical incision, from the woman's sternum to a point just above her dark pubic mound.

Her mound, a thicket before a grotto.

Max closed her eyes and floated. When she opened her eyes again, she saw she was now surrounded by trees as tall as skyscrapers. It was afternoon in the Forest, but the sky was obscured.

Off to her left, Max watched a young woman laying at the base of an ancient Oak tree. The woman was cloaked in a red woolen, hooded coat. Her legs were apart, and a young man with flowing copper hair had his face buried between her thighs, his tongue teasing her clitoris.

The woman grasped the stranger's mane and moaned deliriously, pulling him closer. His lips encircled her pearl, and he slipped a hairy finger, two knuckles into her anus. She came in waves of overwhelming pleasure, bucking her hips against the stranger's rough face.

When calm had returned to the Forest, the stranger lifted his head from between the young woman's thighs. He paused and sniffed at the air. A moment later, his head swiveled and his yellow eyes locked on to Max. His smile revealed a perfect set of Coyote teeth, featuring three-inch long canines.

Max stared at him as a million thoughts rushed at her. Images and flavors, scents and sensations, memories and lies.

When she found her voice, she had but one question: "Why?"

"All the better to eat you with, my dear!" the Coyote replied with a boisterous laugh, his yellow eyes shining."

*****

Max's eyes snapped open, and she sat bolt upright in bed, breathing hard and sweating. She tossed off the covers, ran hands over chest and belly, and felt immense relief that all was intact.

She glanced at the clock and noted the time. It was almost eleven.

As she was pulling the bedspread over the pillows, the hyperactive woodpecker sound of her phone vibrating across the night stand distracted her thoughts. Just as it plummeted towards the carpet, she snatched it mid-air and held it up to her ear.

"Good morning," said the warm masculine voice on the other end of the line.

Max detected traces of a southern accent, Texas maybe, or possibly Tennessee.

"Good Morning," she replied. "This is detective Max Calderas. Am I speaking with Roy Healey?"

"The one and only," came the response. "But my friends call me Goldy."

"Thanks for getting back so quick, Goldy."

"I was curious," he replied honestly. "First time I ever got a message on my machine from a homicide detective. So what can I do for you?"

"Any chance you could come down to the station house this afternoon?"

"What's up?" Goldy asked cautiously. "Am I gonna get charged with something?"

Max chuckled. "If that were the case, someone would be knocking on your door right now, instead of calling you on the phone."

Goldy thought about that for a moment and laughed. "You've got a point. So what is it exactly you want?"

Max turned up the charm a couple of notches. "Your help with a case. I need your professional opinion on a piece of evidence."

"Well, if you wanna see me, it'll have to be later this evening, and you'll have to come out here. I just got back from a fishing trip with my granddaughters. We still have to unpack the camper."

"Not a problem, Mister Healey. What's the address?" she replied, readying pen and writing pad.

*****

"You sure about this?" Calderas asked from behind the wheel of the unmarked cruiser.

"I'm just reading what you have written down here," London shot back. "This a doctor's handwriting, not a detective's."

"You know, I actually studied proctology for a couple of semesters," Max replied straight-faced. "But I changed majors and went for law enforcement, instead. It's all pretty much the same when you get down to it. One way or the other, you spend most of your time dealing with assholes."

At that precise moment a quintet of leather-clad bikers roared by the cruiser on custom Harley low riders, exhaust pipes generating ear-splitting decibels.

"It's the fuckin' third world out here," London complained.

"Kinda makes you lonesome for the 'hood."

London made a pointing motion under Max's nose. "There! That's it! Left, right there!"

Rather than overshoot the unlit street, Max whipped the wheel hard.

Greg's eyes widened as the ass end of the big cruiser started to fishtail off the highway.

"Yeeee-Haaaa!" Max yelled, then gritted her teeth and counter-steered out of the spin. She left a cloud of dust in her wake.

Fifteen minutes later, Max pulled onto a gravel driveway. It was seven-fifteen and still light out.

Goldy Healey's house was a California ranch style, situated smack in the middle of five acres of kitty litter, on the outskirts of Palmdale.

Palmdale, a high desert community populated by lizard-people. Hell on Earth in the summer, and prone to snowstorms and sub-freezing temperatures in the winter. Center of a thriving crystal methamphetamine industry, and refuge to undesirables of every ilk. It was also a home for hermits; suspicious folk who placed a high value on privacy.

Goldy had purchased his acres early on, long before the first wave of refugees fled life in the flatlands and invaded this peaceful moonscape. He remembered when the desert was a lot more isolated and longed for those good old days that were gone forever.

London noticed two girls, obviously Goldy's grandkids, currying ponies in a pipe corral, across from the residence. The girls waved at the detectives and pointed towards the house.

London smiled and waved back, and then the two detectives crossed from the vehicle

Goldy met them on the porch, offered up his hand. Max immediately noticed his fingers. They were long and slender, and the rich burnished brown of hazelnuts. The man possessed the digits of a concert pianist, or perhaps a cardiac surgeon.

"C'mon in," he offered.

The detectives followed Goldy through the foyer into a crowded family room. A river rock fireplace took up most of one wall, and opposite that was a picture window, with a view of a cactus garden and the hills to the east. The furniture was earth tones, old and comfortable.

"So how'd you enjoy the drive up here?" Goldy asked, his nimble fingers preparing a pipe.

"It was adventurous," London replied without missing a beat.

The old man chuckled, shook his head. "Goddamn Pear Blossom Highway gets worse every year."

The old man produced a heavy silver lighter, lit the pipe and puffed. A blue plume of fragrant smoke rose toward the ceiling.

"Can I offer you something wet?" I got all kinds of cold pop in the fridge."

Thanks," Max said. "That'd be great."

"How about you?"

"Well yah know, a cold Coke sounds real nice," London replied.

Goldy smiled. "Make yourselves at home. I'll be right back."

As he adjourned to the kitchen, Max crossed to the piano, examined a collection of photos perched atop the instrument. Black and white images from the Nineteen Fifties. Little boys with crew cuts and little girls in frilly dresses, birthday parties and family outings. Christmases and Easters, proms and weddings. Family history frozen in time.

"Here yah go," Goldy said, returning to the family room with two sweating cans of Coke.

"Thanks," London replied, popping the tab.

Goldy crossed to where Max was standing, handed her the beverage.

"So what is it you wanna show me?"

Max produced the plastic evidence bag from a pocket, and Goldy's long brown fingers extended, grasped the corners and withdrew.

Goldy held the bag closer to his eyes, examined the contents.

"Can you tell us anything about that, Mister Healey?" Max queried.

"Well, it's one of my best works," he answered, a note of pride in his voice.

Calderas brightened.

"See there," he said, pointing to the intricate chased pattern along the perimeter of the toe-guard. "That kind of work takes time and patience, and a human hand. No goddamn machine'll ever be able to equal that!"

Goldy smiled behind a reddish-grey beard, black eyes glinting. "The piece you have here is real unique. It's eighteen carat gold. Very heavy and very expensive. A set of these puppies goes for forty-eight hundred dollars. I don't get a lot of orders for that kind of quality. People just don't appreciate fine craftsmanship anymore. They want it fast, and they want it cheap. It's a crime, I tell yah."

The old man was beginning to digress, so Max attempted to gently refocus him. She could barely contain her excitement.

"Goldy, can you tell us who you sold this to?"

"Sure," Goldy replied with a snort. Just give me a minute to check my database.

He crossed to a desk and sat down behind a computer monitor. Less than a minute later, Goldy was looking at an inventory screen.

"Let's see now... I sold a pair of these in October of 2000 to a fella in Nashville, Tennessee. His name's Haskins, Charlie Haskins."

"Anyone else? Maybe a little more recent," Max suggested.

"January of 2001, I sold a pair to an Ernesto Valenzuela, in El Paso. Then about four months ago I shipped eight sets to an address in Beverly Hills."

"Eight sets?" London repeated.

"Yup," Goldy replied with a sly smile. "That was almost forty grand wortha boot jewelry. Sold 'em to the guy who stars on that new private eye show... what's the name of it?..."

Goldy paused, scratched his stubbly head with those magnificent fingers, tried to recollect.

"Chuck Dallas! That's it!"

Feeling suddenly ignorant, Max was almost too embarrassed to ask. "Can you give us a name?"

Being something of a Chuck Dallas fan, London jumped in. "Guy's name is Cody Clifton."

"You're right about that," Goldy offered. "Real nice fella, too."

"I don't suppose you happen to have a contact number for this Cody Clifton?" Max enquired hopefully.

*****

When the detectives were back inside the cruiser, Max pulled out her cel phone, punched in a series of numbers.

A machine picked up after the fifth ring and informed the good detective she'd reached the offices of the Monroe Talent Group, Limited, and that their office hours were Monday through Friday, nine 'til six. Max disconnected without bothering to leave a message.

"Got his agent's answering machine. Nobody around 'til tomorrow. What do you think?"

London smiled. "Tomorrow's another day."

On the way back to Pear Blossom Highway, the detectives disturbed a young coyote, loitering at the edge of a dirt road. Max made eye contact with the handsome beast just before he turned and loped off into the desert night.

"Nothing is good or bad but by comparison."
Thomas Fuller

36

On Monday morning, Jimmy Bodine's alarm went off at eight-thirty. He rolled out of bed and trotted toward the bathroom. A minute later the shower faucet switched on, and soon thereafter the bathroom filled with steam.

Jimmy stepped from the shower, toweled himself off, and stood before the opaque mirror. He wiped the glass with circular motions and stepped back for an appraisal. He assumed a weightlifter's pose, grimaced, and flexed his biceps.

He dressed in jeans and a black tee-shirt, wolfed a breakfast of Twinkies and Yuban. Then he spent the next fifteen minutes in a frantic search for the slip of paper he'd written the address of the interview on.

At ten after nine, with address in hand, he exited the apartment and rode the elevator down to garage level. A short while later, he was behind the wheel of his beloved pickup truck, ascending a concrete ramp towards morning light. Jimmy slid on a pair of Ray Bans and attempted to nose out into the gridlock.

A woman in an olive green BMW, with an iphone squashed against one ear, was blocking Jimmy's egress. He waited patiently while the woman rambled on, utilizing frequent hand gestures as if someone was in the front seat with her.

Finally, Jimmy politely tapped his horn.

The woman's head snapped in Jimmy's direction, glossy lips curled into a snarl. Then she extended a middle-finger salute.

Jimmy smiled and nodded his head. "Just pull it off the road, bitch, and I'll be happy to oblige yah. Orifice of your choice."

The phenomenon known as Morning Rush Hour was in full swing. Imagine trying to stuff twenty pounds of shit into a bag designed to hold ten. Then multiply that image by several million, and put it all in motion, at roughly five miles per hour.

Ah, nothin' quite like the smell of diesel exhaust in the morning.

As Jimmy drove towards Hollywood two thoughts weighed on his mind, insisted on being heard, on being addressed.

The first was the typical actor affirmations; I studied hard and learned my lines, and this could be the role that makes me. This could be the Holy Grail. Make me a star!

The second thought was not nearly as insistent, but simmered just below the surface. Jimmy was thinking that maybe the time was ripe to look for new representation. In the last six months he'd been on seventeen interviews. That figured to less than three a month! There had to be an agent out there who could do better than that! Someone with better connections. Someone who could Package him. Someone who could see how special he was.

Fuckin' agents were basically all the same. They were your best buddies as long as you were makin' them money. But the moment the checks stopped coming in, the pretension of friendship dropped quicker than a prostitute's panties.

"... Yeah, that's right. First off, land this gig. Right after that, start making phone calls and sending out pictures and resumes."

Jimmy figured it couldn't take more than a couple of days to get the word out, and then he'd have to beat them back with a stick.

Nah, shouldn't be hard at all. Not with this face.

He lowered his sunglasses to get a better look at a brunette in an old Caddie convertible in the next lane. Jimmy shot the babe a self-confident wink, and she responded by pressing the button that rolled up the tinted passenger-side window.

*****

Irv spent another sleepless night, most of it in a prone position, stubbornly staring up at the cottage cheese ceiling. The Rat-Brain inside Irv's head was running in circles and talking in nonsensical sentences. Another man would have thrown in the towel by three am, climbed out of bed, turned on the TV, or picked up a book. Done something! But no, not Irv. Uh-uh. He was determined to get some sleep even if it killed him. God, what he wouldn't give for a handful of muscle relaxers.

But when four-thirty rolled around, his eyes were still open, and his aural acuity was heightened to where he could hear hair leaping from his scalp and crashing onto the pillow.

And as he laid there, he re-ran the scene with Shelly, over and over in his head. And he wondered how he managed to get himself involved in this nightmare. He should have told her right then and there where she could stuff her partnership arrangement

But that wasn't what happened. The interior Irv, the bold and brazen one, the Man of Action, had momentarily seized control of mouth and vocal cords, and accordingly, things would never be the same.

Irv could talk the Talk, alright, but it remained to be seen if he could walk the Walk. In school, Irv was the kid who was bullied into handing over his lunch money every day. As an adult, his survival instinct made an art out of avoiding confrontation, and maintaining a low profile. It occurred to him that this was the fundamental reason he found Shelly so magnetic; the woman was utterly fearless.

This Cody Clifton situation was a black hole whose crushing gravitational pull was threatening to suck Irv into the dying star. His role would require him to commit half a dozen felonies, any one of which could land him in state prison. Horrific images of the urban legend known as 'The Tossed-Salad Man' filled his imagination. Three-hundred, fifty pounds of bald, black, booty-bustin' convict, with a hankerin' for fresh Hollywood Jewboy.

Not a relaxing thought.

Unfortunately, Irv had quite a vivid imagination, and he could easily concoct far worse possibilities than becoming an unwilling sex slave to a mass murderer. Like the possibility of going back to the Way Things Used To Be, for instance.

Back to scraping by, booking C-list clients for under-fives, and then chasing the ungrateful deadbeats for the commission. Back to doing business out of a dingy shit-hole of an office, and driving to and fro every day in a twelve year old vehicle, with a fucked-up air conditioner. McDonald's drive-through for lunch. As far as he was concerned, that was the worst case scenario.

And then, when he began pondering the 'No Mores', his temples started to throb. At the top of that list was No More Brentwood Pussy Palace! Number two had to be No More Beemer convertible. Followed closely by No More great tables at Five Star restaurants! No More A-List parties. No More. No More!

So, like it or not, the time had come to step up to the plate. What was it Shelly had said? Gotta pay if you wanna play. That was it. Well, it was time to Pay. Time to show some chutzpa or perish in the attempt.

Irv climbed out of the sack at seven, showered, drank three cups of coffee, and made himself a couple of scrambled eggs. After breakfast, he rinsed off the dishes, placed them in the dishwasher, and crossed back to the bathroom. He gazed at his reflection in the mirror, took a deep breath, steadied himself.

"I can do this," he said, with not nearly enough conviction.

He slid open a cabinet drawer and removed a plastic box about the size of a deck of cards, placed it on the vanity. Then he reached into the medicine cabinet and removed a small brown bottle of Spirit Gum.

Irv unscrewed the cap from the bottle. And brushed some liquid on his upper lip and chin. Caustic fumes rose into his sinus and he felt suddenly light-headed. When the feeling cleared, he unsnapped the lid from the plastic box, and removed its contents.

He'd acquired the human hair goatee from a makeup artist friend of his, a couple of years back. Its original use had been for a Halloween party, icing for Irv's Devil costume.

His nose twitched as he pressed the fake mustache into

place and held pressure on his upper lip. Next he applied the chin whiskers, delicately pressed the edges down. He checked his reflection once again and smiled.

"Not bad," he commented. "I can do this!"

He slipped on a pair of Elvis style, oversized aviation sunglasses, and finished off the ensemble with a blue Dodgers baseball cap.

He studied his transformed visage in the mirror.

"It's Showtime!"

He was out the door by eight, and parked across from Jimmy's building by nine, nerves strung tight, stomach acids well churned.

When he spotted Jimmy's pickup pull out of the underground garage and turn into traffic, the adrenaline surge overwhelmed the nausea.

The Director in Irv's head screamed, "… And Action!"

Irv exited the BMW, popped the trunk latch and gathered two bags of 'groceries' into his scrawny arms. He waited for a break in traffic and crossed the street.

Irv entered the building and walked through the courtyard, a man on a mission. He wasn't halfway to the elevators, when one of the residents, a well dressed woman in her sixties, carrying a miniature poodle in a basket, stepped from her ground floor apartment. The poodle took an immediate interest in the thin, bearded stranger, and began a high-pitched yapping.

Irv took a quick detour towards the mailboxes. He turned his back on the old woman and her companion and pantomimed checking his box.

When the woman and the dog left for parts unknown,

Irv headed for the elevators, whistling self-consciously. He pressed the 'up' button with one pasty knuckle, a move he saw executed once on late-night TV. Better safe than sorry when it came to leaving any incriminating evidence, like fingerprints.

He got off on the ninth floor and walked down a long hallway, paused at the very last door. He glanced casually over his shoulder and saw that the coast was clear. Putting the grocery bags down, he produced a key from a pants pocket, and a wadded up pair of latex gloves from another. He snapped the gloves over his knobby fingers and inserted the key into the deadbolt. Irv glanced once again down the vacant hallway, thanked God for economic boom times and felt perspiration trickle down his neck. He turned the key, and the lock snicked open.

Irv picked up the grocery bags and stepped inside just as if he owned the place. He closed and dead-bolted the door, turned and crossed to the master bedroom. All business.

Irv set the grocery bags down on Jimmy's unmade bed and scratched feverishly under his nose. He surveyed the bedroom and felt his heart rate start to slow.

He hadn't been inside the condo since Jimmy had gotten back from the Phoenix shoot, and the squalor simply amazed him.

There were piles of clothes laying in at least seven areas of the room. The night stands were littered with beer bottles and various drug paraphernalia; a gold razor blade, several empty, gram-sized bottles, and a couple of oily marijuana roaches. On the coffee table, across from the TV, the remnants of the previous night's meal lay festering. Half-eaten bags of french fries, their paper containers completely transparent, cheese-encrusted hamburger wrappings, and yet more beer bottles.

He headed for the bathroom. Feeling a need to satisfy his curiosity Irv checked the medicine cabinet. He spied plastic containers of antacids, nasal sprays and eye wash. There were a dozen prescription bottles with names on the labels like Skelaxin and Vicodin, Diazipan and Percodan. And on one shelf was an industrial size tube of Astroglide, as well as packets of various condoms. Alongside the personal lubricant there were three bottles of Rogaine Extra Strength.

Jimmy's telephone rang and Irv levitated, smacked his knee into a handle on the vanity.

"Shit!" he cried out, trying to massage away the pain with little success.

Irv closed the medicine cabinet and removed Jimmy's hair brush from the counter.

He padded back into the bedroom, opened the grocery bags that contained Cody's boots, and held the brush extended over the opening. With the thumb and index finger of his opposite hand, Irv coaxed several strands of hair from the brush, and watched them descend.

When he was finished he returned the brush to its place on the bathroom vanity.

He went back to the bedroom, snatched the grocery bags from the bed and crossed to the closet. It was time to exchange one pair of cowboy boots for another. Only he wouldn't be leaving the boots he brought with him in plain sight. No, that just wouldn't do at all.

*****

London abandoned the unmarked cruiser in a red zone in front of the Beverly Hills office building, stepped into the street and wrinkled his nose.

"Smell that, Max?"

"What?"

London inhaled deeply, let it out slow.

"That's the smell of money, honey... Let's check it out."

"Right behind you."

*****

The detectives stepped into the waiting area of The Monroe Talent Group, LTD., and approached the opaque partition window. London tapped on the glass.

A minute later, a shadow appeared behind the milky surface, and then the partition slid open.

Sylvia peeked out and locked eyes with London, smiling her approval.

"Can I help you," Sylvia purred.

Max suppressed an urge to roll her eyes. Men were so predictable.

"Absolutely," London replied, piling on the charm. "I'm detective Greg London, and this is my partner, detective Max Calderas."

"Pleased to meet'cha," Sylvia replied.

London grinned like a puppy.

Sylvia glanced furtively at her purse and made a mental calculation of the various felonies enclosed therein.

Max said, "We'd like to speak with Ms. Monroe."

"I'm afraid Ms. Monroe is in a meeting," Sylvia lied. "If you'd like to leave a number, I'll be sure and have her get back to you as soon as possible."

Sylvia's eyes never left London. She looked him over,

up and down, as if she was appraising a side of beef.

Calderas bent over, put her face close to the girl's. "Now listen up, sweet-cakes," Max began quietly. "Be a good little girl and tell your boss we're here. Otherwise, I may want to get a look at your ID. You know, the one in that purse over there." Calderas motioned with a hand.

Sylvia didn't flinch.

"Just a moment," she replied softly. Then the partition slid shut.

Whatever was going on was definitely juicy, and Sylvia was just dying to know more. Information was power after all.

Raymond poked his head from around the corner and asked, "What's going on?"

"Nothing that concerns you," was Sylvia's terse response.

"Bitch," Raymond cursed under his breath, hunching his shoulders and returning to the Tombs.

Sylvia put the headset on and actuated the Intercom button.

"Ms. Monroe, there are two detectives out front to see you. What would you like me to tell them?"

Shelly closed the script she was reading and put it down on the desk. Poor Sylvia sounded rattled. Probably had a couple of grams of blow in her purse, or God knows what.

"It's alright, Sylvia. Bring 'em on back, please."

Shelly disconnected the Intercom, removed the headset, and ran fingers through her hair. She glanced at the diamond-studded Rolex on her wrist and smiled inwardly.

The fuckers were right on schedule.

Moments later, Sylvia's delicate knock.

"Come in," Shelly said, rising from the chair.

The door swung open and Sylvia stepped inside, followed closely by two of El Lay's finest.

Sylvia excused herself, leaving Shelly to deal with the plain clothes heat however she saw fit.

"Good morning, detectives," Shelly offered, taking note of their attire.

Plain clothes, indeed!

"Good morning, Ms. Monroe."

It was the woman who'd responded. She looked directly at Shelly with penetrating brown eyes, while her partner swiveled his head around, memorizing the décor.

"I'm detective Max Calderas," she continued, extending her hand. "And my partner, detective Greg London."

Shelly shook hands with the lady detective.

"Nice to meet you," Shelly responded, retracting her hand and returning to her chair. "So what can I do for the El Lay P. D.?"

"We're working on a case, and we'd like some information on one of your clients,"

"Well, dear, you're going to have to be a lot more specific than that," Shelly replied, feeling Calderas out. "Like what kind of information are you looking for, and on which client? I represent nearly two-hundred actors and actresses."

London was on the other side of the office, examining Shelly's Awards shelf. "Tell us about Cody Clifton," he said, with his back towards the women.

Even though Shelly knew it was coming, the mention

of Cody's name made her pulse quicken. How much did they really know? And how much was a fishing expedition?

Though her insides were in upheaval, Shelly responded evenly. Her expression and manner betrayed nothing.

"Cody?" she repeated. "Why are you guys interested in Cody Clifton?"

"We're not at liberty to discuss that."

Again it was the woman doing the talking. Shelly wondered if it was that way all the time, or if they switched off, depending on who they were interviewing.

"We could get a court order, if you prefer," London rasped.

Shelly eyed the rumpled detective appraisingly. Probably had unresolved issues with his mother. And he was playing the old Good Cop-Bad Cop routine. How predictable.

"No need to go to all that trouble, detective," Shelly replied warmly. "I always do my civic duty and cooperate with the police. What do you want to know?"

"A residence address and telephone number would be a good place to start," Calderas began. "And then we'd like to get a look at Mister Clifton's employment records for the past year or so if that wouldn't be too inconvenient."

Shelly laughed out loud at the detective's request. "You been living under a rock somewhere, or are you just one of those quaint folk who don't own a TV? Cody Clifton's only the hottest star of the season!"

Shelly slid a copy of TV Guide across the desk towards Calderas. It was the issue with Cody's picture on the cover.

"That's what he's been working on the last year!"

Shelly shook her head and scratched down Cody's address and phone number on a piece of stationery, handed it to Calderas. Five minutes later, the detectives were a fading memory, although it would take another three solid hours for all traces of London's Aqua Velva to finally dissipate from the office.

*****

Cody checked his watch for the fifth time in as many minutes. It was almost ten am and there still wasn't any sign of Irv.

Cody had gathered from Shelly's note that her plan, while feasible, wasn't entirely foolproof. It had an element of serious risk, and hinged on two distinct occurrences, the most important of which involved Irv. That, in and of itself, was enough to give Cody some serious concerns. Having his future in the hands of someone like Irv was a monumental gamble. There were so many ways Irv could fuck up his part, it boggled the imagination. And Cody knew first hand how rapidly things could turn to shit. Murphy's Law.

So many things could go wrong. So many things already had. And Cody wasn't in control of any of it. Not anymore. He didn't even warrant a vote.

Just do what I tell you, exactly like I tell you, and you might slide out from under this.

The note was explicit if not diplomatic. Cody figured Shelly was pretty much beyond diplomacy at this point. It was a whole new ballgame now, and Cody needed her. And that could wind up being a monstrous problem. It all boiled down to an issue of Trust. How much did he really trust Shelly? How much could any woman be trusted?

His mind raced through the possibilities.

269

What if Shelly planned to rat him out all along, collect the reward and recreate herself as some kinda Hollywood Heroine?

He could see it now: His former agent on the daytime talk circuit: Ellen and Wendy Williams and The View! Shelly might even roll it into a few guest appearances on shows like 'NBC News: Dateline' or 'E Hollywood True Stories'.

Christ! What if the cops were on their way right now?!

Overcome with sudden dread, Cody jumped off the couch, scaring Blue, who'd been soundly sleeping. Cody ran into the bedroom, opened the closet and retrieved a duffel bag from a shelf, He started to stuff clothes into it. His heart pounded as a voice inside his head yelled, Get Outta Dodge! Now! Before it's too late!

Cody tossed the duffel onto the bed and crossed quickly to the desk. He opened the top drawer and re-moved a manila envelope. He undid the clasp and in-spected the contents; rubber-banded, thousand-dollar stacks of currency. Better than eighty grand in cash. He smiled in spite of himself. Bobbi had always said one should always keep some 'emergency' money close at hand. Stuffing the envelope into the duffel, he started for the front door. Whistling for Blue, his eyes glanced at his framed TV Guide cover, hanging over the couch: "Cody Clifton is Chuck Dallas."

As he paused, another voice spoke up inside his head. This calm and reasonable voice said, "Hold up there, cowboy! Give Shelly a chance. She'd never turn you in. Not in a million years. You're her Golden Boy, and if you run now, you're throwing it all away. Pull yourself together and think!"

He stood there for what seemed like ages, holding the

duffel in one hand and the keys to the Suburban in the other, just listening to his beating heart. He thought about how hard he'd worked to get where he was, all the pitfalls and missteps along the way. An image of Bobbi flashed across his mindscape, and for a moment he swore he smelled jasmine, It was at that moment Cody decided to play the hand out. He returned the duffel to his bedroom and crossed back to the living room, holding a deck of cards. He sat on the couch beside Blue and began shuffling the deck.

"So what's it gonna be? Poker or Gin Rummy?"

Blue yawned a response and rested his head on his front paws.

"Well, then poker it is," Cody replied brightly.

He dealt out hands for himself and the hound and waited to see who showed up at his door first. Was it going to be Hollywood Irv arriving in the nick of time, to save the day? Or, was it going to go the other way, with the cops showing up ahead of schedule, forcing Cody to improvise.

Cody closed his eyes and mumbled a quick silent prayer. A remnant from a misbegotten childhood. Five minutes later, the doorbell rang, and Cody got his answer.

And apparently God had a soft spot for sociopaths... Cody opened the door and Irv stepped inside, wiping the sweat off his forehead with the back of his hand.

Cody would have liked to bitch-slap Irv for letting him twist in the wind for so long, but the Actor took over and went for the ego-massage, instead.

"Everything okay, good buddy?" Cody asked with genuine concern. "Didn't have any trouble, did yah?"

"No, no trouble at all," Irv replied, a coldness to his tone.

Raping and killing prostitutes was bad enough, but as far as Irv was concerned there was nothing lower than a man who would betray a friend to save his own ass. Even an agent had more scruples than that! When Irv looked at the handsome cowboy, he saw the face of Judas.

He handed Cody the grocery bag that contained Jimmy Bodine's boots.

"I've done my part," he stated mechanically. "Shelly said I should tell you, it's all up to you now... And that she's counting on you to pull this off."

Cody was genuinely moved. He made an attempt to place a consoling hand on Irv's shoulder, but Irv pulled away before Cody could make contact. Even though Irv did his best to hide his revulsion, Cody picked up on it just the same, and pretended not to notice.

"Yah be sure to tell Shelly not to worry," Cody said, cranking up the Southern charm.

Irv was anxious to be gone, but felt it necessary to say something further. To do otherwise seemed rude.

"Break a leg, Cody," he said finally. Then he turned and left.

"You can fool some of the people all of the time and all of the people some of the time…
-Lawrence J. Peter

37

It was almost one in the afternoon and Cody was in the living room with Blue curled up at his feet. A DVD of 'Dirty Harry', one of Cody's all time favorites, was playing on the big screen. Clint Eastwood had just shot Andrew Robinson in the leg, and was stepping on the shattered bone in an effort to get him to tell where the girl was stashed. Ends justify the Means, that sort of thing. It was just background noise to Cody, something to keep the silence at bay. His mind was elsewhere.

Blue stirred, sat up and sniffed the air. A deep growl started at the back of his throat. It was something primal, a sound Cody had never heard before.

"What is it, boy?" Cody asked quietly. "Do we have company?"

Blue started to bark and then he lunged for the front door.

Cody chased after the hound, managed to get a hand on his collar just as the doorbell rang.

"Be with you in a second," he called out. "Settle down, Blue!"

Blue dialed it back to a growl and planted his rump by Cody's feet.

Cody paused to steady himself and take two deep cleansing breaths before cracking the door. He saw two strangers standing on the porch, a man and a woman. He eyed the woman appreciatively and grinned. The pair flashed their badges. Standard protocol.

And... Action!

"Good afternoon. I'm detective Max Calderas, El Lay PD, and this is my partner, detective Greg London. Are you Cody Clifton?"

Cody flashed the smile that had made him America's newest sweetheart. "Yes, Ma'am."

"Would it be alright if we came in and asked you some questions, Mister Clifton?" Calderas probed.

"Sure. C'mon in. You're not afraid of dogs, are you?" Cody replied, opening the door wide and stepping back. "Only nobody calls me Mister Clifton. Name's Cody."

He was well prepared, secure with his Motivation, dialogue rolling right off his tongue.

Calderas and London stepped inside, took mental notes on the furnishings and décor. The place looked like the Maid's month off, with clothes and plastic DVD covers scattered about, and beer bottles sitting atop old pizza boxes.

"'Scuse the mess," Cody apologized. "I'm startin' work on a new film tomorrow morning. Never can seem to keep ahead of things."

"I know what you mean," Calderas said.

Blue looked up at the detective, and recognizing a soft touch, smiled and wagged his tail.

Cody watched Calderas as she squatted and began stroking Blue's back. His eyes followed her, and he imagined her more intimately clad. His pulse quickened. This bitch was wastin' her time workin' for the El Lay PD. She had a better bod than J-Lo! Prettier face, too."

"Handsome animal," Calderas commented.

"His name's Blue," Cody replied, locking eyes with the lady detective. "I think he likes you."

"Ah, he looks pretty friendly to me, "London interjected gruffly. "I bet he's like that with everybody."

Cody ignored him, never averting his eyes from Max. "Sit down if yah like. Make yourselves at home. Mi casa es su casa... Can I get y'all somethin' to drink?"

Cody the cordial host.

Max shook her head. "Thanks, just the same."

London grunted something

Cody smiled, sizing up the pair, Carney to Marks.

"So what's this all about, officers?"

"It's detectives," London corrected as he prowled around the room. He paused by a rack of esoteric audiophile gear and bent over to take a closer look.

"We're investigating a series of homicides of young women," Max replied, watching for Cody's reaction.

"Yah talkin' 'bout what's been on the news?" Cody asked, a measured sadness injected into his tone.

Calderas nodded.

"How can I help?"

Max handed Cody the plastic bag that contained the toe-guard. "Do you recognize this?"

Cody remained in character and held the bag up to the light. He turned it this way and that, narrowed his eyes.

"Sure. It's a toe-guard. What's this gotta do with me?"

"We had a conversation with the man who made it," Calderas replied. "His name's Roy Healey, and he told us you ordered eight sets of these."

"That's right. I did," Cody admitted. "Yah know Healey is the best in the country for this kinda work. The man's a genuine artist."

"Yeah. We heard," London replied, over easy on the sarcasm. "Mind telling us where you were Thursday night?"

About fuckin' time they got down to the nits and grits.

"I was havin' dinner with my agent," Cody replied calmly, following Shelly's script to the letter.

"What restaurant did you eat at, and about what time did you get home?" London probed.

"We had dinner here," Cody parried. "We hadda lot of business to discuss, what with the new movie, Chuck Dallas and these endorsement deals she's been linin' up.

London raised an eyebrow.

Cody continued in his best 'aw shucks' manner, "We needed some peace and quiet so we could go over our game plan for the year. Seems like I can't go anywhere these days without being hounded by all those paparazzi."

Cody's tone turned confidential. "I know they're just doin' their job, but sometimes all that attention can be overwhelming for a small town boy like me."

"So Cody, what do you say? Would it be possible for us to get a look at your cowboy boots?"

Now Calderas was doing the probing.

Cody glanced at the detective's thighs and thought about probing her. He scratched his head, all cornpone charm. Shelly had anticipated all of this.

"Anything for El Lay's finest," he replied.

At that point, Calderas couldn't figure out if the actor was naive or just plain stupid. Anybody with any knowledge of The System would be asking for an attorney right about now... except, perhaps, a stone cold killer with nerves of steel.

Cody crossed through the living room with the detectives bringing up the rear. Not wanting to be left out of the parade, Blue tagged along.

Cody led them through the duplex to the master bedroom. He opened the closet door and stepped aside.

"There yah go," Cody said, pointing towards the floor.

Cody's boots were lined up along both sides of the closet. There were more than thirty pairs, from the common to the most exotic.

"Damn!" London exclaimed. "That's a helluva collection."

The detective bent over to retrieve a pair of pale blue lizard skins.

"Help yourself," Cody replied from his position in the doorway.

Calderas joined London on the floor, and the detectives examined Cody's entire collection.

"I only count seven pairs of boots with the custom gold guards," Calderas commented.

"That's right, Ma'am," Cody replied, feigning embarrassment. "One for each day of the week."

"So what happened to the eighth pair?" London enquired suspiciously.

"It was a present for an actor buddy of mine."

"Pretty swanky gift," London commented.

277

"He's a helluva good friend. Introduced me to his agent when I was just startin' out, and she signed me up. The rest, as they say, is history."

"History. Yeah…" London parroted. "This good buddy of yours got a name?"

"His name's Jimmy Bodine," Cody replied.

"Can you tell us where we can find him?" London asked, intimidation factor nine.

Cody looked at London like the detective had lost his mind. "There must be some kinda mistake. Jimmy'd never be involved in this."

Calderas turned up the warmth, playing the Good Cop. "I'm sure you're right, Cody. But we need to talk to him in order to get this straightened out."

Cody took a dramatic pause, thought about what Calderas said, nodded his head.

"I don't know the numbers off hand, but I can give you the cross streets. It's a condo complex on the Westside. Our agent, Shelly Monroe should have his exact address."

A couple of minutes later, Cody showed the detectives to the door. He watched Max walk back to the cruiser, and thought again how much he'd enjoy a closer, more private interview with her.

All the better to eat you with, my dear.

Oh yes!

He felt relieved as he watched the cruiser accelerate down the street. He closed the door and crossed into the kitchen, picked up the phone and dialed Shelly.

Everything was proceeding according to her plan.

*****

"So what was your impression?" Calderas queried from behind the wheel of the cruiser.

London shrugged. "Oh, I don't know. Seemed like a nice enough guy, considering."

"Considering what?"

"Considering the sonofabitch makes more money in one week than either of us earns in two years! How about you? Get anything off him?"

"Well, Cody Clifton may be just what he looks like; a not-too-bright pretty boy who caught a lucky break."

38

It was almost three in the afternoon, and the blackout curtains were pulled. The only light in Jimmy Bodine's living room emanated from flickering images on his big screen TV.

The images were of a man and a red-headed woman engaged in rough sex on a king-sized bed. The bedroom was set awash in candle light, a mirrored headboard reflecting the heated dance. Elvis, the bear, looked on benevolently through pink, John Lennon sunglasses.

The dead don't complain.

Megan was spread-eagled, legs up on the bed. She bucked her hips in unison to Jimmy's thrusts and cried out as another climax approached. Jimmy gritted his teeth and picked up the pace.

As Megan started to come, she let her legs drop to the bed. She reached for Jimmy's hands, placed them on her throat.

"Do it!" she commanded, her voice filled with lust, her hips rocking violently.

Jimmy drove his meat in to the hilt and tightened his grip around her lovely freckled neck.

"Harder!" she groaned, writhing like an eel beneath him.

Jimmy pressed his thumbs against her windpipe, cutting off oxygen to her brain. Her eyelids fluttered and her body trembled beneath him. Oh, sweet asphyxia!

At the last possible instant he relaxed the tension across the girl's throat, and she sucked in a wheezing breath. All the while Jimmy continued pounding her while Megan whimpered under the onslaught. When Jimmy finally exploded, her elastic muscles gripped him and milked every drop.

"Ohhh Jeesus!"
Jimmy withdrew and rolled onto his back, his heart thrashing his ribcage, his mouth dry.

"Was it good for you?" Megan rasped, rubbing one tapered hand over her battered pussy.'

Jimmy laughed.

When his heart rate had returned to near normal, he stood up and crossed to his trusty video camera. Jimmy had it set up just inside the doorway of his bedroom.

"... And cut! That's a print," he called out playfully.

He put the camera in 'pause' mode and crossed to the coffee table in the living room. He snatched the red and white straw from the mirror and partially inserted it into his right nostril, bent over the mound of Columbia's Finest, and inhaled deeply. He repeated the process for nostril number two.

Megan popped out of bed and glided toward the coffee table.

"How about me?" she pouted.

Jimmy scooped some blow onto his semi-rigid staff and pointed it at the redhead.

"Help yourself, baby."

Megan smiled and dropped to her knees. "Don't mind if I do."

The knock on the door made them both jump.

"Are you expecting someone?" Megan whispered, frozen like a deer in front of an SUV's headlights.

"Get serious," Jimmy responded irritably as he headed towards the door. "Some fuckin' security building. I'm gonna call the manager and ream him a new asshole!"

More knocking. Whoever it was, wasn't going away.

"Who is it?" Jimmy yelled.

"Is this Jimmy Bodine's residence?" the feminine voice on the other side of the door inquired. Megan stood up, placed her hands on her hips and frowned.

"What's it to yah?" Jimmy replied rudely.

"My name is Max Calderas. I'm a detective with the Los Angeles Police Department. My partner and I would like to ask him some questions."

Jimmy turned to Megan, motioned toward the mirror full of white flake, and whispered harshly, "Get that shit outta here!"

Megan's eyes grew wide as she processed the information. Detectives at the door and mounds of coke on the mirror-in plain view! She sprang into action, snatched the mirror off the coffee table, and scooted towards the bedroom.

Jimmy shook his head and checked the peephole, got an eye full of badge.

"Hang on a second. I'll be right with you," Jimmy said. He sprinted for the bedroom, unconsciously wiping under his nose as he went.

Calderas and London exchanged a look as they heard scurrying sounds inside the condo.

Jimmy crossed from the bedroom, buttoning his jeans as he went. He slid the deadbolt and cracked the door a couple of inches, stood shielded behind it.

"What's this about?" he demanded, peering at the two detectives through bloodshot eyes.

"Are you Jimmy Bodine?" Calderas asked.

"Yeah," Jimmy replied.

The detectives did a double-take. The resemblance between Jimmy Bodine and Cody Clifton was remarkable. The two could easily have been brothers.

"Mind if we come in and talk with you for a moment?" London asked innocently.

"I'm kinda in the middle of somethin'" Jimmy replied. "You'll have to come back later."

Loud snorting sounds began wafting from the bedroom, and Jimmy's blood pressure ascended.

London turned to Calderas. "Sounds like Mister Bodine is declining, Max. He doesn't want us to come inside. Perhaps there's something in there he doesn't want us to see."

"I'm entertainin' right now, if you catch my drift," Jimmy replied with a conspiratorial wink.

London's eyes narrowed and he pressed. "I don't suppose you were entertaining last Thursday night?"

Jimmy was getting annoyed.

"Look, what's this about?"

"We're investigating the homicide of a young woman," Calderas replied calmly. "Happened sometime Thursday evening."

This conversation was rapidly ruining Jimmy's high. "What's that gotta do with me?"

Max tilted her head, locked eyes with the suspect. "That's what we're trying to ascertain, Mister Bodine."

By this time, several of Jimmy's neighbors had opened their doors to investigate the commotion in the hallway.

"I don't know nothin' about no homicide," Jimmy insisted in a stage whisper, cocaine and adrenaline surging through his blood stream.

"Then you shouldn't mind talking to us and clearing up a few questions," London concluded.

That tore it.

"I already told yah, now's not a good time. I got company over," Jimmy replied hotly. "And I've seen enough cop shows to know y'all can't just waltz in anywhere you please, without a search warrant... Do yah have a warrant?"

"No, Mister Bodine. We don't have a warrant."

Jimmy was pleased with himself.

"Then y'all won't mind if I get back to what I was doin'."

"Not at all. Have a nice day, Mister Bodine," Calderas replied.

"And thanks for your cooperation," London added, as the door closed, and the deadbolt slid home.

As the detectives hiked back towards the elevators, Calderas turned to London and grinned. "This guy is hiding something. I know it."

"Like a pair of fancy cowboy boots with a missing toe-guard, perhaps?"

Max's grin began to fade.

"But we don't have enough to get a warrant."

"No we don't," London concurred. "Not right at this minute."

"Sounds like you have something in mind."

"Just some basic detective work, Max. Let's just see what we can dig up on Mister Bodine." A sly smile spread across his handsome face.

"One of the biggest lies in the world is that crime doesn't pay. Of course, crime pays."

-G. Gordon Liddy

39

Shelly was enjoying a smoke on her private balcony and marveling at the five o'clock traffic on San Vicente. It was proving to be a bad month to quit nicotine. An expert at multi-tasking, she was also in the process of negotiating a deal. She wore a wireless headset and spoke with practiced emotion.

"I'm sorry, Al. I really tried... I know, believe me. If it were up to me, I'd close the deal at twenty-eight, five, and call it a day, but Carlton won't budge..."

The Intercom sounded a tone over the headset.

"Don't go away. I'll be right back."

Shelly clicked a button on the hand-piece that sent Al between the circuits, where a Muzak version of an old Barry Manilow tune wheezed limply in the background.

"Ms. Monroe, those two cops are back," Sylvia said. "What do you want me to tell them?"

Shelly had figured the probability of a second visit from El Lay's Finest at roughly ninety percent. It followed a fairly logical sequence. They came to her for information about Cody Clifton, and now they were back to see what they could learn about Jimmy Bodine. Closest distance between two points, that sorta thing.

"Send them back, Sylvia."

Shelly ground the butt out in an overflowing ashtray and returned to her desk. She clicked the handset.

"Sorry about that, Al... Let me talk to Carlton again and I'll get back to you."

Moments later there was a rap at the door.

"It's open."

"Good afternoon, Ms Monroe," Max began. "Sorry to be bothering you twice in one day."

"No bother, detective, but where's that good looking partner of yours?"

"I think he's investigating something up front," Max replied, shooting Shelly a knowing look.

"Our Sylvia gets a lot of attention. She's such a lovely girl. So what else can I help you with today?"

"Just a couple more questions?"

The phone rang and Shelly glanced down at the hand-piece, saw that all the lines were lit.

"Excuse me. I gotta take this," she apologized as she clicked the hand-piece.

"This is Shelly... Uh-huh. Yes... Of course." She scrambled for her Mont Blanc and began scribbling on a message pad.

"What time do you want him there?" No problemo, Curtis."

Shelly clicked the hand-piece and finished writing down the information. Then she looked back at Max. "You were saying?"

"I have a few more questions," the detective replied.

"About Cody? I don't know what else I can tell you."

Calderas shook her head. "No, not Cody... What can you tell me about Jimmy Bodine?"

287

Shelly felt a surge of triumph. Oh yes! Hook, line and sinker!

"Jimmy? Let me see… He's been a client for three years. He hasn't hit much, although Cody got him a regular gig on Chuck Dallas. They're good friends. Matter of fact, it was Jimmy who brought Cody in to meet me. You don't think Jimmy has something to do with this?"

"It's routine, Max replied. "We just need to clear something up. Would you happen to have Mister Bodine's employment records handy? If it wouldn't be too much trouble," detective Calderas added as a polite afterthought.

"No trouble at all, detective. Just a couple of mouse clicks away."

Shelly tapped at the keyboard and a page of information appeared on the monitor.

"Would you like me to print you out a hard copy?" Shelly asked.

"Thanks. That'd be great," Calderas replied.

Shelly punched a button on the keyboard, and a minute later the printer kicked out two sheets of data.

Shelly handed the papers to detective Calderas and smiled. "Here you go."

Max took the sheets and began to scan them.

A minute later, Shelly noticed the lady detective's facial muscles tighten.

"Everything alright, dear?" Shelly asked. "Is that of any help?"

Calderas looked up from the pages, smiled thinly. "Everything's just fine," Calderas replied, trying to conceal her excitement. "Thanks again for your help, Ms. Monroe. We appreciate your cooperation."

"Glad to be of assistance, detective."

Before she excused herself, Max suggested Shelly keep their little chat confidential. And that was when Shelly knew for certain there was something of interest to the El Lay PD in those records. What it was she couldn't imagine, but her instincts told her she'd just scored major bonus points. As soon as she was clear of The Heat, Shelly planned to spend some time studying Jimmy Bodine's files to see what she might have missed.

But first, she'd put in a call to Cody. Check up on him and let him know all was well, and that the sharks had taken the bait.

*****

London was less than thrilled when Max showed up to yank him away from the creamy receptionist. But once again, Duty called. He was elated when Sylvia scribbled her cel on the back of an agency business card and tucked it in his palm.

"Call me," Sylvia said with an alluring smile.

As soon as the two detectives were in the hallway, Calderas turned to London.

"Check this out," she said, handing him the documents.

London scanned the papers.

"Sonofabitch!!" He exclaimed.

"Jimmy Bodine's our guy, chief! I knew it as soon as I laid eyes on him. Fucker was shooting a movie in Phoenix when that local girl turned up dead."

"Shouldn't be a problem getting a warrant now," London assured her, breaking into a wide grin. "And I know just the judge..."

40

It was almost ten pm when Jimmy picked up the phone and speed-dialed Cody.

Cody picked up after the third ring and grumbled, "Yeah?"

"Hey buddy, did I catch yah at a bad time?" Jimmy asked, put off by Cody's tone.

"No, bro'," Cody apologized. "I though you were some-one else. What's up?"

"I was kinda in the mood for a little prowlin' around. Thought you might wanna join me."

"Sorry Jimmy-Bo, I'm just hittin' the sack. I gotta 6 am makeup call for 'Ballistic'. Maybe tomorrow night, if we wrap early, okay?"

"Sure Cody," Jimmy replied, feeling somewhat let down. "Tomorrow's good..."

"Okay, Bro'. Talk to yah tomorrow."

"Later," Jimmy said as the line went dead.

*****

It was eleven p.m. when a parade of police cruisers pulled up in front of Jimmy Bodine's apartment building, light bars flashing. More than a dozen officers deployed, with Calderas and London taking up point. The team moved en masse to the building's security door, and Cal-deras buzzed the manager. Less than a minute later, they were trotting through the courtyard towards the elevators. Ultimate destination: The ninth floor.

Jimmy had a hell of a buzz on. Since hanging up with Cody, he'd spent the better part of the last hour sitting motionless in front of his aquarium, mesmerized by the ever-changing colors and textures of the fish. The shrill ring of the phone broke the spell, but he let the machine pick it up. There wasn't anybody he cared to talk to at the moment.

Jimmy, it's me, Kathy. Pick up if you're there..."

He leaned against the couch and pressed the remote control. A moment later, the big screen fired up and bathed the living room with colored light. A tight close-up, gynecological in nature, and then a slow pull-out reveal-ing a young woman bent over a plush leather chair. The camera simply loved Megan.

Jimmy took a pull off the half-empty bottle of Cuervo he found clutched in his hand, swished the fiery liquid around in his mouth, swallowed hard.

He gazed up at the big screen through fuzzy lenses, recognized his posterior enter into frame. His erection grew rigid as he watched himself have oral sex with Me-gan. Jimmy, the Virtual Voyeur.

His mood was shattered by a pounding on the door.

Jimmy levitated from the floor, his heart hammering.

"Who is it?" Jimmy demanded.

"Police! Open up!"

Jimmy cursed under his breath as he made a mad dash through the living room. When he got to the bed-room, he slipped and slammed his shin into the desk so hard, he literally saw stars. He sucked in a breath and yanked a drawer open, inadvertently scattering papers and office detritus across the floor. Dropping to one knee, he retrieved a plastic baggie filled with shiny white powder. Then he sprinted towards the bathroom and locked himself in, just as the front door splintered.

As a dozen cops deployed throughout the condominium, Jimmy took one final snort from the stash before he tearfully, emptied the baggie into the toilet.

Calderas and London were standing in the hallway with weapons drawn when they heard the toilet flush. The detectives exchanged a glance and trained their weapons on the bathroom door.

"C'mon out of there, Jimmy! You got nowhere to go!" Calderas demanded.

"I'll come out. Just don't shoot me, damnit!"

"Nobody's going shoot you," London assured. "Just open the goddamn door and come out with your hands up!"

The detectives kept their weapons leveled just in case.

When Jimmy cracked open the bathroom door, a hand reached in and grabbed him. A second later he found himself pinned, face down, on the floor.

"Fuckin' relax, will yah?!" Jimmy protested.

"Put your hands behind your back!" Calderas yelled.

Jimmy complied.

"What the fuck is all this about?!" Jimmy demanded. "And who's gonna pay for my door?"

As soon as he was cuffed, a burly uniformed officer hoisted him to his feet.

"Hey Jimmy, you missed a little," London said, wiping white flakes from under Jimmy's nose.

"Y'all can't just come bustin' in here like that! I have rights, you know." Jimmy protested.

London smacked Jimmy in the forehead with some rolled up papers. Puppy Punishment.

"This time we brought along a search warrant, pal. And do you want to know what's funny?"

Jimmy blinked.

"Dope's got nothing to do with it."

"Detectives! In here!" A voice boomed from the master bedroom. "I think we found something."

"Sit on him," London told the uniform. "If he tries to run, shoot him."

The uniform nodded and Calderas and London adjourned to the master bedroom. "Check it out," said the rookie with the blonde buzz-cut, pointing towards Jimmy's bed. "Found it stashed in the back of the closet."

There was a nylon bag resting on the bedspread, its zippered lips gaping wide. Within its maw there was a collection of wadded towels, old socks, boxer shorts, and one pair of scraped up, python skin cowboy boots.

When Calderas took a closer look, she noticed the snake skin around the right toe was shredded, and she could make out where the toe-guard had separated from the boot. A wave of triumph washed over her.

"Yeah baby!" London howled, high-fiving Calderas. "Told you we'd get the son of a bitch!"

Calderas smiled at her partner.

"Don't you think someone ought to read Mister Bodine his rights?' London queried.

"Be my pleasure, chief," Calderas assured him.

"There is only one thing worse in the world than being talked about, and that is not being talked about."
                                                    -Oscar Wilde

41

Shelly stepped off the elevator Tuesday morning in a deliriously good mood. She was singing her favorite Beatles tune, all the way down the hall.

Your love gives me such a thrill,
But your lovin' won't pay my bills.
Give me Muh-uh-uhney, That's what I want.
It's what I wah-ah-ah-ahh-ahhahhant,
That's what I want.

Shelly opened the Agency door and stepped into the reception area, crossed quickly into the Inner sanctum. Every phone line in the place was either lit or ringing. Poor Sylvia was beside herself trying to keep up with the flow. Shelly glanced at her Inbox and was surprised to see ten full message sheets, each containing dozens of notations and return phone numbers.

"What's all this?" Shelly asked.

"Phone hasn't stopped ringing since I got in this morning," Sylvia complained. "Half of those I picked up from the service."

"Where's Raymond?"

"Off pouting somewhere," Sylvia replied, exasperated. "Never around when there's work to be done, that's for sure."

Shelly chuckled. "Well, round his skinny ass up and throw a headset on him," Shelly suggested. "Tell him he's on the phones 'til he hears otherwise from moi."

And then as an afterthought, "Is Irv here?"

Sylvia shook her head.

"Well, when he comes in, tell him I want to see him."

"Yes, Ms. Monroe."

Shelly proceeded to her office, closed the door and plopped down on her cushy executive chair. She lit up a cigarette and began to peruse the message sheets, ninety-five percent of which had to do with her brand new Mega-Star, Jimmy "The Coyote" Bodine. She rolled the phrase around on her tongue. Kinda had a ring to it.

The calls were mostly from media concerns, from rag sheets like The Inquisitor and TMZ, all the way to the other end of the scale, with Time and Newsweek. There were messages from representatives of the three major networks, all interested in the same thing: TV rights for a Movie-Of-The –Week. Ditto HBO and Showtime. There was a call from the Fox network as well. They were interested in doing a segment on The Coyote, on one of their Reality Cop shows.

About eighty percent of the messages were marked urgent, call back as soon as possible. Shelly smiled at those. Presumptuous and desperate at the same time. How charming.

"Come in," Shelly called out to the closed door before Irv even had a chance to knock.

He stepped inside.

"I hate when you do that," Irv stuttered. "It creeps me out!"

"Then you oughta consider springing for a pair of loafers that don't squeak. Sounds like a pack of rodents approaching every time you skulk down the hall... Sit down, Irv. Take a load off. Relax."

Shelly clicked the remote control and the big screen lit up. The tuner flipped through the channels, past an array of soap operas and talk shows.

Shelly paused surfing when she spotted an ex-client on a commercial, touting a new feminine hygiene product: 'April Clouds', makes you feel as fresh as Spring time.

"Oh, I remember her!" Irv snarled, pointing an accusatory finger. "Had to chase that one for every dime... Haven't seen her around in years."

"Rene Lamm," Shelly replied with a laugh. "Now that's what I call Type Casting. Hire a cunt to promote a douche spray..."

Shelly clicked the remote, halting on a local news channel. A blonde, with high cheek bones and an expensive nose job, reported the top story of the day:

"Good morning. I'm Beverly Crescent, reporting to you from our news studio in Hollywood." She shuffled some papers for effect. "The citizens of Los Angeles can breathe a weary sigh of relief today..."

The Image Window behind the newscaster cut to footage taken the night before, of Jimmy Bodine being hustled into the back of a police vehicle and whisked from the scene.

Beverly continued. "At a press conference conducted in front of Parker Center this morning, Police Chief Robert Vasquez had this to say."

The Image Window slid into full-screen, revealing a

stern-faced Chief of Police flanked by several well fed, high ranking brass. The Chief bowed his head and read stiffly from a prepared statement.

"Good morning... I am pleased to announce that a suspect was taken into custody last night in connection with the Coyote Murder investigation. The suspect, Frances James Bodine, aka Jimmy Bodine, thirty-eight, was placed under arrest at around eleven o'clock, last night. Mister Bodine is being held at the Twin Towers jail in downtown El Lay, pending his arraignment on capital murder charges, tomorrow morning"

The Image Window retracted and Beverly Crescent eyeballed the camera.

"Police conducted a search of the suspect's residence and vehicle, and turned up, what investigators are calling, extremely provocative evidence."

"My God," Irv mused. "It actually worked."

Shelly muted the sound, feeling quite pleased with herself.

"Now, it's on to the next step, Irv, my boy. Time to capitalize, and with a little luck, cross-collateralize!"

Irv looked confused. "I don't get it."

"See all those sheets sitting in my desk?"

Irv nodded. "I was gonna ask you about that."

"Sylvia handed me those when I walked in the door. Apparently the phones started ringing late last night, after word of Jimmy's arrest leaked to the media."

She pointed to the pile.

"Reporters wanting interviews, Irv. Newspapers, magazines, TV and radio commentators. There's a message from Diane Sawyer for chrissakes!"

She grabbed the sheets and fanned them out under

Irv's nose, then handed him half. "Here you go, partner. That oughta keep you busy for awhile.

Irv squinted to read Sylvia's writing, shook his head. "Morley Safer wants to talk to us? The View? This is unbelievable! We're getting more hits off of Jimmy's arrest than we did when Chuck Dallas took off."

Shelly laughed. "What's so unbelievable, Irv? This is what Show Biz is all about. And remember what they say: 'There's no such thing as bad press'."

"Americans do love their homegrown psychopaths," Irv added, shaking his balding head.

A tone sounded and Shelly slipped on her headset. "Yes?"

"Sorry to bother you, Ms. Monroe," Sylvia began. "But I was pretty sure you'd want to take this call. You have Jimmy Bodine on line four."

"Thank you, dear," Shelly replied.
She clicked the hand-piece.

"Jimmy! How are you?" Shelly began, oozing in her most maternal of tones. "I'm glad you called. I've been so worried!"

Irv rolled his eyes at Shelly's performance. She responded by extending her stubby middle finger.

On the other end of the line, Jimmy's voice was cracking with emotion. "I need you, Shelly! This is a horrible mistake."

"Don't you worry about a thing, honey," Shelly soothed. "Everything is gonna be alright. We'll get this straightened out."

"I didn't do it, Shelly. I swear I didn't," Jimmy insisted.
Now it was Shelly's turn to roll her eyes.

"Of course you didn't ,sweetheart. It's all just a terrible mistake. Believe me, this kinda thing happens all the time."

"I need a real lawyer, Shelly. A heavy hitter like Tom Mesereau or Mark Geragos."

"Don't worry," Shelly assured him. "I've got just the guy."

42

(Three Months Later)

Jimmy Bodine was stretched out on the lower bunk of a six by eight foot cell, reading a copy of the National inquisitor. The cover shot was a photo of him looking through the rear window of a police cruiser. There was an inset photo taken from Jimmy's high school yearbook, and the headline that screamed: Faces of The Coyote. Beneath the bold headline print, the capsule stated –An Intimate Portrait of an alleged Serial Killer.

Jimmy's face was expressionless as he read the articles in the rag sheet, seventy-five percent of which featured The Coyote, and one-hundred percent of which was unadulterated bullshit. It didn't matter. Reading helped pass the time.

Cody hadn't been by to visit once, but he had arranged for a care package to be sent every week. Jimmy appreciated the gesture but would have much preferred the company. Being something of a celebrity, Jimmy was housed, along with a handful of prisoners, in a special isolation wing of the jail. They were locked down twenty-three hours a day. No sunlight. No human contact. Jimmy was slowly dying of boredom.

As he scanned the latest issue of his favorite rag sheet, he contemplated his options. They were few.

Debra Lazaro, the illustrious defense attorney Shelly had hired on Jimmy's behalf, had a reputation as a fierce advocate. At their first meeting, Ms. Lazaro had assured him the prosecution's case was thin. No DNA evidence, no eye witness. The bite mark impressions and hair samples had all come back inconclusive. And even though the forensics in the case in Phoenix were still pending, Jimmy's attorney explained that the damaged cowboy boots found in his residence were the only evidence the prosecutors had that linked him to any crime. That, and the fact he happened to be shooting a film in Phoenix when an Arizona State University freshman turned up raped, strangled and gnawed upon.

"Their case is circumstantial," Ms. Lazaro had concluded in an assured tone. "Believe me. I've created reasonable doubt with a lot less than this to work with."

The lawyer's assurances aside, Jimmy's spirits remained in the cellar. He wasn't a fool. He knew perfectly well one could never predict what twelve jurors might do.

*****

The visiting room of the El Lay Twin Towers jail was, as usual, filled to capacity. Friends and family members of the incarcerated conversed over telephone handsets, separated by a partition of wire-reinforced glass. Babies wailed amid conversations carried out in Espanol and Farsi, Mandarin and Russian. If you closed your eyes, you'd think you'd been teleported to some third world bazaar.

Shelly was seated on a metal chair facing the partition, with what appeared to be a laundry bag resting beside her overstuffed Prada shoes.

Seated to Shelly's left, a walrus of a woman, with three unruly tow-headed offspring, chatted into her handset. Judging from the expression of the heavily muscled man with the neck tats Walrus-woman was talking to, jail really wasn't such a bad place after all.

An overly perfumed Latina in her early twenties was seated to Shelly's right. Her hair was shiny black and hung in ringlets that spilled onto a sheer purple blouse. For some reason the girl made Shelly think of Shakespeare's tragic character, Juliet. The girl was cooing Spanish words of love into the receiver, and her hand was pressed to the partition. On the other side of the glass, Romeo had his hand matched with hers. Cruel and Unusual Punishment.

Shelly shook her head as a random thought flew by her periphery. Poor Romeo. He was too small, and far too pretty, to last long in El Lay County.

Shelly's mood brightened when Jimmy Bodine finally appeared from around a corner. He was attired in an orange jumpsuit, handcuffed, and shackled at the waist. He was ushered to the seat across from Shelly by two stone-faced deputies, one of whom uncuffed him.

Shelly smiled and picked up the handset.

"Hey Jimmy. How yah doin'?" Shelly asked in her most upbeat tone.

Jimmy's beard had grown out over the last ninety days. He unconsciously tugged at his calico chin hair.

"Long time, no see, Shell," he grumbled.

"What can I say, Jimmy. The office is jumpin'. I seldom get out of there before eight," she lied.

Jimmy nodded his head.

"So how 'bout my pal, Cody?" he retorted facetiously. "Sonofabitch hasn't visited me once! Not one goddamn time!"

Shelly knew this was coming, was fully prepared. "Listen, Jimmy. If you gotta be pissed at someone, be pissed at me. I told Cody to stay away."

"Why'd yah do that? Cody's the best friend I ever had."

"You gotta understand, Jimmy. It's just not a good idea right now. The press would have a field day."

Jimmy shook his head and gazed sadly through the partition.

"...Anyway, on to a more pleasant subject," Shelly continued, setting the line. "I got a call the other day from the editor of People Magazine. And guess what? They wanna do an interview with you."

"Why?" Jimmy snapped, the muscles in his jaw flexing. "I keep tellin' everyone I had nothin' to do with killin' those girls. It just doesn't seem to matter."

"Jimmy, it's PEOPLE magazine, for chrissakes," Shelly implored. "And believe me when I tell you, it's not about you. They want 'The Coyote',"

"But I'm not the Coyote!" Jimmy screamed. "I'm innocent!"

Neck tats shot Jimmy a look of pure malice.

"Of course you're innocent, honey," Shelly soothed. "And I'm sure when all the facts in the case are heard, the jury will feel the same way... But in the meantime, Jimmy, You know the old saying-there's no such thing as bad publicity."

Jimmy was baffled. "Huh? I don't understand."

Shelly continued, attempting to clarify. "Look, you definitely don't want to confess to killing those girls. The trick is, you just don't deny it, okay? We need to create an air of mystery to this Coyote thing."

He looked at her dumbfounded.

"What're you sayin', Shelly? I thought you were on my side."

"I am on your side, but you gotta trust me. It's called making lemonade out of this lemon!"

She kicked the laundry bag by her feet.

"Do you know what's in the sack?"

Jimmy shook his head, not really caring.

"Fan mail!" Shelly burst out, dumping the contents so Jimmy could see. "You've been averaging three letters to every one of Cody's."

That little trinket of information got Jimmy's attention. "At last count, there were twenty-nine websites dedicated to you, er –I mean, The Coyote. You've got letters in here from as far away as Georgia, and I mean the country, not the state. There are even marriage proposals, Jimmy, some from women who look like this."

Shelly fished around the floor, retrieved several photographs, and held them up for her client to inspect. Some were boudoir shots of scantily clad, buxom young women. The majority left less to the imagination. Several of the packages contained personal items as well; panties, bras, and the like.

Neck Tats's eyes narrowed as he attempted to steal a surreptitious glance.

Walrus-Woman's face grew several shades pinker, and she hammered against the glass with one massive fist.

Jimmy sat mesmerized by the glossy photos.

"You're a World-Wide celebrity, Jimmy! You couldn't buy this kinda name recognition with a platoon of PR agents, and hundreds of thousands of dollars! Isn't this what you've always wanted?"

Jimmy thought about that, his eyes never leaving the photos. "Shell, I wanted to be a star."

"Look Jimmy, I'm not gonna bullshit you. I will always tell it to you straight.The truth is, you were never going to be a star. You were always going to be a second string, C Lister. You're a good looking guy and a decent actor, but it's not enough. This town is full of good looking, decent actors, but there are only a handful of real stars. Either the camera loves you or it doesn't. You're either born with that magic or you're not. Do you want to know what the feedback has been on ninety percent of your auditions?"

Jimmy looked at her, too shell shocked to respond

Shelly leaned into the glass. "The feedback is 'nice job, but he's not interesting. He just doesn't 'pop'. The verdict is in, Jimmy. The camera doesn't love you. And as soon as the media made the connection between Jimmy Bodine and The Coyote, your acting career, such as it was, is now DOA, finished, stick-a-fork-in-it, DONE. On the bright side, the phones in the office haven't stopped ringing. Most with offers for The Coyote. So, you see, it really doesn't matter if you're innocent or not. The fact is, you're hotter right now than the Cast from 'The Voice'. The Coyote is Dangerous. And dangerous is Sexy... And Sex Sells!"

Jimmy sat frozen.

"You wanted to be a star? Well, this is your Fifteen Minutes!" Shelly continued. "And right now's the time to capitalize on it, before they realize they have the wrong guy. Are yah with me?"

Jimmy listened to Shelly's pitch, not once averting his eyes from the semi-nude photos held to the partition.

Shelly had given it her best shot. She leaned in for the kill.

"So, what's it gonna be Jimmy? What do you want me to tell People Magazine?"

Jimmy took only a moment before answering.

"Tell 'em The Coyote's agreed to give 'em an interview.

Shelly beamed a smile. "Now you're talkin' cowboy!"

"Character is a journey, not a destination."
-Bill Clinton

43

(One Month Later)

It was the second week in December, and the Santa Ana's had arrived. Fierce, dry winds, gusting up to fifty miles an hour, blew in from the northeast. The mercury hovered in the mid-eighties, and the humidity index was just above nil. It was the kind of weather conditions that gave arsonists wet dreams.

Cody Clifton lounged on the couch in his trailer. The Ballistic crew had been on location for the past three weeks and Cody was enjoying a rare break in the action. A copy of The National Inquisitor lay open on the coffee table.The cover was a candid shot of Jimmy Bodine being escorted from the court house, surrounded by a herd of beefy deputies. An inset image in the right corner featured Megan McKinnon, a highly photogenic redhead who, thanks to Shelly's sense of publicity, was rapidly becoming a household name. The Headline shrieked: I Survived The Coyote! –The Girlfriend Talks!

Cody was in a contemplative mood. He missed having Jimmy around to shoot the shit with. Missed a lot of other stuff, too. There were people around to run lines with him, but they were just employees. Cody appreciated their contribution, but he certainly couldn't relax around any of them. Still, he knew it was for the best.

His musings were interrupted by a knock at the door.

"Hey Cody. You're needed in five."

Cody swept The Inquisitor into the trash.

"Be right there!" he said and strode from the trailer with a smile.

*****

The sign on the office door was brand new. Fancy gold lettering scrolled over a black background proclaimed: The Monroe/Birnbaum Talent Group, LTD.

It was a little before five p.m., and Sylvia had just turned the phone lines over to Raymond.

Down the hall in Shelly's office, the big screen was dialed in to the five o'clock news on channel six. The Boss Lady was reclined on the couch, with one hand propped behind her head, and a Camel filter dangling precariously from the corner of her mouth.

Irv was slumped in the chair beside her, with his stocking feet propped up on an ottoman, his Gucci loafers resting nearby.

On the screen, Beverly Crescent stood outside the court house in downtown El Lay, and reported on the top story of the day:

"Reporting to you on the recent turn of events in the closely watched trial of Jimmy Bodine, the alleged Coyote killer. Today, in a move that stunned many in the legal community, August Cisneros, the assistant DA in charge of The Coyote murders prosecution, agreed to a special request from the Maricopa County District Attorney's Office, to extradite Jimmy Bodine to Arizona.

According to our sources, defense counsel for Jimmy Bodine entered into negotiations with the Maricopa County District Attorney's Office more than three weeks ago...

In a tearful address to the court, the accused Coyote killer admitted to strangling Angela Peterson, a freshman at Arizona State University, and agreed to be extradited to that jurisdiction, A plea agreement is allegedly in the works. When asked what all this meant for her client, Mister Bodine's attorney, Debra Lazaro, had this to say…"

"Well, that's that!" Shelly said brightly, muting the sound. Irv continued staring at the TV, lost in his thoughts.
Shelly glanced at him.

"Now what's wrong?" she asked irritably.
"Nothing."

"C'mon," Shelly complained. "Something's been eating at you for weeks. So what's your problem?"

"What's my problem? It's not my problem, Shell. It's our problem. Partners, remember?"

Shelly fixed him with a steely gaze. "Alright already! So spit it out, partner," Shelly demanded.

"Doesn't it bother you that Jimmy's gonna do time for something he didn't do?'

"What're you talking about, Irv?" Shelly began. "Weren't you listening to the news just now? Sounds to me like our Mister Bodine wasn't so innocent after all. He did kill someone! So yah see, Irv, that means we did a public service. You know the saying 'God works in mysterious ways'? Well, just think of yourself as one of God's little instruments," Shelly concluded brightly.

Irv wasn't finished. He had other questions that were keeping him up at night. "And what happens when Cody starts killing again, and the cops realize they have the wrong guy? I was wondering what our long range plans were."

Shelly laughed and stubbed out her cigarette, examined her face in a compact, touched up her lipstick. "Long range plans? Please, Irv. I thought you knew me better than that."

Now Irv was irritated.

"Illuminate me, please."

Shelly started thumbing through a copy of 'The Reporter'.

"It involves a deal I arranged through a friend of a friend; a Mexican National. The guy sets up shell corporations in Latin America and the Caribbean."

"And?"

"And not so long ago, we, meaning you and I, became silent partners in a chunk of real estate down on the Mexican Riviera. A lovely little villa with a view of the ocean and the mountains. The perfect place to go on vacation."

"I don't get it," Irv replied, stymied. "How's a villa in Mexico solve our problem? I don't even like Mexico. Every time I've gone down there, I've gotten sick."

Shelly shook her head impatiently. "That's your problem, Irv. You don't have any imagination... Now, if you'll just shut the fuck up, I'll explain how it solves our problem.... You see, I already worked this out with Cody. He assured me his little problem was under control. So our long range plan goes like this: We keep the bastard working. He's a good boy when he's working. –No unstructured free time, and we continue to collect our commissions."

"C'mon Shelly," Irv argued. "You know as well as I do there's no way to keep a client working all the time! Shows get cancelled. They go on hiatus. And every actor has slow periods. What then?"

"What then? Let me tell you what then... Whenever it looks like Cody's going to be unemployed for any length of time, he's on a private jet to Mazatlan. From now on, that's gonna be his vacation destination. Comprende?"

"Not really," Irv replied.

"You disappoint me, Irv. You're so dense sometimes!" Shelly proceeded to draw him the picture. "If Cody resumes his little hobby down south, so what? How much press you think dead hookers get in Mexico, Irv? Nada is how much. Nobody down there gives two shits about dead hookers. Hell, killing women is part of the culture, for chrissakes."

Irv digested that piece of information.

"What happens if he gets caught?"

"End of problem," Shelly summed up. "If Cody is careless enough to get caught, there are only two scenarios down there. One: he winds up getting planted in a hole with a big bag of lime. Or two: He rots away in a Mexican prison, where they really don't like rich, pretty gringos. Either way, Irv, we're in the clear."

Shelly's private line began chirping.

"Hang on a second, partner. I've been waiting for this call." She crossed to her desk and picked up the receiver.

"This is Shelly... Yeah, uh-huh... Certainly... What time would you like me there? Not a problem."

Shelly hung up the phone and turned to Irv, beaming a smile.

"You're not gonna believe this! That was Quentin Tarantino's office. They want me to do a cameo in his next film, playing myself! What do you think about that?"

"Fine by me as long as you plan on paying commission."

"Very funny, Irv."

"Well, it sounds like you've got us covered, Shell."

Shelly smiled. "Any more questions?"

"Just one," Irv began. "Don't you feel any guilt about what happened to Jimmy?"

"Why the hell should I? Jimmy got exactly what he'd wanted all along. We made him famous, a bona fide celebrity. People actually want to know what he thinks. I've gotten him interviews on 20/20 and Sixty Minutes, and I smell a book deal in the near future... And even though the law prohibits Jimmy Bodine from making money off his crimes, there's not a goddamn thing written anywhere, that says we can't collect our Ten Percent off of the victim's proceeds. God, I just love America."

Irv shook his head. "Shelly, you're amazing."

And yah know what else, Irv? I've been doing a lot of thinking the past couple of months, and I've come to a conclusion about the future."

"I'm all ears," Irv replied.

"After dealing with these whiny cocksuckers for a decade now, I've come to the conclusion that the Talent Agency business is too much work for far too little compensation. The future's in Management, Irv. No more horseshit Guild regulations hampering our every move, and no more caps on commissions. Whadda yah say, partner? How does Twenty Percent sound?"

Irv smiled like a happy ferret.

*****

The setting sun reflected in the building's windows as a sparkling new butter creme Bentley pulled up alongside the curb. The license plate read: KILR-MGR.

Moments later, a man emerged from the drivers side. He was dressed to the nines and resembled a sharkier version of Alec Baldwin. He crossed to the passenger side of the Bentley and opened the door. A long, lean set of legs appeared and soon thereafter, a long lean woman stepped onto the sidewalk. She was stunning even by Hollywood standards. She looked like a red-headed Sharon Stone. She referred to a piece of paper in her hand.

"This is the place, Jake. Monroe/Birnbaum Talent Group."

"Now Bobbi, once we're inside, please resist the urge to run your yap. Let me do the talking. I deal with these kind of people every day," Jake lectured.

"Whatever you say, dear," Bobbi replied.

She smiled to herself and thought: "Men! They always think they're the ones running the show."

They entered the building and took the elevator to the seventh floor.

44

It was a quiet weekend morning in January, and Max stood alone on the archery field. The air was crisp, and heavy with the smell of eucalyptus and freshly mown grass. She inhaled slowly and held the bow string taut, concentrated on the target.

In the time it takes to blink an eye, the aluminum shaft covered the distance, the point striking close to dead center.

Max brushed her ponytail off her shoulder and notched another arrow. As she was drawing the string, she became aware of a presence.

Someone was watching her.

She attempted to put the feeling aside and concentrated on the task at hand. She let the arrow fly and watched with disappointment as the tip struck the target's outer ring.

She cursed under her breath and swung around to face the interloper.

A hound dog bounded up to her, tail wagging ferociously. Max smiled, squatted and patted the dog on the head.

"Well hello there," she crooned sweetly. "My, you're a handsome boy. You're not lost, are you?"

Max looked towards the running track, checking to see if any of the joggers was missing a pooch. A sandy-haired man, dressed in gray sweats, was loping in her direction. He lifted an arm in a friendly wave. A minute later, Max recognized the face.

"Mornin' detective," Cody said in his most charming of tones. "Funny runnin' into you here."

Max scratched Blue behind the ears.

Cody smiled warmly at Max.

My, what pretty teeth you have!

All the better to eat you with, my dear.

THE END

DL Bruin was born in Los Angeles, California.

At the ripe old age of five he began his career as an actor, and spent his childhood working on numerous TV shows and feature films, under the name Lindy Davis.

After high school, DL joined the US Air Force and served as an air traffic controller, specializing in RADAR approach control.

Upon completion of service, he returned to Hollywood and a career behind the camera as a photographer and writer.

Preferring to just visit Hollywood these days, DL currently resides with his family in beautiful, rural northern California.

CPSIA information can be obtained at www.ICGtesting.com
Printed in the USA
LVOW11s0424200216

475943LV00001B/46/P